## "You're dead."

A low, hoarse voice shattered the s~~ill~~ locker room. Who was it? Shannon strained to see into the darkness.

The outline of a person stepped into a vague beam of light from the windows. He was dressed completely in black, down to his ski mask, and he held up leather-gloved hands and flexed them menacingly.

Grabbing the only weapon she could find, she threw her shoes at him and bolted for the door, without looking back. Footsteps followed her as she ran up the stairs two at a time. She tried not to think of those large hands reaching out to grab her, to pull her back into the darkness.

Then the figure lunged for her. Shannon pushed on the gym door, but it was locked. Frantically, she looked around her...but there was no way out....

## ABOUT THE AUTHOR

Heather McCann read her first Agatha Christie novel by age seven and that's when she knew she wanted to write mysteries. It took some time, but Heather found success with the sale of her first book to Intrigue. Now having penned two novels, Heather feels that writing a romantic mystery affords the luxury of combining the best of both fields.

## Books by Heather McCann

HARLEQUIN INTRIGUE
207—THE MASTER DETECTIVE

Don't miss any of our special offers. Write to us at the following address for information on our newest releases.

Harlequin Reader Service
901 Fuhrmann Blvd., P.O. Box 1397, Buffalo, NY 14240
Canadian address: P.O. Box 603,
Fort Erie, Ont. L2A 5X3

# Whispers in the Dark

## Heather McCann

# *Harlequin Books*

TORONTO • NEW YORK • LONDON
AMSTERDAM • PARIS • SYDNEY • HAMBURG
STOCKHOLM • ATHENS • TOKYO • MILAN
MADRID • WARSAW • BUDAPEST • AUCKLAND

To my dear friends and kindest critics,
Mary and Mark

Harlequin Intrigue edition published July 1993

ISBN 0-373-22236-X

WHISPERS IN THE DARK

# BOXFORD, MAINE

Boxford Beach

Ms. Viola Tibbs

The "Y"

Police station

Ocean Road

Warehouse

Library

Cemetery

Congregational Church

Main Street

Cottages

Mountainvale St.

OCEAN

Bowling alley

Market

School

Leslie and Paul Wagoner

Pond

Field

Old cellar hole

Harry Clarke Conservation Land

Wild Goose Farm

Penny Royal Lane

Tim Carver Carriage House Barn

Shannon and Nick

# CAST OF CHARACTERS

*Shannon Hollister*—She was targeted for murder by an unknown killer.

*Mike Finnegan*—His new neighbor was in need of a protector, and he was ready to take on the role.

*Mrs. Brennan*—She knew too much.

*Tim Carver*—He mysteriously arrived in town... and then the fires began.

*Nick Hollister*—Shannon's son was a junior Sherlock Holmes.

*Andy Finnegan*—Mike's son also fancied himself to be a master sleuth.

*Christie Finnegan*—She kept her brother and friend in line before they got into too much trouble.

*Paul and Leslie Wagoner*—Good thing Boxford's newest residents didn't plan on staying long.

# Prologue

He had murder on his mind. Standing concealed in the grove of maple and scrub pine, he looked down the slope toward the clearing below. He was watching the old woman and the dark-haired boy. Meddling old fool, he thought angrily.

Utterly motionless, he studied the old woman and boy in the distance, his mind racing with various grisly possibilities of murder. He knew the old woman walked back country roads. He could arrange a hit-and-run accident one of these evenings when fog was rolling in along the coast as if a great cold fire burned out on the ocean. The fog would be thick in some places, thin in others, getting denser all the time and making it hard to see.

Run her down with the car. He could picture her standing there in the road, hands spread, wide-eyed, screaming. And then he'd floor the accelerator. He imagined the stark terror in her eyes as she realized there was no escape. He could almost feel her slick warm blood and smell the slightly bitter coppery odor of it.

As the vision filled his mind and took command of all his senses, he gripped the trunk of a nearby pine tree so hard his knuckles whitened with strain.

He was sweating.

Mrs. Brennan. Meddling old fool couldn't keep her nose out of things that were none of her business. Well, he'd show her.

The neckband of his shirt was damp, and he loosened his collar, but he couldn't remove his jacket without the risk of being seen. If that happened, he might be forced to kill the old woman now, and he'd have to kill the boy, as well.

He considered that possibility without emotion, his blue eyes calmly studying the boy and the old woman moving about down below. Common sense told him to get rid of any possible witness. The boy was expendable, merely someone unlucky enough to get in his way. Too bad. He recognized the kid. Hollister, that was his name. Lived in that big farmhouse with the antique sign out front. Wild Goose Farm, that was it. The kid's mother was dark-haired, too, and good-looking. He'd seen her around town. She was a stunner, all right. Too bad if her son had to go.

The wood was very still except for the flitting of midges and fluttering of birds high in the treetops. Down below, the old woman's voice murmured indistinctly as she showed something to the boy. The man watching moved farther off the path and froze behind a clump of bushes that lay in shadow where the path descended the stony slope.

The old woman was coming closer. If they climbed up the path... He reached for the knife tucked in his waistband. He could cut their throats, a single slash from behind, left to right, cutting through the trachea to the vertebrae. Silent, deadly, and over in seconds.

He sank carefully to a crouching position on the litter of pine needles and, rocking gently on his heels, waited.

# Chapter One

It was getting dark. Five o'clock, and the woods were full of creeping shadows and somehow, an atmosphere of suspense. Black tree trunks stretched in the distance, and the leaves stirred nervously. In daylight, they looked spring-green; but now the gathering dusk had leached away their color, leaving them black.

Eight-year-old Nick Hollister started as his elderly companion, Nonie Brennan, grabbed his shoulder and hissed, "Shh, he's in that big oak across the clearing. Use the binoculars."

He lifted the binoculars, adjusted the focus and squinted. Nothing but a maze of black branches and head-high tangles of bramble and wild raspberries, then with startling clarity, a huge oak tree appeared in the lens. Where the main trunk branched, about thirty feet up, a dark hole.

Something was inside. He could see it move, a feathery form of brown and gray. At that moment, the huge barn owl emerged from its nest, perched silently on the edge of the hole for a second, then flitted off through the trees.

"Did you see that?" he whispered excitedly. "Mrs. B., it was *gigantic!* Wow!" He raised the binoculars again and tried to see where the owl had gone, but it had disappeared. "Gosh, he flew fast, didn't he?"

After a few seconds, he realized Mrs. B. hadn't answered and turned to see what was more important than the owl. She had moved a step or two away and was concentrating on something beyond the fringe of tangled brush and twisted trees. "Mrs. B.?" She still didn't answer, and her silence scared him. It wasn't like her. Ordinarily, she was full of energy, talking a mile a minute, teaching him about birds and nature, ecology and the way all life on earth was interconnected.

But she was frowning and had forgotten about the owl they'd come into the woods to see. It was weird, her acting like that.

He tried again. "Mrs. B., what's the matter?"

She started, her hand going to her breast. "Wha—oh, nothing, nothing at all." Looking at her watch, she went on, "My goodness, it's past five. The sun will be down soon. We'd better go." Her expression set and serious, she turned and walked ahead, a black silhouette among the gathering shadows.

"Which way do you want to go?" he asked. "The shortcut up the hill? That's where the owl went."

She shook her head. "No, I'm tired, and the owl's long gone at this point. Let's take the lower path."

She was already a good twenty feet ahead, and he had to walk fast to keep up with her. He wondered what the big deal was. So what if it was after five. They still had plenty of time. He wanted to stop and eat the chocolate bar in his knapsack. Enough for himself and Mrs. B. Enough for him, anyway. She probably wasn't all that crazy about chocolate. How come she was suddenly in such a hurry?

This problem called for scientific analysis. Luckily, he was good at stuff like that. His friends didn't call him "The Brain" for nothing. He went over what they'd been doing. They'd been looking at a dead tree, half-gutted and spongy with rot. Mrs. B. had been energetic and animated, pointing out small round pellets at the base of the tree. "Sure signs of owl," she'd told him. "Those are mouse pellets."

He'd picked one up. It was small and gray. Regurgitated fur and bone. Then she'd spotted the oak across the clearing and told him to use the binoculars. But when the owl came out of the nest and flew off, she hadn't even cared.

He frowned. It didn't make sense.

Suddenly, Mrs. B. stopped in the middle of the path and looked over her shoulder. "Did you hear something?" she said in a voice barely above a whisper.

He yawned and shook his head. "Nope."

She looked around worriedly. "Where did I leave my knapsack? Oh, there it is, by the cellar hole."

Wind swirled among the leaves and took his breath. He shivered and pulled his wool cap down over his curly dark hair. It was cold for March and getting colder. Darker, too. There was hardly any light by the old cellar hole. Mrs. B. looked like a black cutout shrugging into her knapsack; a black stick figure with wisps of white hair dancing in the wind.

As she hurried toward him, he saw the fright in her eyes. Which was crazy. Adults didn't get scared for no reason.

"Let's hurry," she said distractedly, urging him ahead of her through the trees. "It's cold. Your mom will worry if I keep you out much longer."

"How come you don't feel cold when you're moving?" Nick wondered out loud, his mind still busy with the knotty problem of Mrs. B.'s being scared. Maybe she was worried about the fires, he thought. Last week another barn had gone up in flames, and the local paper ran the headline: Arsonist Strikes Again! The story had been full of words like "suspicious origin" and "accelerant". Nick was pretty good with words, but he'd had to look that last one up in the dictionary.

Sure, that had to be it. Mrs. B. was scared of the arsonist.

"Kinetic energy causes heat," she muttered. "Get a move on, Mr. Science. Your mom's probably got supper on the table." Her hand urged him forward, almost pushing him along the path. "Think about how hard she works, raising you all alone and running her antique shop. It's not easy. Try to be considerate once in a while."

"It's not even five-thirty. It won't get real dark for ages," he complained. "We've got time."

"Maybe you do," she replied briskly. "But I've got things to do."

"I'll bet Mom's made meat loaf. It's Tuesday, and she teaches aerobics tonight. She always makes meat loaf on Tuesdays because there's enough for Thursday, when she's got another aerobics class. I hate it." He screwed up his face. "Yuck, it looks like dog food." He grinned suddenly as he thought of something funny. "Want to know how to make a tooth look like it's been knocked out?"

"No, and meat loaf's good for you," she said grimly. "Nourishing. Full of vitamins and minerals."

"Put a raisin on your tooth, and it looks black. I learned that last year in third grade. You could use lots of raisins, then it'd look like you had no teeth."

"Wonderful, I'll have to remember that." She pushed aside some scraggly raspberry canes. "Watch your head."

He climbed through the brambles and glanced backward. Behind them stood the far reaches of the woods and a looming mountain range thick with pine, fir and birch, lighted only along its crests by the sinking sun. Then he thought he saw movement. Something, not hurrying, but moving, slouching really, reminding him of the mummy in *The Mummy's Curse,* that film that had scared him when he was a little kid. One hand out, dragging its leg behind him. Out in the gloom somewhere, watching, waiting.

Mrs. B. put a hand on his shoulder, and he almost jumped out of his skin. Her hand was trembling.

He caught her fear. This time there was no mistaking it.

"Mrs. B., what's wrong? Is it that guy setting those stupid fires? Mom says he must be crazy." He looked up at her face, saw the direction of her eyes and turned to look again at the woods behind them. Nothing.

"Perhaps it wasn't such a good idea, coming here while the arsonist's loose. He could be hiding in these woods," she said thoughtfully. Then she took a shaky breath and went on, "No, that's not it—but never mind, it's probably nothing."

Frowning, he took another look. There was nothing there, no arsonist, not even the terrible vision of a mummy among the windblown branches.

Mrs. B.'s footsteps quickened, and Nick had to struggle to keep up with her until they came to the rutted dirt road where she'd left her car. She found her car keys, unlocked the door and opened it, urging Nick to slide in. Her face looked white and strained in the car's interior light.

"What's the matter? Don't you think the police will catch the arsonist?" he asked, leaning forward on the seat.

"I'm sure they will. It's just a matter of time." She smiled, and he could see she was struggling to regain control of herself, to remain calm and not panic.

Something back there had scared her, badly. What? He hadn't seen anything, at least he didn't think so. Not really.

"I'm taking you home," she said as evenly as she could. "Lock your door."

Why? They were in the middle of Conservation Wood in Boxford, Maine. Way out in the sticks. Nothing exciting had ever happened around here except that lately someone had started setting fire to a few old barns and outbuildings. Big deal. Nobody'd even got hurt, for crying out loud. He yawned again and rubbed his hand across his freckled nose. Same old boring small town, some deer, raccoon and an occasional moose. Real scary.

But Mrs. B. was fumbling with her ignition key. She dropped it and groped around on the floor. "Oh, no!" Her fingers closed around it and inserted it in the ignition. The car started up with a roar.

Nick stared at her, examining her expression with a mixture of fright and awe. As they backed out into Blacksmith Lane, her elbow hit the horn, sending a shrill electronic scream through the growing gloom. She stepped on the gas and the car slammed into reverse, skidding, scraping the back bumper against a tree trunk.

She turned on the headlights, illuminating the temporary signpost in front of the car, ghostly, flapping in the wind, like a sign in a horror movie:

Harry Clarke Conservation Wood.
   No littering, please. What you bring in, take out with you. No trespassing after dark.

Nick, a great reader, addicted to print, repeated the lines in his head as they drove away.

What if something really exciting happened? Something really scary, like in that mummy movie! Images flashed through his mind. Mummies roaming the woods, their rotting bandages falling away, littering the trails. Distorted masks of death and horror. Mournful groans in the rising wind.

But all he could hear was the thumping of his heart, the insistent pounding of a pump that wouldn't stop. Swallowing hard, he forced himself to look out the side window, half fearing he'd see a mummy's grotesque face pressed against the glass. From the corner of his eye he imagined clawing hands on the window, spread out as if to force it open. The thought of those clutching fingers increased the thumping in his chest. A feeling of panic tingled up his spine, creeping, crawling fear that drained him of energy. Gasping for breath, he turned his head and stared out the window. There was nothing.

Though he was frightened, his brain still worked all right. What a dope he was. It had been his imagination. The whole thing, thinking he'd seen a mummy, thinking Mrs. B. was frightened. No, he'd acted like a silly kid, scaring himself out of his wits. Mrs. B. was fine, a little quiet, maybe, but she was tired. And she was seventy-two. That was old. Old people got tired.

After a few moments, the entire incident blurred in his mind. He relaxed a little, yawned and turned the binoculars over in his lap, wondering if he should build a periscope, sort of a scientific experiment. He was good at stuff like that, and the barn behind the house was full of interesting junk that'd be perfect for such experiments. Wire, old bottles, switches, rusty nails, crowbars, all kinds of great junk.

IN THE SHADOWS at the edge of the conservation land, the man stood watching the rear lights of Nonie Brennan's car until they disappeared. His blue eyes were almost transparent, and his smooth face reflected no emotion save intent, animal-like watchfulness. He fingered the knife tucked in his waistband. Something would have to be done, and soon.

"HELP YOURSELF, Nick." Shannon Hollister pushed the broccoli across the table toward her young son. "It's good for you."

"Come on, Mom. Meat loaf and broccoli at the same time?" He turned imploring blue eyes toward her. "I'll get sick. I could even die."

"No one ever died of meat loaf poisoning," she said dryly.

"That's what you think."

Shannon gave an impatient sigh. "Nicholas, you will eat every bit of dinner," she said, articulating each word carefully so there'd be no mistake. "I don't want any more nonsense. Julie's coming any minute to keep an eye on you while I run over to the Wagoners' before aerobics class.''

It was almost six-thirty. They were seated at the old pine table in the kitchen of Wild Goose Farm, his mom's business establishment and their home. Wild Goose Antiques: bow-backed Windsor chairs, blue transferware plates, cranberry glass, coin silver flatware and a worn Oriental rug on the pine floor.

All the comforts of home. But Nick was blind to them as he was to the comeliness of his mother, Shannon.

She wore her dark hair in a short, curly cap. Her wide blue eyes, so like his own, were fringed extravagantly with long, black lashes. Twenty-seven and extremely capable, she was divorced from his dad and doing pretty well running the antique shop and teaching aerobics twice a week at the local Y.

From Nick's point of view, life wasn't fair. His mom could outrun him any day of the week and was always two steps ahead of him when it came to figuring out whatever he was up to. ''The advantages of a misspent youth,'' she'd said once with a sly grin. ''There's nothing you can try that I haven't already done.''

And he believed her. Just as when he was little, he believed she had eyes in the back of her head. If that wasn't bad enough, she could do his math homework standing on her head, but made him figure out the answers anyway.

And sometimes the list of chores she gave him seemed endless. Showering when he wasn't even dirty, cleaning his room on Saturdays. While contemplating these injustices, he casually covered the meatloaf and broccoli with the napkin.

''Nick, eat your dinner,'' she said.

He gave her a wary look. She was glaring at him, those blue eyes shooting sparks of temper. His attempt to slide the food off his plate and into the open mouth of his dog, Max, waiting patiently underneath the table, hadn't gone unnoticed.

With the distinct feeling that things would get worse before they got better, he tried changing the subject. "Uh, Mrs. Brennan and me, I mean, I saw a barn owl today in the woods. We found the tree he was nesting in and mouse pellets. That's what he throws up after eating mice...."

He paused to draw a breath. "You saw a barn owl?" Shannon asked. She smiled, but reached down and swept the napkin from his plate. "Eat."

"Well, I could be wrong. It could have been a great horned owl. We really didn't get a good look at it," he explained. "It flew off too fast and it was getting dark. Anyway, Mrs. B. got scared all of a sudden and said we had to come home. I think she saw that guy who's setting the fires."

She drew a sharp breath. "What?"

"Sure, the arsonist." His eyes glistened. "Only it probably was a mummy, just like in *The Mummy's Curse*. I'm gonna call Andy and tell him."

"You're making that up," she said, frowning. Andy Finnegan was Nick's best friend. Along with Andy's little sister, Chris, they formed The Martian Spaceship Society, the secret club that met in Nick's tree house in the backyard. When they weren't playing in the nearby woods, they were busy drawing up secret plans for inventions or planetary exploration.

Up until now Shannon had considered the woods a safe place to play, but she also knew Nonie Brennan wasn't the type of woman who frightened easily. If she'd cut their nature walk short and hustled Nick home, there was a good reason.

Just then, the doorbell rang, and, grateful for the interruption, Shannon went to answer it. She felt slightly sick at the thought of Nick and Mrs. Brennan at the mercy of the arsonist. So far, no one had been hurt in the fires, but it was only a matter of time.

JULIE THE BABY-SITTER, of course, Nick thought sourly. Well, so what. He disposed of the despised meat loaf beneath the table, and seconds later was rewarded by the sound of Max licking his chops. Mom and Julie were coming down the hall toward the kitchen, so he quickly dumped some of the broccoli on the floor. Not all of it, Mom'd never believe he'd eaten the whole thing, not in a million years. He left enough on the plate to look convincing, then slid off his chair and went to call Andy from the telephone in the hall.

Sitting at the foot of the staircase he dialed the number, and made a mental note to look up mummies in the card file at the library. They'd probably have lots of creepy stuff about ancient Egypt. With great colored pictures of dripping blood and rotting bandages. While the phone rang at Andy's house, Nick wondered idly if mummies drank blood, sort of like vampires. Yeah, they probably did, he thought, imagining the mummy's half-open mouth fixed in a rictus between a smile and a sneer; the dead eyes seeming to shrink in their sockets like black marbles; the grasping hand with its long, grisly fingers, the palm thick with blood—   Andy's voice came on the line after only two rings. "Hullo?"

"It's me—Nick," he said, looking over his shoulder to see where Mom and Julie had gone. From the clink of plates and the sound of water running, they were washing the dishes.

"What's up? D'ja finish the math homework?" Andy asked. "I had trouble with problem five. What'd you get?"

"I'm gonna do it later. Multiplication's a snap. You just gotta learn the tables."

Andy sighed in resignation. "I guess so, but they're boring. I hate 'em."

"Me, too," Nick replied. "But they're pretty easy once you get 'em down pat. Listen, the reason I called, uh, my mom's going over to the Wagoners' for a while before her aerobics class. Want to come over? Julie's gonna be here while Mom goes over to the Wagoners'. She knows Mrs. Wagoner's sister. That's the lady who inherited old Harry Clarke's house by the conservation wood."

"Oh, yeah," Andy said thoughtfully. "I heard he left a lot of money, too. Some kind of trust fund, a couple of million."

Nick whistled. "No kidding. I didn't know that."

"Well, my dad's been working over there, renovating the house. It was built in the early 1700s or something. Harry Clarke liked things just so, and he hired Dad to rebuild some paneling and stuff in the library before he died. Mr. Clarke, that is, not my dad—Dad's not dead, he's fine."

"I know he's not dead—I'm not stupid," Nick retorted, at that point hearing a slight scuffling noise at the other end of the line.

"Would you let me talk to Nick in peace, for cryin' out loud? Okay, okay." Andy sighed and added impatiently, "Chris says 'hello.'"

"Tell her 'hi' back. Hey, you know anything about mummies or vampires?"

"Sure, I know all about that stuff. Mummies smell awful and their heads can come off and they walk around, blood everywhere, coming after you with an ax."

Nick's mouth fell open, and his heart started pounding like a drum. He knew instantly, and with absolute certainty that he'd had a narrow escape that afternoon in the woods. "No kidding," he gasped. "I didn't know that." He pressed his back against the wall by the stairs, grateful for the support of its post-and-beam construction. But neither its strength nor his tightly closed eyes could shut out the horror.

That mummy had chased him and Mrs. Brennan with an ax! And the creature had been headless, probably.

"Yeah," Andy went on, unconscious of the effect his words were having on his listener. "Just like slitting your throat, only they chop you up with an ax. It's real neat." He gagged and made a horrible gurgling noise, like warm blood gushing up in his throat.

Nick swallowed hard and put a hand to his neck, which he found reassuringly whole. Menacing images of headless mummies swam before his eyes and when he spoke, his voice squeaked with fear. "Uh, Andy, I think there's a mummy on the conservation land. It was stalking me this afternoon, watching and waiting to make its move. I *saw* it."

"Honest?"

"I think so. Something was there."

"Okay, but not a mummy. In my experience, I've found they're generally after some lost arktifract or other, like something a museum would have. Does your mom sell ancient mummy arktifracts in her shop?"

"No," Nick snapped. "In my experience," nuts, he thought sourly. Andy was always saying that, like he'd been everywhere and done everything. And who'd had the adventure with the mummy this afternoon, anyway?

"Well, he's probably still there, hiding in the woods with his ax," Andy said gleefully. "Maybe we could catch him, lay a trap. We could dig a deep pit and lay branches over it. They did that in one of my comics, and the mummy fell right in. In my experience—"

"Never mind that," Nick interrupted. "And don't bother coming over tonight. Julie probably won't let me have company. We'll have to meet tomorrow at the fort."

"Okay, and we're gonna need shovels, a big net and a saw to cut branches with."

Nick was aware of a shadow looming beside him. He looked up, his mind a tangle of mummy traps and axes dripping blood, and saw Julie. He almost moaned with relief as he took in her familiar dimpled cheeks and wide smile. "Oh, hi."

"Your mom just left. She said to hang up and do your homework." Julie tilted her blond head and added with a sigh, "Don't bother telling me you already did it, because I know you haven't."

"Okay." He told Andy he'd see him on the school bus in the morning and hung up. Then he followed Julie back to the kitchen. She was putting the kettle on for tea. As she turned the water off and switched on the gas stove, he said, "Um, I wanted to ask you something."

She turned around and wiped her hands on the dish towel. "Okay, shoot. What did you want to ask me?"

"Do you know anything about mummies? Like, can you scare them off with garlic?"

## Chapter Two

Mentally, Shannon was kicking herself for not having called Mrs. Brennan before leaving for the Wagoners'. One thing for sure, she thought, as she backed the car down the driveway and headed for Pomfret Road. She'd get to the bottom of Nick's mummy story before the night was over.

The wind was rising and raindrops whispered at the windshield. On the seat beside her lay a gaily wrapped package tied with gold ribbon. The end result of a somewhat harried long-distance phone conversation that morning with her old college friend, Linda Clarke.

"I'm in Chicago, at O'Hare Airport, on my way to Amsterdam," Linda had said, sounding frantic. "Would you believe it? A two o'clock flight. All I could get was standby, damn these buying trips!" She took a breath. "How are you? Did you get my letter?"

"Fine, and no. You probably forgot to mail it," Shannon said, trying not to laugh. "How are you? We haven't talked in ages—"

"Work work work, all the time. Damn, I thought I'd written—anyway, how're things? Last I heard, you were still wondering if you'd done the right thing, dumping Tom."

Shannon sighed in exasperation. Linda hadn't changed a bit. Same gravelly voice, same conversational style. She plunged right into the subject at hand with no time to waste.

"I'm not wondering anymore," Shannon replied tartly. "And second thoughts are normal when you're going through a divorce."

"He was a jerk. You fell for that all-American smile of his. He just wanted a household slave. Thank God you had the gumption to kick him out."

"Actually, he walked out on his own," she admitted.

"A minor technicality. You would have kicked him out sooner or later. Listen, I have a big favor to ask—"

"What?"

"It's my sister Leslie's birthday. I haven't seen her in almost a year, since she married Paul Wagoner. Remember Harry, the rich uncle I used to talk about when we were in college, the one paying my tuition? He died and left Leslie and me everything. A few days ago, she moved into Uncle Harry's old house in Boxford, Maine, which is why I called—"

"What a coincidence," Shannon said with a smile. "I happen to live in Boxford, Maine."

"Exactly! Oops, I dropped my purse, wait a sec—" Linda said breathlessly. After a moment, she went on, "Where was I? Oh, yes, did you ever meet Leslie while we were in college?"

"No."

"Well, you'll love her. She's a lot of fun. Pretty, too, she inherited all the beauty while I got the brains."

Shannon laughed. "The only picture I ever saw of her, she was six months old and bald."

"Believe me, she's changed. Anyway, I meant to write and let you know she was moving to town, but I've been so busy!" Linda paused for breath before resuming. "To make a long story short, Uncle Harry's estate was split more or less in half. I got the place in Palm Beach, and Leslie got the Boxford house, which, as I recall, was a showplace, crammed with antiques. Lucky Leslie." She sighed gustily. "The Palm Beach house needs fixing up. A bomb wouldn't hurt, it's a complete mess. That's where my half of the interest on the trust fund will go. New roof, painting, landscaping, air-conditioning, God only knows what else. It looks like something out of a Tarzan movie, overgrown vines everywhere."

"Sounds like you'll need more than the interest on a trust fund," Shannon pointed out.

"You've got that right. Trouble is, I can't touch the capital unless Leslie dies, or the other way around," she said grimly. "Never mind all that. Could you possibly pick out a birthday present for Leslie from your antique shop, something nice for, say—three or four hundred? I'll send a check from Amsterdam, first thing." Announcements of airport arrivals and departures blared from the PA system in the background. "They've announced my flight—before I forget, I found an old photograph of Leslie and me, taken years ago. I'll send it with the check. Try to find a nice old frame for it. She'll really get a kick out of it."

"Okay," Shannon agreed.

"Don't let me down, now. I'll call from Palm Beach next week when I get back. Bye!"

The sudden rumble of thunder and gusting wind buffeting the car brought Shannon's mind back to the present and the subject at hand, Leslie's gift. She glanced across the seat at the prettily wrapped package. It was a small nineteenth century oil portrait of a young woman. Miss Henrietta Pingree, age sixteen, of Bath, Maine. Lace ruffles at her white throat, a fan in her hand, she stared ahead solemnly. Utterly charming. Leslie would love it.

It was raining harder now, and Shannon adjusted the wiper speed. Black tree trunks flashed by in the headlights, a tumbledown stone wall, and a hundred yards ahead on the right, a large red two-story frame dwelling with its barn looming against the hillside.

She parked in the driveway. A gray Volvo station wagon was parked up near the barn, and a light had been turned on by the front door. The Wagoners were expecting her.

She got out, tucked the package under her arm and ran up the path. She rang the bell, and after a moment, a pale face appeared in the window to the left. Rain running down the glass blurred the face into a a dream-image. Shannon couldn't tell if it was a man or a woman.

The door finally opened, and a slant of light fell across the stone steps. A tall woman stood there, smiling, "Hi, you must be Shannon. I'm Leslie, Linda's sister. Come in."

Leslie reminded her of a well-trained athlete. She was slim and sleekly muscled, and moved gracefully. Expertly cut dark brown hair with russet highlights framed her face, and her brown eyes were large and tilted upward at the corners, with long, curling lashes.

Low murmuring voices came from a nearby open doorway. It sounded oddly like a very polite disagreement. She recognized one of the voices as that of Nonie Brennan. "More than three months ago," she was saying, her voice edged with anger. "There's no point in prolonging this. I won't change my mind. It's what Harry wanted. If you have anything more to say, you can tell it to my lawyer."

A man's voice Shannon didn't recognize replied, "We've every intention of complying with Harry's wishes." He stopped speaking as Shannon followed Leslie into the large sitting room. He rose from a slightly crouched position by the fireplace where he'd been putting another log on the fire. He was tall and blond, with deep-set eyes.

Firelight flickered on the walls of the room, and Leslie urged Shannon forward. "Darling, look, it's my sister's friend, Shannon Hollister. She's brought my birthday present from Linda!"

Paul Wagoner smiled. "Have you met a neighbor of ours, Mrs. Nonie Brennan?"

"Of course," Shannon said, smiling at the white-haired lady sitting in the wing chair by the hearth. "We're old friends."

"I was going to call you, my dear," Mrs. Brennan said as she got up and pulled on her mackintosh and scarf. "Nick and I found an owl's nest today."

"He told me all about it." Shannon put the portrait down and unbuttoned her jacket, realizing all at once that Mrs. Brennan must have walked from her home or she would have noticed the older woman's car parked in the Wagoners' driveway. "If you'll wait a few minutes, I'll give you a lift home. It's raining cats and dogs out there."

Leslie leaned over and pulled the window curtain aside. "It's pouring! Have a drink and stay until it lets up. Coffee or a hot toddy? Paul makes a terrific Cajun

Special, just the thing on a night like this. Shannon, Mrs. Brennan, please stay a while.''

Mrs. Brennan looked at her watch. "I really must go, I'm sorry."

"In that case, I'll take a rain check on that drink, Leslie. Why don't you open the present now," Shannon said, buttoning her jacket.

Leslie picked up the package, tore off the paper and ribbon, and squealed with delight as she tilted the portrait to the light. "It's marvelous! I love it! Paul, darling, isn't she perfect?" She showed it to her admiring husband. "Where shall we hang her? Between the windows? Or would she look better in the dining room?"

"Oh, one more thing, Leslie," Shannon added. "Linda asked me to frame an old photograph of the two of you. She's sending it from Holland. It should arrive in a few days."

Leslie turned away from her husband and looked back at Shannon, her face lit with pleasure, "Wonderful! I'm probably in pigtails and covered with freckles. Linda always said I was the world's biggest tomboy."

Smiling, Shannon picked up her purse and moved toward the hall door where Mrs. Brennan was waiting. "I don't know. She didn't tell me what it looked like, just said she'd mail it to me."

Leslie went with them to the front door, chatting amiably. They'd both have to come to dinner soon. Leslie would call them next week. With a cheery, "Drive carefully!" she waved good-night.

Mrs. Brennan was silent until they were in the car and Shannon had started the engine. Then she sighed and said, "Ordinarily, I'd walk home. I try to get in five miles a day, but the weather's been so cold lately. And my legs aren't as young as they used to be." With a smile, she added, "Nick and I got in a mile or so this afternoon."

Shannon put the car in gear and drove on. "I wanted to talk to you about that. He said something had upset you while you were out walking." She gave the old lady a worried glance. "He said you'd seen the arsonist—"

"No, at least I don't think so." For a moment, Mrs. Brennan seemed to hesitate, then said slowly, "It was probably nothing. I had a vague sense of unease, call it a premonition, if you will." She shook her head and added, "There was something else—but I must have been mistaken."

"Not a mummy, I hope. Nick had the most ridiculous story," Shannon said with a smile.

"No, nothing like that." Mrs. Brennan shook her white head. "The truth is, I've had better days. Today was one thing after another. I didn't mean to frighten Nick, but it was getting late and I knew supper would be on the table." She sighed. "To top it off, I had to deal with Paul Wagoner. He's not my favorite person. Smokes like a chimney, a habit I gave up a good many years ago. Cold turkey, I might add."

"Good for you. It must have taken willpower."

Mrs. Brennan sighed and admitted, "That's never been one of my failings. No, Harry Clarke said my blunt tongue would be my downfall. But I can't abide hypocrisy or lies—it just puts my back up." Glancing at Shannon, she chuckled. "I'm turning into a curmudgeon. I rub everyone the wrong way these days. My next-door neighbor's been fighting me over the property line, threatening to sue. It's ridiculous."

Shannon smiled. "Isn't that Mrs. Prouty? Her bark is worse than her bite."

"You're probably right." Mrs. Brennan shrugged. "Maybe it's me. I just don't understand what's happened to moral values these days. My niece's husband—they're divorcing—wants me to take care of his monetary obligations. My niece, Dana, and her son, Bart, are staying with me." She raised a quizzical eyebrow. "Only four years old, too young to be friends with Nick, I suppose."

"Probably," Shannon agreed. "They wouldn't have a lot in common."

"They'll be here for the next month or two, until the divorce is settled. Dana's husband hired a private detective." Mrs. Brennan gave her a sober look. "A big, burly man wasting time poking his nose into things that are none of his business." She shook her head and added grimly, "You can't miss him. Baby-faced, curly blond hair and the coldest blue eyes I've ever seen. Enough to chill your blood."

Shannon smiled. "Sounds like you've got your hands full."

"That's not the half of it," Mrs. Brennan snorted. "I caught two loggers cutting timber illegally on Harry Clarke's conservation land last week. Evidently planned to be in and out with the skidder and power saw with no one the wiser. I soon put a stop to that! You know how I feel about the few acres of wilderness we have left in town. It's a matter of principle. Harry and I tramped through those woods every day of our lives—until he fell ill. You'd be surprised at the things we found. Arrowheads, bits of pots. Nothing of intrinsic value, but they're part of our heritage. Nick's probably told you, I plan to offer them to the historical society."

Shannon pulled up and parked in front of Mrs. Brennan's house. On impulse she said, "Thanks so

much for taking an interest in Nick. He's learned a lot
about nature on his walks with you.''

Giving Shannon's arm a pat, Mrs. Brennan heaved
herself forward and opened the car door. "He's a great
youngster. No complaints on my part. We have a fine
time, exploring together. But if Paul Wagoner has his
way, there won't be much more of that. He's terrified
of a lawsuit, thinks I'll break a leg over one of his stone
walls and sue." She snorted. "Tell you another thing,
he lacks good old-fashioned common sense. I get
around quite well, thank you." Fumbling in her coat
pocket, she held up a delicate gold locket and chain.
"Goodness, I forgot to give this to Leslie. I found it in
the woods the other day." It dangled from her fingers,
a tiny glittering garland of flowers surrounding an or-
nate *L* inscribed on its round surface.

"Are you sure it's hers?"

Mrs. Brennan shrugged helplessly. "I don't know.
The Wagoners' property borders the conservation land.
I assumed it was hers, because of the initial. It could be
anyone's, I suppose."

"I'll see if it's hers," Shannon suggested. "I have to
frame and deliver that photograph from her sister."

A light sprang on in an upstairs window in Mrs.
Brennan's house. With a sigh, the old lady got out.
"Looks as if Dana's home. She said she was going away
for the weekend. I thought she was leaving tonight instead of Friday, but evidently not." Mrs. Brennan
frowned. "She's seeing another man in spite of the
messy custody battle and that detective looking under
every rock for a scandal. She's a silly fool. If her husband finds out about the other man, she won't have a
leg to stand on." She shook her head and added wryly,
"Her four-year-old son acts more mature than she

does." Leaning across the open door, Mrs. Brennan smiled. "Thanks again. Good night."

Shannon waited until Mrs. Brennan had waved and gone into the house before driving away.

A FEW MINUTES LATER, turning into her own driveway, Shannon noticed a familiar blue-and-gray Bronco parked by the back door. It belonged to Mike Finnegan, Andy and Chris's father.

She was tempted to sneak into the house and pretend she hadn't seen the car. Absurd, of course—but she'd had a long, tiring day, and still had to run the aerobics class in an hour. Talking to Mike, no—*fencing* with him wasn't exactly what she'd had in mind for the next sixty minutes.

In her opinion, Mike Finnegan was the most irritating, maddening man she'd ever had the misfortune to meet. Rude, opinionated and obnoxious, he was outspoken about things that were none of his business: how she raised her son, where she went, and with whom. To hear him talk, she was the worst parent in town. She didn't run here, there and everywhere with Nick. No, she'd worked damn hard teaching him to be self-sufficient, to think for himself. It hadn't been easy, not by a long shot.

Head bowed against the rain, hands in her jacket pockets, she trudged up the path to the house, wondering what he could possibly want at this time of night.

A widowed architect specializing in the renovation and restoration of old houses, Mike worked at home when he wasn't on-site somewhere. Keeping an eagle eye on his two kids, she thought sourly. Ordinarily, he wouldn't have been caught dead in her driveway. He acknowledged the explosive chemistry between them. It was as plain as the slightly crooked nose on his lean face.

He didn't like her anymore than she liked him. One of those things. She frowned, remembering their latest skirmish, over the Cub Scout spaghetti supper that had been held on the same night as her aerobics class. She'd called to ask if he'd take Nick with Andy—the brakes on her car had died, and besides getting a ride for Nick, she had to beg a ride to aerobics class from somebody else—and Mike had acted as if she were out of her mind. The ensuing argument had raged for a good ten minutes.

"Not going to the spaghetti supper?" he'd snapped disbelieving.

"That's right," she'd said quietly. Anger is nonproductive, she'd told herself. Anger accomplished nothing. Especially when dealing with a Neanderthal mentality.

"I suppose it's your night for aerobics."

"Yes, my car is—"

"Can't you get a substitute?" he interrupted without listening. "Have them shove a tape in the VCR. This supper means something to the boys. Cub Scouts. Does the name ring a bell? Den meetings, badges, projects like Pinewood Derby. Which, correct me if I'm wrong, you missed two months ago."

The night of the derby she'd been flat on her back in bed with the flu, but she was damned if she'd remind him of that! Instead, she'd snapped, "A simple yes or no will do. Are you taking Nick with Andy, or not?"

After a moment, he'd said coolly, "How many functions have you missed so far this year? Four, five, or have you lost count?"

It was two, with legitimate reasons for both, but unfortunately, that's when she'd lost her temper and called him a few names better left unsaid. She'd banged down the receiver, and when Nick had asked if he was going to the spaghetti supper, she'd told him no.

Naturally, Mike had rung the doorbell at ten to seven the night of the supper and informed her tersely that he'd stopped by to pick up Nick.

Blank-faced, she'd stuttered, "Oh, I didn't expect you."

"I'm not here for you. I came for Nick. I happen to be very fond of him." A faint ghost of anger lurked in his gray eyes, and his words rang with casual contempt.

It took an effort, but she gritted her teeth, got Nick ready and waved as they backed out of the driveway. Her bright smile had almost cracked her face. Mike Finnegan had the most extraordinary capacity to catch her off balance. Six feet three inches of bully. She hated him, she'd decided as she watched the car disappear. She'd gone back into the house and slammed the door as hard as she could. As a result, two very nice old plates had fallen off a shelf and broken.

That episode had occurred two weeks ago, and in the intervening days, she'd kidded herself into thinking she could handle Mike Finnegan. All she had to do was be calm and practice square breathing.

She concentrated on breathing in and holding, one, two, three, four. Out, one, two, three, four. Feeling numb, she eased open the back door. Mike was by the refrigerator, reading cartoons she'd cut out of the Sunday paper and stuck on the door with magnets. His expression was intent and slightly frowning; clearly, he didn't think Garfield was funny.

When the ringing in her ears subsided, she heard him call out to Nick, "Your mom's home. Come down to the kitchen."

She'd been sure, a few minutes ago, that her spirits had sunk as low as they possibly could. She'd been wrong.

He turned to her, moved his eyes deliberately from her damply curling hair, down her body to the tips of her muddy running shoes. "I've seen you looking better."

Ignoring that crack, she wiped the rain off her nose with the back of her hand. "To what do I owe the honor?"

He shrugged. "The kids and I were going out for ice cream. We thought we'd ask Nick along. It's your night for aerobics, right?"

Her voice, when she found it, was calm. "I have a sitter. Julie Shaw is here."

"What the hell, she can come, too. The more, the merrier." He smiled then, a genuine, heart-melting smile, and Shannon forgot all about square breathing. "Why don't we drop you off at the gym on the way?" he added casually. "We'll pick you up after class and save you a trip." His bland assumption that she'd go along with this plan would have made her laugh under other circumstances. While she was trying to decide whether to give in or invent an excuse, he went on, "Nick said you were having trouble with your car battery. Get that fixed soon. You don't want to be stranded."

She flushed and muttered, "The car runs well most of the time, but it hates rain. I was lucky it started at all today." She looked at him as he leaned against the counter, arms crossed; he seemed quite prepared to stand there all night. Taking a deep breath, she went on, "Okay, I'd love a lift to the Y, thanks."

His expression didn't change, but for some reason, he looked like the cat that swallowed the canary. "Fine," he said. "Let's collect the kids and go. They disappeared upstairs a few minutes ago. Looking for comics or some darn thing."

Suppressing irritation at being preemptively ordered around in her own house—after all, it was late and he was doing her a favor—she nodded and went to the foot of the stairs to call them.

HALF AN HOUR LATER, Shannon was in the gym dressed in a black leotard and tights and leading her class in warm-ups. They began with a mile run on the small upstairs track; afterward, they concentrated on their workout. Keith Jarrett's recording of Bach's *Goldberg Variations* played softly in the background. Stretching, bending, turning to the beat of the music, the group moved to the easy rhythm.

Shannon had been walking around the perimeter of the floor, checking everyone's balance and mobility. She moved to the front of the group. "Bend," she said. "Don't think about anything but moving. Let go. Push, go with your energy. That's it."

Backing away slowly, she watched the class. They were doing fairly well, although chunky Nancy Davis in the front row still had a long way to go. Embarrassed and tentative when she'd first started coming to class hoping to lose thirty pounds, she talked in self-deprecating terms. But Shannon was less interested in helping her shed pounds than in helping her shed her poor self-image.

The session lasted another twenty minutes and ended with a quarter-mile run around the track. Shannon was silent, knowing her voice couldn't be heard above the thud of their feet. She let herself go mentally, and only then found herself thinking about Mike, that fleeting smile she'd seen, and something in his voice—

She forced herself to look at things realistically. Give him credit. He'd sensed that ill will and quarreling between them would only hurt the children. At least he was honest. He'd met her more than halfway, dropping by tonight to offer a lift. Well, if he could be polite and pleasant, so could she.

That decided, she moved over beside Nancy who was red-faced and panting, but doggedly trying to keep up. "You're doing fine," Shannon told her.

Nancy managed a nervous smile. "You didn't think I'd give up so easily, did you? No way. I'm in this for the duration!"

"Good for you," Shannon told her as they slowed to a walk. "You'll make it, I know you will."

When class was over, she showered and dried herself with a big blue towel, then pulled on her jeans and a green sweater. She glanced at her watch as she came downstairs and went outside, deciding she had time for a tranquillity exercise. Mike and the kids weren't due back for another five minutes.

She sat down on the front steps of the building and closed her eyes, letting tension flow from all her muscles, starting at the top of her head, downward over her face, neck, shoulders. Breathing slowly, passively—an image of sheep eating grass in a green meadow came to her. Cows, a fence and barn, a wide blue sky. She reached up in her imagination, feeling lightness flood over her. A floating sensation, upward to the blue sky,

higher, higher, then for a moment she felt the peaceful-
ness of nothing at all.

Her moment ended with the arrival of Mike Finnegan's Bronco. He rolled down his window. She could
hear the children laughing in the back seat. "Too many
late nights?"

She drew a deep breath and stood up. "No, just re-
laxing." Trailing wisps of fog curled in the Bronco's
headlights as she walked around to the passenger's side
and got in. Wind must be blowing in off the ocean, she
thought absently. One of those nights when the mist
condensed into a layer of solid fog obscuring trees and
houses; nearer shapes shone ghostly, weak yellow beams
of light from oncoming traffic, streetlamps shining like
dim torches in the banks of drifting fog as they drove
toward home.

"Not a fit night for man or beast," Mike remarked,
flicking on the windshield wipers. "Want some pizza?
It's probably still warm. The ice cream made the kids
hungry, so I got some takeout."

Nick leaned over the back of the seat and handed her
a napkin-wrapped slice. "It's great!" he announced.
"The works—onions, mushrooms, hot peppers, hamburger and some kind of green stuff."

"Green beans," Mike said. "Give your mom a cola,
too." He threw her a questioning look. "Do aerobic
instructors drink cola?"

"No, we don't," she told him between bites of pizza.
"This stuff's strictly verboten, too. Don't tell my class."

Mike smiled a little, then said, "How did you get
started teaching aerobics?"

"By accident, really. I was taking a class, and one
week the instructor didn't show up. We decided to exercise anyway, and someone had to lead us through the

routines, so I did. The next week, the same thing happened. Turned out the woman had quit." She shrugged and added, "To make a long story short, the class thought I did a good job, so I continued. The Y paid me, and it was worthwhile exercising. Not just for the money, which I needed, but for the sheer joy of it."

"Joy of movement?"

"Yeah, but Nick doesn't buy it. I've brought him to the gym once or twice, and he just gets bored," she said, finishing the last bite of pizza. She wiped her fingers on the napkin. Mike was silent. The only sound was the whisper of tires on the road and the occasional murmur of conversation from the back seat. Something about ancient Egypt, the pyramids, mummies and plans to check the library for books about them.

"I see you and that scruffy mutt, Max, out jogging early in the morning," Mike said after a moment. He glanced over at her, then looked back at the road and the faint red taillights of the car ahead. "Sure you're not getting obsessive about exercise?"

"I like running," she said quietly. "I went through a bad patch when I divorced Tom. Depression, tension—I needed to relax, to learn self-control, meditation. Exercise has been all that for me." She turned her head and studied his face. He wasn't aware she was looking at him. His attention was focused on the fog and his driving; he peered intently at the narrow road before him.

The faint green glow from the dashboard dials and gauges illuminated his face. He wasn't handsome in the classic sense, but he was good-looking in his own way. Broad forehead, tousled dark hair. Deep-set gray eyes. His nose was slightly crooked, his mouth well formed over a strong jawline. His face unquestionably contained both power and appeal—and more than a hint of unyielding single-mindedness.

A man who wouldn't give up easily.

They had reached Wild Goose Farm. As the split-rail fence by the road appeared out of the blanket of fog and they bumped up the driveway, she resolutely put thoughts of him out of her mind. Or at least tried.

# Chapter Three

Despite all her resolution, the memory of Mike's beguiling grin was Shannon's last conscious thought that night before she fell asleep and dreamed.

Rolling green hillsides, a bucolic landscape covered with stately trees, rich farmland and meandering country roads. One led uphill to an abandoned farmhouse that loomed dark and ominous. There was a painted sign creaking in the wind, but though she studied it intently, she couldn't make out the words. Finally, she caught a glimpse of a man walking near the ruined house. She called out, but he disappeared into the trees. As he moved, something silver gleamed at his shoulder. An ax.

She heard the rhythmic chopping sound as it bit deep into a towering tree. The tree swayed slightly, then fell, shaking the earth.

The hand shaking her pulled her out of sleep, every muscle knotted and tense. Max was at the window, barking, his paws scraping the glass. Nick shook her again, then ran to the window and pushed it open. "There's a fire! Mom, wake up, I can see it through the woods."

Oh God, no, the arsonist! She struggled to sit up and fumbled for the lamp. It seemed to take forever to find the switch. Outside, except for sullen streaks of crimson flaring over the trees, the skies were dark. The fog had cleared somewhat; it was windy, and she could smell the smoke.

Grabbing the phone, she dialed the fire emergency number. It rang twice before it was answered. After giving a garbled account of seeing flames through the trees, she told Nick to get dressed. The fire looked as if it was blazing near Mrs. Brennan's house, and God only knew if the old lady had escaped in time.

When she glanced at the clock on the bedside table, she expected it to be two or three in the morning. It was just past midnight.

Since she was wearing her normal and favorite sleeping clothes, an oversize YMCA T-shirt and a pair of underpants, she paused at the bureau to pull out some sweatpants and lace up her running shoes while Nick ran to his room to dress. Then they hurried downstairs.

"Keep Max in the house," she said, snatching up her purse and making sure she had the car keys. A cool night wind touched her face as she opened the door.

"Mom, grab him!" Nick yelled as the dog scampered downstairs and tried to squirm through the opening. She pushed him back with her foot, and Nick yanked him away from the door. "Sorry, I tried to grab him, but he got past me," he said, holding the squirming bundle of fur.

"Never mind," she said. "We have to hurry."

Max's barking grew fainter as they ran to the car and got in.

"Is Mrs. B. gonna be okay? What if she's asleep? Do you think we called in time?" He peppered her with frantic questions as she turned the key in the ignition and prayed that the car would start. It did, reluctantly, coughing and spluttering; but she kept her foot down on the accelerator, and after a moment the engine steadied.

Her hands shook on the wheel. If felt as if she were back in that awful nightmare. She gripped the wheel harder, willing the trembling to stop. Then she took a deep breath and said, "We don't know for sure it's her house burning. There aren't many houses at that end of Pomfret Road, but maybe the fire's farther away than it looks. Distances are confusing, especially at night." She drove as fast as she dared, the car headlights carving a tunnel in the darkness. Nick's window was open, and the acrid smell of smoke was stronger now. She had a terrible feeling of dread, but did not want to frighten Nick. "Don't jump to conclusions. We just don't know—" Her voice stopped as she looked away from the road and into his eyes. She could see he already knew the terrible possibility she didn't want to put into words.

As they turned onto Pomfret Road, she became aware of waves of shimmering heat above the trees. The wind hit her face, and she felt a bead of perspiration on her upper lip vibrate and tickle. She wanted to turn around and go back home, but she kept on up the hill toward Mrs. Brennan's house. The sky was rosy-red, and she heard the sound of glass breaking. "Nick," she said, reaching over to put her right hand on his leg. "Whatever happened, we did all we could. We called the fire department. There's nothing else we could have done."

He didn't answer. She saw his lower lip tremble, but he didn't cry.

Just ahead, there was a line of parked vehicles, fire
trucks and police cars. Shannon pulled over and parked
behind a battered blue pickup truck at the foot of the
driveway. People were milling around. Flames glowed
like liquid curtains in an upstairs window of the house,
and thick black smoke spilled outward, curling up
around the roofline.

She saw Mike's Bronco. He stood near another man,
his eyes fixed on the burning house. "I got her out, but
she was already gone," he was saying. "God knows—
it must have been the smoke, or maybe she struck her
head somehow. There was a bump on the back of her
head." Even as he was speaking, two more fire trucks
pulled up and men piled out, unrolling hoses, and di-
recting streams of water at the flames.

A man wearing a baseball cap brushed past Shannon
in a hurry to get into the blue pickup and drove off.
Shannon barely noticed him; all her concentration was
on Nick by her side, unnaturally silent and still. She
kissed his cheek and hugged him tightly. A terrible sick
feeling knotted the pit of her stomach. They'd been too
late.

Finally, she said gently, "I'm sorry. Mrs. Brennan
was a wonderful person. I know how you felt about her.
We all loved her, honey."

NICK GLANCED UP at his mom. Her face looked white
and tired. The world had changed for him in the last few
minutes. It was there, and yet wouldn't ever be the
same. He was still part of it, but his mind had gone
numb. He could see the firemen still hosing down the
smoking house, but to him there didn't seem much
point. Mrs. B. was dead.

He leaned into his mom's body, willing himself not to hear. Maybe then it wouldn't be real. But he couldn't shut out the shouts of the firemen, the snap and crackle of the flames. His mom's hand gripped his shoulder so tightly it hurt, but he didn't mind the pain.

For some reason, he remembered something Mrs. B. had told him once, her eyes sparkling with humor and spirit. "Life's too short for might-have-beens. Make the most of it. You never know when your time's up." She'd handed him an arrowhead, its surface shiny and gray, chipped at the edges. "Here, keep it. A gift from me to you. Found it out by my back porch, just lying there, some twenty years ago. Frost heaves probably worked it out of the ground. It's an Abenaki, or I'll eat my hat."

Standing in her driveway now, surrounded by the smell of burning wood, he reached into his pocket and touched the arrowhead, feeling the sharp edge nick his finger. It stung a little.

MIKE FINNEGAN TURNED and noticed them standing there. "Shannon, Nick, you all right? You look white as a ghost."

She shook her head slowly, then looked up at him. "I can't believe she's dead. I never met anyone so alive."

"I know. She was a special lady, unforgettable." He sighed and said, "I saw the flames and managed to get here before the whole wing went up." The blanket-shrouded shape on the lawn was being loaded onto a stretcher and carried to the waiting ambulance. Mike led them toward a nearby tree, gently moving them away from the sight.

"What happened?" she asked, casting an uneasy glance back at the house.

"Mrs. Brennan was upstairs in her room. Lying across her bed, already dead. It looks like she was smoking there and accidentally set the room on fire. It's a wonder I got her out at all."

Shannon frowned and looked at the gathering crowd. "What about her niece, Dana, and Dana's little boy, Bart? Mrs. Brennan said they were staying with her."

"One thing to be grateful for," he said grimly. "No one else was in the house."

He could see Shannon was still shaky and a little disoriented. She swallowed and said, "Mrs. Brennan said Dana was going away for the weekend, that she was leaving tonight with her son. But what if she changed her mind?"

He slid a comforting arm around her. "No, I checked. Mrs. Brennan was the only one home. The rest of the house is empty."

A uniformed policeman approached with a pad and pencil. "Mike Finnegan?" he said briskly. "Want to tell me what happened when you got here? What did you see when you went inside?"

"She was upstairs, lying on her bed as if she'd been trying to escape when the smoke overcame her. She must have fallen and hit her head. There was a bruise by her temple." He sighed and said, "I tried to revive her, but it was too late."

The policeman nodded, writing this down. "Did you see cigarettes beside her bed? Sure looks more like a tragic accident than the work of our resident arsonist. So far he's gotten his kicks from torching unoccupied buildings. Setting fire to a house with an old lady inside isn't his pattern." He shrugged. "Maybe he didn't know she was home, but it still doesn't look like his work. Why go all the way upstairs to start the fire? It could have been faulty wiring, or—this is a very old house, built in 1744. It's not uncommon for limestone mortar in brick chimneys to turn to sand after many years, leaving gaps where heat and fire can get into air space around the chimney or behind interior walls. Could be it was spontaneous combustion." Turning to look at the house, he added grimly, "Over the years, the wooden beams are continually exposed to heat. Eventually, that changes their chemical composition and you've got a fire waiting to happen. We see it all the time." He shook his head. "An old house with an old chimney."

"That can be checked out, but Mrs. Brennan kept the house in good repair otherwise," Mike said quietly. "I saw a pack of cigarettes on the bedside table. And an ashtray, a big clamshell."

Shannon stood quietly by Mike's side, her right hand tight on Nick's shoulder. She was numb with shock and sorrow. What a waste. Mrs. Brennan had been so full of life and energy, young at heart. She felt the muscles in Nick's shoulder tense and thought wretchedly, *how do I explain this to him?* How do I make it hurt less?

The confusion of her thoughts added to the difficulty of everything, but she managed, wordlessly, to comfort her son.

But something else niggled at the back of her mind. It wasn't until she'd taken Nick back to the car and told him that they were going home that she remembered what it was: A few hours earlier, the rainy windswept dusk and Mrs. Brennan saying about Paul Wagoner, "Not my favorite person. Smokes like a chimney, a habit I gave up a good many years ago. Cold turkey, I might add."

She told Nick she'd be right back, closed the car door and turned to Mike. "Mrs. Brennan wasn't a smoker," she said flatly. "That's not how the fire started. She told me she'd quit years ago."

Raking a hand through his tousled hair, he sighed. "Look, I didn't see ashes in the clamshell by her bed, but there was a pack of cigarettes. It's a tough habit to give up. Maybe she slipped back."

She shook her head. "It's so hard to believe. She was so alive. Now she's gone. Oh, I don't know. Maybe it was a chimney fire or even the arsonist, damn him."

"I don't think it was him. The police seem to have ruled that out." Mike frowned and added, "Of course, he might have thought the house was empty."

"Damn him, I'd like to—" Shannon began, and then broke off. "What if it was a bungled robbery? If someone broke in and killed her accidentally, then started the fire to cover it up. What if he was looking for money, jewelry, and she woke up? If he had his arms full of things he could hock, and she confronted him . . . Maybe he hit her too hard. You said there was a bruise on her head. He could have gotten scared and panicked, then used kerosene to start the fire."

"Look, I was in the bedroom," he said patiently. "There was no sign of a robbery. She had a TV and a VCR out in the open, on the bureau and no one touched them. No drawers pulled out, no disorder, nothing disturbed. Frankly, you wouldn't have needed kerosene to start that fire. She had piles of combustibles all over the place, stacks of magazines, mending, pillows, rugs, curtains."

Paul Wagoner drove up and parked behind Shannon's car. He got out and stared at the charred wing of the house at the top of the driveway. Part of the roof collapsed, and he let out a soundless whistle. "What is going on? I saw the glow through the trees and heard sirens."

"Mrs. Brennan is dead," Mike said bluntly. "They think it started with a chimney fire. Or smoking in bed."

"My God," Paul muttered. "My God." He walked off to talk to the firemen, leaving Mike and Shannon alone.

Mike laid a hand on her arm as she turned to open the car door. "There was no sign of forced entry. I had to smash a ground-floor window to get in." For the first time, she noticed he'd tied a handkerchief around his left hand to make a rough bandage. It was grimy and stained with blood. "I wasn't very accurate with the damned rock. It was pitch-black." He gave a grim smile. "If there'd been anyone else in that house, I'd have seen him. But there wasn't. She was alone."

She stood motionless beside him, and he could smell the petal-fresh scent of her hair. *Violets,* he thought absently. "God, it's so awful," she said in a faltering voice. "We may never know how Mrs. Brennan died. If it was accidental or not."

"We may clear it up when the arsonist's caught. No one's really safe until then."

How long would it take to catch him, she wondered. And how many people would die? She was frightened.

THE DAY of Mrs. Brennan's funeral, Shannon crawled out of bed at dawn as usual, showered, dressed and woke Nick to tell him to get ready for school. He was groggy and sat up, rubbing his eyes.

"Mrs. B.'s funeral is today," he said with a wide yawn. "Can I go?"

Her first inclination was to say no. He was only eight. But Mrs. Brennan had been a special friend. "Aren't you doing something special at school today?" she asked.

He looked at her blankly for a moment, then nodded as he remembered. "Yeah, the bird museum. We're holding it in the school cafeteria. Everyone's made models of birds and painted shadowboxes. Mine is the great horned owl."

"I know." She smiled. "I supplied the cardboard box and paint."

He climbed out of bed and headed for the bathroom. "I worked on it for two whole weeks. Andy's bird was a cinch, the Franklin gull. Owls are harder to do."

"I didn't know that." She picked up his rumpled jeans and shirt and put them in the clothes hamper. He was brushing his teeth. She could hear water running. Then the water stopped, and he padded back down the hall, his blue eyes round and solemn.

"Mom, Mrs. B.'s funeral. Can I go?"

She sighed. "Yes, if you really want to." He nodded.

"You still have the best part of her friendship, what you shared together. Walks, things she taught you about nature and wildlife."

"I know."

"Well, I'll drop you off at school afterward, okay?" Picking up his sneakers, she carefully untied the double knots.

"Okay."

He looked so forlorn, she reached over to touch his cheek. "I know it's hard, and it's going to be a long day, but things will get better."

"All days are the same in longness," he corrected as he dragged a T-shirt over his head and climbed into jeans. "All the days are twenty-four hours."

"Right, Nick," she agreed with a smile.

THE WHITE CLAPBOARD Congregational Church of Boxford gleamed in the sunlight as the steeple bell tolled eleven o'clock. As the funeral service ended, Shannon and Nick came down the front steps. She noticed Mike Finnegan talking to a small blond woman a few feet ahead of them. She was dressed in black, and a boy about four years old stood by her side. Dana Jennings and her son, Bart, no doubt.

"There's Mike," Nick said. "Can we wait for him?"

"No, you've got to go to school." She unlocked the car and got in, noticing a pickup truck with peeling blue paint parked nearby. The driver raced his engine and backed up with a screech.

"Wow! Look at that!" Nick cried as the truck leaped out onto the main road, barely missing a red Izuzu Trooper. Someone in a big hurry, she thought, frowning. She couldn't make out his features as the truck's sun visor was down, casting a shadow over his face. He was fair-haired, young and muscular. His left arm hung out the window. He wore a red plaid shirt rolled up to the elbow.

She watched as the truck made a rolling stop at the intersection and turned right past the drugstore, tires squealing. After turning on the engine, she backed up with a quick look in the rearview mirror, then pulled out onto the street and braked at the intersection, taking a moment to roll down the car window before turning right.

Oddly, the blue truck had made the same turn only seconds ahead of her, but now it was gone. The truck had disappeared.

Feeling strangely unsettled, she dropped Nick at school and continued home. She dismissed her jitters as understandable; after all, she'd just attended a funeral for a wonderful old woman who shouldn't have died so horribly. Visions of the terrible house fire filled her head. Leaping, devouring flames. Sparks flaring upward in the black night sky, hissing like demons.

She tried to concentrate on the day's schedule. Maybe she'd strip that old pine cupboard in the barn. But the upstairs back hall needed wallpapering. There was time to scrape off the old paper and maybe get in an hour's run before Nick came home from school. Business had been slow lately. Anyway, her part-time assistant, Angela Wallace, had a little boy, Steven, home with the chicken pox. There was a good chance she wouldn't be able to work today.

She eased up on the accelerator as several cars overtook her and drove by. A station wagon, a Bronco II and a gray van with white markings on the side— Something Vision. Probably the local cable TV truck.

The phone was ringing when she got home. It rang twice, and she had her hand out for it when she paused. It might be Mike, she thought. She had asked him to call and now wasn't sure she wanted to talk to him. He was too attractive, sexy, and maddening. Part of her wanted—what? There was an electricity between them, a kind of chemistry she'd been denying all this time. The sound of his voice—low and husky—made her heart pound in a way she hadn't felt in a long time. She admitted she wanted something more. The trouble was, what did Mike want?

"Okay," she said to herself and reached for the phone. "Hello."

"Shannon," said Angela. "I just got back from the doctor's. Steven's better, so I dropped him off at my mother-in-law's. She'll take care of him till suppertime. Want me to work today?"

"I wasn't going to open the shop. Business has been slow in the middle of the week. I thought I'd get in a run, then strip wallpaper in the upstairs hall."

"That old house will fall down around your ears before you're done."

"Right," Shannon agreed ruefully. "Those layers of wallpaper might be all that's holding up the wall."

"Where were you about an hour ago? I called, but got your answering machine."

"Mrs. Brennan's funeral. She had a lot of friends, the church was crowded."

"Charlie told me the medical examiner's report came in. She died of smoke inhalation," Angela said with a long pause. "My mother-in-law thinks our arsonist set fire to the house thinking no one was home. I'm not sure but I think it was an accident. Charlie says you'd be surprised how many times crimes look as if they're related, and they're not."

Charlie was Angela's policeman husband. He was sure to have the most reliable information, Shannon told herself, biting on her lower lip. She didn't want to sound as if she was pumping Angela, but she had such a weird feeling about Mrs. Brennan's death, and she wanted to know everything about it.

"What about the bump on Mrs. Brennan's head? Is there any chance she surprised a burglar who knocked her out, then set the fire."

"Come on, be serious," Angela said. "Everybody knows Nonie Brennan had nothing to steal."

"I don't know," Shannon replied, her mouth prickly and dry. "I just have this feeling—"

Angela sighed. "Listen, it was an accident. Old houses go up in flames sometimes. I don't think the arsonist had anything to do with it. Up till now he's been torching empty sheds and barns. This would be a radical departure in his behavior. Besides, Nonie Brennan didn't have an enemy in the world. Why would anyone want to hurt her?"

"I don't know, but thanks."

"You're welcome," Angela answered. "I gather I haven't convinced you."

"Not altogether, but I appreciate the try. I'm sorry I'm such a pain."

Angela laughed. "You're not a pain, just human. We'll all be on edge until the arsonist is caught. Forget about it. There's nothing you can do, anyway. Want company while you run?"

"Sure, you coming over soon?" Damn, Shannon thought. She sounded as if she was begging for company.

"One o'clock sharp. But don't expect a dazzling new running suit. I've got one pair of running shorts, and my old favorite sweatshirt."

"We're running, not modeling," Shannon said.

"How about taking a thermos of coffee along?"

"Caffeine's not good for you."

"I don't care," Angela said.

"Decaf?"

"You're a hard woman, Shannon."

"You've got that right. See you soon." Shannon hung up first and knew she'd made a decision. She would try to believe Mrs. Brennan's death was an accident, that it had nothing to do with the arsonist. She would believe it until she had no choice. And if that was sticking her head in the sand, so be it.

She glanced at the clock and decided that she had enough time to get started on her stripping project. She collected scrapers and a bucket of water and sponge and lugged them to the upstairs hall. A short while later, she'd torn down almost a quarter of the wallpaper on the left wall. She looked around. A crumpled pile of pink cabbage roses and blue stripes lay at her feet. The right wall was still intact, but stained and bumpy in patches. It wasn't good enough to save, even if she liked the hideous paper, which she didn't.

Downstairs, the back doorbell rang. She put the scraper in the bucket and went to answer it.

A young blond man wearing sunglasses stood outside. He was lean and muscular, dressed in jeans and a red plaid shirt, the sleeves rolled up to his elbows, revealing an elaborate dragon tattoo on his left forearm. Behind him in the driveway was parked a blue pickup truck. The same man she'd seen tear out of the church parking lot in such a hurry. Now he removed the sunglasses and looked at her with unblinking blue eyes. Something about his stare completely unsettled her.

"The shop's closed for the day," she said, quickly, moving to close the door but it wouldn't move. He was holding it back, leaning on it, giving the clear message he would not be leaving until he got what he came for.

# Chapter Four

"I'm answering your ad. About the apartment."

She'd forgotten about the ad she'd placed in the Boxford paper last week. "Furnished apartment in barn in exchange for skilled carpentry and rough yardwork at Wild Goose Farm."

"My name's Tim Carver. Looks like your barn needs a new roof," he said with a grin. "I can do that, no problem. Order the shingles, I'll take care of the rest." He smiled again, and she felt her edginess subside. He was just a man looking for work and a place to stay. Times were tough. A lot of people were looking for work.

He waved at the canvas-shrouded shape in the back of his truck. "I got my own tools, a table saw and most anything else I need to fix your roof. I've got references, too. My Uncle Don owns Lucky Dry Cleaners downtown, and I've done a lot of work for the high school and the Congregational Church."

She smiled politely. "I thought I saw you down there this morning."

He shrugged. "Just finished working on the staircase in the bell tower."

Maybe he wasn't a good driver; well, she'd settle for a workmanlike carpenter. But—with the arsonist loose, she wanted to make sure he was who he said he was. So she copied down the names and telephone numbers he gave as references and made a few phone calls to the high school principal and the congregational minister and Tim's uncle. They all had high praise for Carver. Several minutes later, satisfied, she offered him the apartment and the job. "There's a woodstove and a bath. You can move right in, there's fresh linen on the bed. Oh, and there are shingles in the barn. You can get started on the roof right away."

She found the key to the apartment in the rack by the door, stepped out onto the porch and gestured for him to follow. "The apartment's in the barn."

They walked across the driveway. Grass and weeds poked through the stones beneath their feet. He glanced at her sideways. "You owned the farm long?"

"About six months," she said. "It still needs work."

"Outside could use painting," he replied, looking at the side of the barn. The old red paint was faded and peeling.

"The apartment might give you a surprise." Smiling, she unlocked the door and stepped back so he could go in first.

It was a three-room apartment, well-windowed and spotless. She had furnished it with antiques from her shop and the effect was warm and inviting. She pushed open the door on the right. "The bedroom."

He gazed around and nodded, satisfied. "Looks great. I'll get started on the barn roof right away, long as you already got shingles."

She showed him where the ladder was stored. He picked it up and tossed it over his shoulder as if it were weightless. A short while later, he'd begun stripping old shingles off the roof.

She watched him for a while longer. He was about twenty-three. Vivid blue eyes and regular features. But he seemed strung out, tense.

When he came down the ladder, he said he had gone through all the shingles in the barn. He offered to pick up more at the lumberyard.

"Let me call and order them," she said. He followed her into the kitchen while she made the phone call, and as there was a pot of minestrone soup already on the stove and she saw him looking at it hungrily, she offered him some.

Finishing his second helping, he asked if she'd seen the fire the other night, at the Brennan house. "They buried poor Mrs. Brennan this morning." He shook his head. "Bad thing, that."

"Horrible."

He looked around her wood-paneled kitchen. "These old places go up like matchsticks. You gotta be real careful. Guess that Mrs. Brennan just wasn't careful enough." His eyes shifted suddenly, and he caught her staring.

"Last I heard, they didn't know how the fire started." Shannon hoped he wouldn't notice that her voice was a little high.

He shrugged. "Guess fire's as good a way to leave this world as any other." He pushed his chair back and got to his feet. "Thanks for the soup. I'll go pick up those shingles now."

The door banged behind him, and the dog, Max, stirred briefly in his sleep on the rug by the stove. Shannon scratched his ears. "Great watchdog. A

stranger's in the house, and you sleep like a baby."
Max's tail thumped once, and he went back to sleep.

A rap at the back door. It was Angela in a sweat-shirt, shorts and sneakers, ready for their run. They planned to cover about five miles, around the conservation land, down by the pond and back again. About an hour and a half, depending on weather and traffic.

They set off at a good pace, and the time sped past. It hardly seemed possible that it was three-thirty when they rounded the last corner before Wild Goose Farm and eased into a slow jog up the narrow driveway and around back. Shannon slowed to a walk and glanced over at the barn. No sound of hammering, and Tim Carver's pickup truck was gone. Maybe he was still at the lumberyard.

"Let's go slower next time," Angela said, panting.

Shannon looked at her friend, who was drenched in sweat, and grinned. "Okay."

"I've gotta go, I'm late," Angela gasped, looking at her wristwatch. "See you later." She drove off with a wave of the hand, and Shannon unlocked the front door.

In the living room, Nick was munching popcorn and watching a TV documentary about flying saucers. He looked up at his mother, swallowed and said, "Hi, mom. Early release from school today. When I came home, the door was locked. I had to climb in a window."

"I'm sorry. I don't know how I could have forgotten," Shannon said, frowning. Just then the doorbell rang.

It was Mike. He held up a bowl covered with aluminum foil. "I remembered you had class tonight, right? And your car probably hasn't been fixed yet—stop me if I'm wrong. Anyway, I brought my special potato salad, too much mayonnaise and too many onions, the way the kids like it."

"I—I..." she stammered, pushing her hair back.

"Look," he said with a shrug, thinking she seemed tired. "Am I getting the wrong vibrations? Would you rather we did this another time?"

"No, come on in. I'm just a little harassed. I wanted to finish stripping wallpaper in the upstairs hall, and there's never any time." She stood back to let him enter.

"Mom, the phone rang a couple of times, but no one was on the line when I picked up," Nick said, taking another handful of popcorn. He looked around. "Hi, where's Andy and Chris?"

"Right behind me," Mike replied, laughing as the children came in, plopped down on the couch and helped themselves to popcorn.

"Maybe it was one of your pals kidding around," Shannon said, pushing down the scary thought that it was the arsonist checking to see if people were home before he struck.

"No way," Nick said loudly.

"Ssh," Andy muttered, poking him in the side. "This flying saucer stuff is real neat."

"Yeah, I like spaceships," Chris chimed in.

"Be quiet!" Andy said loftily.

Relative quiet descended on the living room, and noticing Shannon giving the phone a long look, Mike said, "Probably just a wrong number."

She turned and smiled at him. "Let me take a quick shower. Beer's in the fridge, or there's coffee or tea, if you'd rather."

He popped two beers while she showered upstairs. When she came down, they sat at the kitchen table, within hearing distance of the end of the program on flying saucers. Shannon found the story about the fire at Mrs. Brennan's on page two of the newspaper, read it quickly and passed it across the table to him.

"The police are being flooded with complaints," he said, looking at the article. "Everyone in Boxford has seen someone suspicious lurking around their house. It's only natural, I guess, considering the arsonist has struck all over town. But the police are having a hard time chasing down every call." He smiled over the paper at Shannon. "I guess it's good that people are keeping a sharp eye out."

"Uh-huh," Shannon agreed. "You think the arsonist will strike again so soon?"

"You want the truth?" Mike said. He picked a green apple from the bowl in front of him, took a bite and chewed thoughtfully before he continued. "Truth is, I don't know what to think. He's got to be a nut. Maybe he watches too much TV. It gives him ideas." She gave him a worried look, and Mike mentally kicked himself. "So," he went on, "if you think the arsonist calls before coming by to set a fire, get yourself an unlisted number. Stay close to Nick. Listen, it was probably just a wrong number on the phone. Whoever it was heard Nick's voice, knew it was just a kid and hung up."

"Sounds reasonable in the daylight, but I'm not so sure about when the sun goes down," she said, with a deep sigh that lifted her breasts under her gray sweatshirt.

He watched lights gleam in her dark hair as she tilted her head back and drank her beer. Her face, her smooth pale skin touched with rose, her fringed blue eyes, all held a subtle reserve where he was concerned. He had only himself to blame, he acknowledged. They'd struck sparks off each other right from the start, but he'd resented her air of independence. That look on her lovely face that said, "I'm living my life on my terms, not yours."

He sipped his beer and wondered what it would feel like to have the length of her body pressed against his, from her breasts to her thighs. To feel her lips open under his.

From the living room, a man's voice intoned solemnly, "Thousands of sightings of UFOs have been reported all over the world. The latest is from our correspondent in Brazil."

"I hate that nonsense," Shannon said, shaking her head. "Sorry."

"I hate it, too," Mike admitted. "May they outgrow UFOs soon. I'm sick and tired of hearing about the Plains of Nazca and the Bermuda Triangle. Come to think of it, they've been on a mummy kick lately. I don't know which is worse."

Just then the phone rang, and Shannon got up and called to Nick, "I'll get it." From the sound of the TV, the children were now engrossed in sightings from Russia.

She picked up the receiver on the fourth ring. "Hello?"

Only silence at the other end of the line.

But someone was there. She could hear him. Maybe whoever it was hadn't heard her. So she tried again, louder this time. "Hello." Still no answer, just a weird silence. "Look, I'm going to hang up," she said through clenched teeth. She waited another second, holding her breath, then there was a little click and the line went dead. Whoever was on the other end had hung up first.

Damn! She slammed down the receiver, telling herself the caller couldn't possibly be the psycho arsonist. No, just a normal, run-of-the-mill crank.

Mike came down the hall. "Who was it?"

"No one, she said grimly. "No one was there."

AT THE SAME TIME, the man with ice-blue eyes turned away from his phone and toward his companion who stood by a window. "She's home now. She answered the phone."

"You've been watching her. That's her usual schedule. Afternoon run, and she's back a little before three-thirty, just before the school bus."

He tried to picture Shannon Hollister in his mind. Strong, slender, pretty. He'd seen her like that maybe a dozen times in the past few days, driving by in her car, walking down to her mailbox, running. Her eyes, deep blue and fringed with thick lashes, magic eyes burning into his brain. Driving him crazy. Why did she have to get in their way? He didn't like taking unnecessary risks. It didn't pay. It was asking for trouble. He poured himself a shot of bourbon and watched the brown liquid swirl in the glass. "Just tell me what you want me to do."

"We agreed. She's trouble. We have to get rid of her, and soon."

He sighed. "I think we've got more talking to do. If Shannon Hollister dies, the heat will really be on. The old lady's one thing. I made it look like an accident. Even if they find kerosene started the fire at the Brennan house, they'll blame it on the arsonist. We're in the clear. But we can't set another fire so soon, it'll look suspicious. That's not the arsonist's pattern. No, we have to think of some other way to get rid of her."

"Run her down while she's out jogging. Make it look like a hit-and-run accident. Just be sure she's dead." A pause, then "What happened this afternoon? You said you were going to do it today."

"I couldn't. She wasn't alone. Someone else was running with her."

"We can't wait too long."

The man with blue eyes glanced up, annoyed, *"I told you she wasn't alone. I couldn't do it."*

"Getting cold feet? It's a little late for that."

He took another swallow, the bourbon burning all the way down. "The other woman could have given a description of the car to the police. I'd have to get rid of it sooner than we planned."

"What's the difference? You smeared mud on the license plate, right? So the woman would have seen a car hit her friend. All her attention would be on her friend. She'd be hysterical, half out of her mind, wouldn't remember a thing. Even if she did, eyewitness accounts are notoriously inaccurate."

"What if she's got a photographic memory and saw my face? What if she remembered every damn thing she saw? It'd be just my luck." He put the glass down with a bang and leaned back, folding his arms. "I'd rather do it at night, when no one's around."

"What about her son? Did he see you when he was in the woods with Mrs. Brennan?"

"I don't think so."

"But you're not sure, are you?"

"No, and until I'm damn sure I'm not touching an eight-year-old kid," he said angrily.

"Okay, leave him alone for now. If he causes trouble, we'll get rid of him. But we've got to take care of his mother soon."

"YOU SAID something about stripping wallpaper. Let me give you a hand with it." Mike propelled Shannon toward the stairs.

"Well, if you don't mind—"

"If I minded, I wouldn't have suggested it," he said, smiling. Keep her busy and she'd forget about that crank phone call, he thought.

As he followed her upstairs, they passed the window on the landing, and he paused and said quietly, "Who's that on your barn roof?"

Something about the way he said that put her back up. Keeping her voice even, she explained about her having hired a part-time carpenter. Mike nodded, still eyeing Tim's rangy figure skeptically.

"So long as you had the sense to check his references."

"I did," she snapped. "And they couldn't have been better." Who did he think he was, telling her what to do? She glared at him. He shrugged and wandered down the hall toward the pile of crumpled wallpaper.

"You're not using a steamer."

"They cost money," she muttered. "Anyway, the paper comes off with a scraper. Most of it's falling off by itself." She gave an ironic shrug.

Turning, he moved a step toward her. "I said you looked tired, and you do. Using muscles you ordinarily don't. I'm pretty good at massage." One look at Shannon's stormy blue eyes, however, and he backed off. "No?" he said affably. "Then put me to work. Give me a scraper. We'll finish this wall and then feed the kids."

They worked for forty-five minutes, at the end of which they'd stripped one wall completely, and half of the other. They lugged the discarded paper outside to be hauled to the dump. Tim had deserted the barn roof, but his truck was still parked in the driveway.

Mike glanced toward the barn. "Where's your live-in carpenter?"

"How should I know? Maybe he's getting more nails, maybe he's taking a break," she said defensively, hating herself for even giving Mike an explanation. It was none of his business where Tim was. He hadn't hired Tim, she had. She glared at him again, but he wasn't looking her way. He was staring at the front of the house.

# Chapter Five

"You know, there's something peculiar about the proportions of this house," Mike said after a moment. "I can't quite put my finger on it, but it looks like there should be another window. There, in the side ell. The second floor." He pointed to the right side of the house from which jutted a shedlike addition. Shannon could see what he meant. There was a window on the ground floor, but none on the second floor.

"Who knows," she said briskly. "Maybe they turned a small room upstairs into a closet. It doesn't matter."

"It matters to me," he corrected. "Architects are always curious about missing windows, especially in old houses. By rights there should be a window upstairs, and there isn't. Why not?"

"Your guess is as good as mine." She shrugged, and after another thoughtful look at the front of the house, he followed her inside.

He stopped at the back staircase to run his hand down a corner beam. "Nice old construction. Edges still crisp on the moldings. Not too many layers of paint. Do you know anything about the history of the house?"

"Not much," Shannon acknowledged. "The town clerk's records go back to the early 1700s. Jared Ewing built the original cottage of braced frame and brick, clapboards outside and plastered inside. He was the tax collector and town judge." She looked around the narrow back hall. "It seems every owner since has added on to the house."

"You're lucky, though," he said, nodding. "Woodwork's hand-planed, beaded-edged cherry, and most of it's still here. Flooring, doors, mantels, even chair rails. It's a nice old house." He paused at the stairway door, standing on the step above her, and reached his hand down to touch the door latch. "This is special. You don't see many of these, an old tulip-bud thumb latch." His voice held a quizzical note and his eyes smiled down at her. "Do you ever get a sense of the people who lived here in the past?"

"If you mean do we have ghosts floating around and rattling chains, no." She smiled and fingered a worn spot on the banister where generations of hands had rubbed the wood to a polished glow. "But I'd have to be deaf, dumb and blind not to be aware of the past. It's all around me."

He nodded and gazed critically at the walls. "Be careful what you strip away. There could be some historic murals underneath this old wallpaper. Rufus Porter, who worked all over New England in the 1800s, is said to have painted landscapes on the walls of a few houses here in Boxford." He grinned down at her. "You might get lucky and find out you're living with a genuine Porter."

He went up a step and examined the stairway wall carefully, running a hand now and then across the surface. While he studied it, she watched him. His lean cheeks were freshly shaven. His dark hair was clean and a little windblown, curling down over his collar. The bronze of his arms, neck and throat contrasted with the white of his shirt, making him look strong, healthy and male. Suddenly the hallway seemed claustrophobic.

She drew a sharp breath and said, "I'm starved. Want to feed the kids now?"

MIKE GRILLED hamburgers, and Shannon made a tossed salad and fixed a pitcher of root beer. Everything was set on the table just as the three children straggled in, complaining about hunger. Nick poured three glasses of root beer and passed them around. "We need some shovels, Mom, and a net like one of those fishing nets."

"What for?" she asked, doling out the potato salad Mike had brought over.

Andy and Nick exchanged guilty looks, and Chris piped up, "We're playing knights and dragons. We need to dig a dragon trap."

"You kids have seen too many movies," Mike said, after finishing a massive bite of his hamburger. He glanced at Shannon and said with a smile, "Speaking of which, 'I suddenly felt shaken in a way which I had never experienced before.'"

"Shakespeare," Shannon said. It was a wild guess, but the best she could do.

"Ingmar Bergman, *Wild Strawberries,*" Mike said with a laugh. "'An idle mind is the devil's playground.'"

"That sounds like the Bible," she tried in between bites of hamburger.

*"The Music Man,"* Mike said. "'Trouble in River City.'"

"You're too good at this," she accused.

Chuckling, he pushed the remaining hamburger on the plate in front of the children. "Eat." Turning to Andy, he said, "This week we are going to get your hair cut. It's too long."

Andy pulled a long lock of red hair down his forehead. It reached all the way to the tip of his nose. Chris and Nick laughed, and the two boys reached for the last hamburger at the same time. Shannon cut it in half and they devoured it. Chris drank the rest of her root beer and said, "The lady down the street from us had a new baby. Suzanne, she's in my class. She's the baby's big sister."

Andy grinned. "That's not what you said earlier. You said Suzanne had a baby."

"I didn't mean that. Suzanne's only six." Chris put her hands on her hips.

"So?" Andy said, looking superior.

"You're teasing me and it's not funny," Chris snapped. "Suzanne's mom had the baby," she explained.

"Who's Suzanne?" Andy asked solemnly.

"You know," Chris said in exasperation. "She lives down the street. Stop teasing."

He crossed his eyes and said, "Cross my eyes and hope to die, I forgot Suzanne lives down the street."

"Dad," Chris whined.

"Okay, Andy, enough is too much," Mike said, reaching across the table to ruffle his son's red hair. "Cut it out." He glanced at Shannon and said quietly. "We're sure a noisy lot. Are you sure you want to have anything to do with two red-haired kids and their father?"

She didn't answer in words, just a Mona Lisa smile.

AN HOUR AFTER Mike left Shannon off at the Y, she looked around at her assembled students and thought that it was one of those nights. Nothing was going right. Twenty-three bodies were moving more or less to her instruction, but she could tell that their thoughts were elsewhere. To compensate, she turned the volume up on the cassette player as Handel's *Water Music* came on.

She tried to focus on something solid, like the starter problem on her car and the fact that the brakes were going, but instead, she kept recalling the phone call she'd had that afternoon. It was so eerie. She knew someone was there, but he'd said nothing. The only sound he'd made was when he hung up moments later.

It had definitely not been Andy. Nick had already asked him about it, and Andy said, no, he hadn't been home most of the afternoon. Maybe it was just some teenager playing a joke, she told herself. A bad joke. Or it could have been a wrong number, and the caller had been too rude or embarrassed to admit he'd made a mistake.

She was making too much of it, she told herself, and struggled to think about colors, urged her body to absorb thoughts about feeling strong and well, and for the next few minutes fought to banish her fears. Her neck felt hot and gritty, and she rubbed it with her hand.

A woman in front suddenly groaned, "Must be ninety-five degrees in here." It was Nancy Davis, and her face was fire-engine red. She was trying, without much success, to do deep knee bends to the music, which was just ending.

Shannon changed the tape and said encouragingly to the class, "Do what you feel you can. It's warm tonight. If you want to rest a while, we can do that."

More or less as a group, they voted to keep going. She nodded, and they changed the routine to jumping jacks.

Nancy Davis's eyes widened in terror. Her mouth went slack and her cheeks flushed an even deeper red. She looked as if she was going to collapse.

"Nancy," Shannon said softly, moving to her side. Around them, nineteen women and three men worked out to the soft tape of the Mainz Chamber Orchestra playing a Brandenberg concerto.

Nancy stared at Shannon with pleading eyes. Shannon had seen that look many times. It said, let me out of here. Let me go home. If I can't lose weight, at least spare me humiliation before I have a heart attack.

Shannon looked back at her evenly, no smile but no threat, no sign of disappointment. It was relatively quiet except for Nancy's labored breathing, the music and the thump thump of a runner on the overhead track that circled the gym. She preferred no distractions, but the athletic director wouldn't close the track during her class.

"If you quit now—" Shannon said softly so that the knee-benders around her couldn't hear "—you'll hate yourself, me and the world. If you stay with it, there's a new woman waiting in the mirror."

"I just can't," Nancy panted, rubbing her sweating forehead with her forearm.

"I know you can," Shannon said firmly.

"I'll try," Nancy gasped, holding her right hand to her chest, where she obviously thought her heart was. Not exactly a commitment, but it was a step.

Shannon backed away slowly, watching the rest of the class work out. Back in front of the group, Shannon rubbed her hands on her black tights, adjusted the sweatband on her head, and softly said, "Okay, change." They looked up and watched her lean forward, almost touching her head to her knees without bending her legs.

The rest of the session took about twenty more minutes and ended with a final quarter-mile run around the overhead track. Shannon let herself be taken up by the running. The music helped her sense time, know when to come out of the workout.

Besides, Mike had promised to come back and pick her up in the parking lot at nine. He had even arranged for a sitter to stay with the three children.

Just a lift home, she told herself firmly. Casual, friendly, nothing more. She let out a long breath and slowed to a walk. Who was she kidding? Casual had nothing to do with the way she felt about Mike.

When she came back down the stairs, she told the departing class that she'd see them on Wednesday. She considered a special word for Nancy Davis but decided against it. Nancy would have to find the determination to stick to it on her own.

Slinging a towel around her damp neck, she walked through the deserted gym. There was a slight echo now that it was empty. A window was open, creating a slight draft. A wisp of cool night air touched the perspiration on Shannon's forehead. From the weight room came the sound of heavy metal bouncing on a mat, followed by a male voice swearing softly.

Someone had dropped a weight. He needed a spotter. She sighed and checked her wristwatch. A few minutes after nine. The gym was closing, and the staff would be leaving shortly. She had just enough time for a shower.

OUTSIDE in the parking lot, Mike switched off the car engine and glanced over at the Y entrance. Two or three people came out, crossed to their cars and drove off. The light by the entrance flickered out. Must be closing time, he thought. But no sign of Shannon. She was showering, probably. He glanced at the clock numerals glowing on the dashboard. Nine-ten. He hoped he hadn't missed her, and decided he'd give her another fifteen minutes before checking inside.

THERE WAS a night-light on in the woman's locker room. She flipped on the overhead, went to her locker, turned the combination, opened it and pulled out the change of clothes she kept there. She stripped, feeling the moisture on her body, the sticky sweat drying on her skin. A cool breeze, brief but pleasant, came from a slightly open window and rippled over her. She tiptoed to the shower room off the locker area, turned on one of the lights, put her towel, soap and shampoo down and turned on the shower. The water thudded hard and warm against her. She let it hit her shoulders, her back, her neck, and then turned to let it bounce between her breasts and down between her legs. It felt good. Everyone on this side of the building had left for the night. Although there was usually a watchman and a janitor on duty all night, they were confined to the office side of the building, and seldom ventured into the gym. If Mike weren't waiting for her in the parking lot, she'd go through the far door of the shower room and plunge into the pool naked, but she was... And then she heard it.

The sound seemed to come from the locker area but with the water on she couldn't be sure. She glanced toward the door to the locker room and then went back to soaping herself. The second sound was louder, the clanking of metal on metal. She rinsed herself quickly and turned off the water.

"Is someone there? Mike?"

There was no answer. She toweled off rapidly, keeping her eyes on the door. It couldn't be anything to worry about.

She couldn't let her imagination make such a big deal about a creaking locker and a faint breeze.

She rubbed her hair with the towel and told herself to get a grip, and then she heard it again. There was no doubt about the sound this time. It was coming from the locker room. It's nothing, she thought, but edged cautiously to the pool-room door. To her relief, it was open.

Moonlight streamed through the high window, hitting the surface of the water, which lapped gently in the darkness. Visible through lacy tree branches outside, the moon shone in fragments of silver. Shannon looked around the pool and up to the empty balcony. She moved slowly, her towel wrapped around her. The door to the pool office was open, and she walked, barefoot, and paused at the inner door that led to the rear of the locker room. If someone was there, she would be behind him. Opening the door slowly, carefully, she willed it to be quiet, and it obeyed. She heard water running. A faucet in the corner sink. The lights were out, and she tried to remember if she'd turned them off when she'd gone into the shower. She didn't think she had, but that wasn't necessarily anything to worry about. The night janitor might simply have come down, seen the lights on and turned them off... but he would have heard the water running, would have looked in there and turned that off, too. Reaching down, she turned the water off, herself.

The locker room had only two small opaque windows on the far side of the room. Shannon stood for a moment, letting her eyes adjust to the dim light, trying to breathe deeply and quietly. She saw nothing as she moved slowly to her locker in the corner. She stepped into her jeans and sweater and sat down on the bench to put on her shoes when a low, hoarse voice shattered the stillness.

An eerie whisper: "You're dead."

She jumped to her feet, holding her sneaker in her hand, straining to see into the darkness. God, God, no, she said, but she said it to herself. He had to be a madman. Oh God!

The man stepped out of the darkness, into a vague beam of light from the windows. He was dressed completely in black down to his black ski mask. He held up leather-gloved hands, flexing them menacingly. He was tall, well-built, muscular. His shoulders were taut, his arms sinewy. He was about one-eighty to two hundred pounds, and she was no match for him.

There was only one way to go. Shannon threw her shoe at his head and ran for the door to the gym without waiting to see if she'd hit him. She heard the shoe connect with a locker, quickly followed by his footsteps coming after her.

She took the stairs upward two at a time trying not to think of those gloved hands reaching out to grab her, pull her back into the darkness. When she got to the gym level, she pushed on the door. Locked. She pushed her weight onto the door to the gym offices. It, too, was locked. There was only one place to go. He lunged for her, panting as he hit the top of the stairs, and she went up the next flight of metal steps, knowing there was only the track over the gym and the handball courts in front of her. There was no way out.

DOWN IN the parking lot, Mike rubbed the back of his neck, easing away a slight crick. What time was it? Nine-twenty. He glanced at the entrance of the building again. Dark, and there was still no sign of her.

He frowned, wondering if somehow he'd missed her. Could she have come out, not noticed his car and got a lift home with one of her students? She could be home right now, thinking he'd forgotten all about her.

Maybe he should drive down to the telephone booth in front of the drugstore. Give her house a call. If the baby-sitter answered, he'd know she was probably still back at the gym. It'd only take a minute to double-check, he thought. Good idea.

He turned the key and the engine started with a muted purr. Whistling softly, he backed out of the parking lot and headed out onto Main Street, braking as a van whipped by. Soon, the thin vapor of his exhaust disappearing beneath the lights of the parking lot, Mike's car was lost in the stream of traffic.

THE DOOR TO the overhead track was open. Shannon went in, dashed down the banked track and broke into a run. She wasn't used to running barefoot and the track felt weirdly soft and warm under her feet. The windows on the far side of the small track let in light from the parking lot.

She heard the man in black running behind her. She could see that the windows were closed. There was no time to open them and scream. Even if she did, they were on the third floor and Mike would never hear her over the steady roar of Main Street traffic. The walls of the old building were thick and there was no chance that Frank, the janitor, or Cliff, the night watchman, would hear her, either.

When the footsteps behind her faded a bit, she dared to slow and look over her shoulder. The man had stopped, trying to catch his breath. He looked menacing, faceless, terrifying. His chest heaved, and she sensed him glaring at her through his black mask.

She halted when she was on the far side of the track, away from him, and they looked at each other across the unfathomable darkness of the gym below them. He leaned forward on the steel railing, and she did the same. Looking downward toward the gym floor, it felt as if they were standing on the rim of a bottomless pit.

"If you don't stop—" he panted "—you'll regret it."

His voice echoed off the walls, and all she knew was stark, icy fear.

The man pushed away from the railing and took off in the opposite direction. Shannon was paralyzed with fear and anger. It took a remarkable effort to force her trembling legs to move. She noted that he'd stopped again. Shock rippled down her spine as she realized that he had placed himself in front of the only exit from the track.

"I'll get you now, bitch," he whispered. "Bitch, bitch, bitch" echoed faintly from the fathomless darkness. "My partner's coming up here shortly, and we'll have you circled. So, baby, you just stand there and wait."

She struggled to catch her breath as she wondered if he could be bluffing.

"Just stand there, lady. I'll just look at you, and we'll wait for my partner."

While he was talking, hidden in the corner except for the dim shape of his legs, she heard a faint sound from deep below in the locker room. She strained to see if the madman had heard it, too, but in the darkness she couldn't tell. She had to do something, had to act before his partner appeared. A scream wouldn't do any good. It would only echo off the thick concrete walls and expose her hiding place.

She backed slowly to the wall, up the incline of the track, careful to stay in the shadows, her bare toes pushing to keep her from slipping. A slight breeze from behind indicated that a window was open a crack. Another sound came from below, coming closer. The man in black laughed softly, and his voice seemed frighteningly close. "I'll get you, sweetheart. I've got a knife. You'll feel what it's like, *way up inside.*"

She almost gagged in horror.

Her abdominal muscles were tight with fear. Her mouth was dry, and her noisy breathing seemed to fill the gym like a rushing wind. Yet her hearing was so acute she could make out the soft scrape of his shoe on the track as he moved toward her. The window was her only way out.

She sucked in her stomach and forced herself to turn her back on him and focus her attention on the window. Her hands went up and pushed at the window sash. The bottom rail stuck on one side, and she trembled at the heavy thud of his footsteps as he came around the track. Relentlessly coming for her.

It was taking too long! The window had stuck. She forced herself to stop and realign the bottom rail, then threw up the sash, all the while expecting to feel his hands grab her ankles. With a massive effort, she pushed herself through the open window.

There was a narrow ledge outside, about three feet wide, with a three-story drop to the parking lot. Her heart sank as she saw that the lot was empty. Mike's car was nowhere to be seen. Had he got tired of waiting and left? Oh God, she'd have to get herself out of this alone.

The plan came without much thought. She lay back, the gravel of the ledge scratching her back through her thin sweater. She lay with her head over the ledge and her feet pointing at the rectangular darkness of the open window. Above her, the nearly full moon was covered by a slowly moving cloud. Any other time, she might have been able to enjoy its beauty. She could hear the man in black scrambling after her. His fingers curled over the edge of the window in the moonlight, and then his hooded head appeared. He looked out, at first not seeing her until he looked downward. Then their eyes met, and he started to wedge his way through the window.

"I'm gonna enjoy this."

"Like hell you are!" And then she kicked. With both feet, her back pushing against the gravel and with all the strength she had, she kicked at him. Her bare feet caught his neck. She could feel spittle on her heels as he gave a wild, animal cry and tumbled backward onto the track. She watched him fall back down the incline, his mouth open. Startled, he groped awkwardly to stop himself sliding toward the railing, inexorably downward toward the gym floor below.

As she scrambled up to the window to see, she thought she heard someone calling her name. *Mike.*

"I'm out on the window ledge, beyond the track," she yelled, fingers gripping the sill until her knuckles whitened with strain. And she heard another sound from deep within the building. Mike, and he was running.

The masked man stumbled to his feet and moved along the track in the direction of the door. "You're dead!"

"Leave me alone!" she yelled. "Who are you? What do you want?"

"I want you dead."

Tears were on her cheeks, tears of rage and helplessness. Her fists clenched. "Leave me alone!"

The man in black continued to move toward the door. It opened, and he snarled, "I'll get you. I'll get you," just as the door slammed back against the wall. The echo rattled the window glass.

She pushed herself back inside and stood on the track, her breath heaving in gasps of adrenaline and fright. He was gone, thank God!

Just then, a second masked figure appeared, much shorter than the first, standing near the doorway, blocking the way. The man in black took a step backward into the gym. In that moment Mike's voice cut through the darkness. "Are you all right, Shannon? Where are you?" he called, puzzled, muscles tensing as he suddenly saw the short man in the doorway.

"Mike, watch out!" she shouted, as the taller man lunged at him. Too late, Mike saw the flash of silver as it sank into his shoulder. He toppled back, with a muttered curse.

From the track above, Shannon could hear grunting and the sound of something tumbling down the stairs.

"Mike," she shouted, starting to run toward the door of the track, the door leading to the man in black and Mike, who was now bleeding from the shoulder.

She bolted through the doorway and hit the light switch. As she went hurrying down the stairs, she only partly formed an idea of what she'd do if the other man appeared before her. She could leap down at him, trying to knock him off-balance. She tried not to think of what that leap would do to her. All she knew was that something had happened to Mike, and she couldn't stand there on the track and wait for help. There was no one there when she reached the alcove outside the gym. But the lights in the hall were now on, and before she could stop herself, she slipped on a stream of blood.

Darkened steps led downward. She flipped on the light switch. "Mike?" Two small bulbs down the stairway popped on, and at the bottom she could see the crumpled form. Mike wasn't moving. She took the stairs two at a time, holding the railing.

# Chapter Six

"Mike!" No answer, and no sign of life until she knelt next to him. His head was awkwardly leaning against the wall, and blood was seeping from a slit in his sweater, forming a sticky puddle beneath him. He was breathing heavily, but he was breathing.

"Mike," she repeated softly, touching his head and looking around at the door to the locker room.

"Damn punk," he gasped. "I twisted the knife out of his hand, and I managed to slash his arm, but he got away." Then his eyes opened and he looked up the stairs. Shannon turned her head quickly to see what was there, but there was nothing.

"Are you okay?" he gasped, his eyes searching her face.

"I'm fine, but I'm going for help," she said, brushing back his thick, curly hair. "I'll be back in a few seconds."

Mike's answer was to close his eyes. She could see that his skin was pale. A thin film of perspiration covered his upper lip. She had to get help, and fast.

She got to her feet and moved to the locker-room door. Opening it, she plunged into the darkness, not knowing what to expect as she darted across the floor to the stairs. When she reached the upper door, she pushed, sending it back with a slam.

No one at the locker-room desk; well, she hadn't expected to see anyone. She ran past it, down the darkened hallway to the main desk. Maybe the night watchman was on duty.

"Help!" she panted. "There's a . . ."

The watchman looked up at her, frowning. He had a folded cloth in his hands. It fell to the floor. "Something wrong, Mrs. Hollister?"

"Plenty, Cliff," she said breathlessly. "There's a man on the floor outside the gym. He's been stabbed. Did you see another man come out this way? Wearing black, with a ski mask."

The watchman's frown deepened as he shook his head. "Naw, nobody's come this way. 'Course, I been pickin' up trash out by the handball courts. You wouldn't b'lieve the mess some people leave." He scratched his chin and gave her a long look. "You say somebody's hurt? Stabbed?"

She could see it in his eyes. He thought she was drunk or insane. Catching a glimpse of herself in the mirror behind him, she realized she looked crazy. Her dark hair was wild, her sweater filthy with dust and gravel, and her bare feet bruised and stained with blood. There was blood on her hands, too.

"Hey, take it easy," he said, and over his shoulder he called, "Frank, come out here now, will you, quick."

"I'm not crazy," Shannon insisted. "Get on the phone. Call an ambulance—the police—and for God's sake, come and help me. A man's been stabbed."

A nearby door opened, and the janitor appeared, bucket and mop in hand. He looked at the watchman. "What's goin' on, Cliff?"

The watchman shrugged. "Geez, I dunno. Mrs. Hollister says some guy's been stabbed. Better call the cops. Use the phone in the main office. It should still be working."

"Okay, if you say so." The janitor stared at Shannon with some doubt for a second, then put down the mop and bucket with a shrug and moved down the hall toward the main office.

The watchman turned to Shannon and said loudly over his shoulder, "I'm goin' with Mrs. Hollister to check on the guy. Do like I say, Frank. Call the cops first, then the ambulance." He jerked his head down the darkened hallway and said to Shannon, "Show me."

As she padded down the hall, she heard the janitor's yell of surprise from behind them. "We been robbed! Somebody's been in the office, turned the place upside down! It's a guldarn mess in here!" Then came the faint sounds of his phone call to the police.

Shannon and the watchman followed the bloody footprints she'd made, and she wondered if the blood was Mike's. If he'd wounded her attacker, maybe the blood had come during the struggle.

The next hour was a collage: Mike saying things that didn't make much sense; the police taking Shannon to headquarters a few blocks away to question her; and a man she assumed was a doctor giving her two pink-and-white capsules, which she refused to swallow.

"Mrs. Hollister," said a uniformed officer whose name tag read Conway. His hair was thinning and he had a slight cut on his chin where he'd nicked himself shaving. "Your injured friend's been taken to the hospital. The EMTs seem to think he'll be fine, just a flesh wound to his shoulder. He's pretty lucky. For that matter, you are, too." He added gently. "How are you feeling? Do you want us to call someone for you? Friends, family?'' He smiled and handed her a white mug of steaming coffee.

She took a sip and considered the question. Someone had retrieved the rest of her clothes from the locker room at the gym, and she'd cleaned up in the woman's room at the police station. She didn't think she was doing too badly. She was breathing normally, and she'd finally stopped shaking. Best of all, Mike's wound wasn't serious. She shrugged wearily and said, ''I'm all right. I have to call home, though. A baby-sitter's with my son and Mike's two kids.''

He nodded and pushed the phone across the desk, then rose and moved toward the door to give her some privacy. ''You make your call, then we'll finish up and drive you home.''

She punched in Mike's phone number and waited as the metallic burr sounded in her ear. Once, twice…the baby-sitter's light voice, ''Hello?''

''It's Shannon Hollister,'' she said. ''This is Maureen, right?'' Mike had said he usually got a teenager, Maureen O'Neill, who lived nearby, to baby-sit if his housekeeper wasn't available. ''Something's happened to Mike. I'm fine and he's okay, but it'll be a while before I can get there. Is everything all right?''

''Uh, sure.'' Maureen sounded puzzled. ''Are you okay? You sound…''

''I know,'' she cut in. ''I'll tell you about it when I get there. Are the kids all right?''

''They're lying on Andy's bed with a stack of comics. They had a package of Oreos and some corn chips, but I took the corn chips away from them. I was afraid they'd get a stomachache.''

"Okay, I'll be there soon as I can." Shannon looked up as Officer Conway came back in, a question in his eyes. She nodded, said "See you soon" to Maureen and hung up.

The policeman sat down and took out a pad and pen. "What makes you think Mike wounded one of the men? And if he did, where and how badly?"

She shook her head helplessly. "Just before he passed out, Mike said he got hold of the knife and cut him. They struggled, and that's all he knew."

"You didn't see the struggle?"

"No. It was dark, and I was climbing back in off the windowsill." She glanced around as a door opened and she heard murmured conversation. Several uniformed officers were standing around talking. One of them was laughing. Shannon looked at him as if he were an alien presence. How could anyone laugh after what had happened? But, she remembered, it hadn't happened to him, and that made all the difference.

"If Mike's car is still in the parking lot at the Y, I can drive it home," she said. "But I need a ride over there."

"I'll give you a lift as soon as we're through here, ma'am," Conway said, indicating his notepad.

"All right," she agreed wearily.

Ten minutes later, he signed a copy of her statement, had Shannon countersign it and put it in a file basket. "Let's go," he said, getting into his jacket.

They drove in silence except for the low crackle emanating from his police radio. As they pulled into the parking lot at the Y, Officer Conway looked around and frowned. "Dim lights spaced far apart. It's downright crazy!" he said with a shrug. "No wonder they got robbed."

Shannon pointed to Mike's Bronco under a nearby light. "That's it, over there."

He tapped a thoughtful finger on the wheel for a moment, then said, "It might not be a good idea to drive that home tonight. No offense, ma'am, but you're in no shape to handle a strange car on back roads." He smiled. "Come on, admit it. You don't really feel up to driving. Let me take you home."

"I don't care, whatever you say," she conceded, putting a hand to her forehead. "I just want to get home."

So he turned the car around and headed out on Main Street, Shannon giving him directions and the officer saying calmly, "Okay." Ten minutes later, they pulled into the driveway of Wild Goose Farm. She started to get out, and Conway leaned over to keep her from closing the door. "Might not be a good idea to stay here tonight," he said. "You shouldn't be alone, anyway."

"I suppose you're right," she said, feeling an icy shiver snake down her spine. Thank God, Nick and Mike's two children were safe at his house! She shook her head. "Look, I'd like to go to Mike's place. My son is over there with the Finnegan kids. If you'll wait just a few minutes, I'll run inside and get a few things I need."

"I'll come in with you," he said, starting to open his door.

"It's not necessary," she said, motioning for him to stay. "I'll check the house and wave to you from the window over there. If there's anything suspicious, I'll come right out. If I don't appear in that window in two minutes, you come in. I really don't need a keeper."

"Suit yourself, ma'am" he said, and turned back to the police radio. "I've got to call in, anyway."

Walking up the stone steps to the front door, Shannon fished her key out of her purse. As she inserted it in the lock and turned it, she looked over at the barn. Tim's pickup was gone, and his apartment windows were dark. He was out.

The door opened, and she went inside and turned on the light in the living room. Everything was in place and quiet. Max followed her from room to room, wagging his tail. She petted him and checked the basement. Then she went to the window, waved at Officer Conway and indicated with two fingers that she'd be out quickly.

She was on the second-floor landing before she sensed she was not alone. Nothing had been disturbed, nothing was out of place, but something was wrong. Suddenly, she realized what it was. Nick's bedroom was at the top of the stairs, and a thin crack of light shone from under his closed door. Nick never left his light on, no matter what kind of hurry he was in. Common sense demanded that she call Conway, but she proceeded up the stairs as if hypnotized. Cautiously, she opened the door, saw nothing out of the ordinary and reached for the light switch. Suddenly, the door to Nick's closet flew open, slamming against the wall with a loud bang as a man—the same man in black who'd terrorized her only hours ago—charged out at her, grabbing her wrist and pulling her toward him with one hand, slapping her across the face with the other. As she fell backward against the wall, her face throbbing with pain, her right hand groped for something to stop her fall and came away with a drawing Nick had done years ago of Luke Skywalker. It had been taped to the wall, and now it clung to her hand.

She sat on the floor, looking up at the man, trying to decide what to do. Should she scream for help? Try to get to the door behind him somehow? He stood glaring, the ski mask obscuring everything but his ice-blue eyes. He was breathing hard, and there was blood on his left forearm.

"What do you want from me?" she said, starting to pull herself up by the edge of Nick's desk. She tried to let the drawing drop from her hand, but the tape clung, and she had to shake it loose.

He grinned. "I told you, I want you dead. You were unlucky enough to be in the wrong place at the wrong time, so you're dead."

"I don't even know who you are," she cried, fighting to hide her terror.

"Sorry, it makes no difference." His grin widened, and he picked Nick's papier-mâché owl off the desk and crushed it in his fist. "This is how much your life means. Nothing."

One side of her face ached where he'd slapped her. Something warm, from the taste of it, blood, ran from her nose. She wondered how long she'd been in the room, when would Conway come to check on her, but she had already learned this night that time could move so slowly that it didn't seem to move at all. They might have been there for only a few seconds, but if felt like a lifetime.

"Wait," she said as he moved toward her, trapping her between the desk and Nick's bed. But he didn't wait. He moved forward and their eyes met. She bent down, picked up Nick's metal Star Wars wastebasket and threw it at him, but he blocked it with his arm. Then he reached for her.

"Too late. It's all over." He was inches from her. She could smell his breath, and she had the feeling he was getting a kick out of terrifying her, goading her into begging for her life.

She reached up toward the ski mask, trying to gouge his eyes with her nails, but he jerked his head out of the way, put a hand around her neck and began to squeeze. "No, no, let me go!" she insisted. "Help! Help!"

She fought him then, kicking and writhing in his grasp, and below in the house she could hear glass breaking. "It's the police!" she rasped as he tightened his fingers around her neck.

Imperceptibly, the man's grip eased, and he turned and looked toward the door. The sound of a door breaking downstairs, then footsteps crunching on glass. "Mrs. Hollister?" Conway shouted. "You okay?"

"Up here," she said as her attacker released her and ran to the window. "Hurry! He's up here! He tried to kill me! Oh, no, he's getting away!" The man in the mask glared back at her once as he threw up the window sash and climbed out onto the sloping roof. Then he was gone, and there was only the mess on the floor and curtains blowing softly in the rush of cold air from the open window.

"Mrs. Hollister, you all right?" Conway shouted as he came upstairs. "What's going on?"

"In here," she called. "Everything's okay now. He's gone."

Conway stood in the doorway, gun drawn. His eyes ranged over the room, noting the overturned wastebasket, the crushed owl, the open window and the bruises on Shannon's neck. "What happened here?"

"He was waiting for me. The same man who was stalking me at the Y. The same man who stabbed

Mike." Her voice was rough and husky. She put a hand to her throat and touched her fingers to where it was sore. "He tried to strangle me. There," she said, pointing toward the window and blowing curtains. "He went out there."

"Geez, and no backup," Conway said with disgust. "Okay, then," he went on, still brandishing his gun. "I'll just check and see if he's on the roof." He stuck his head out the window and after a second, drew it back in. "We'd better go downstairs. I've got to call headquarters."

He led the way down the stairs, still with a hand on his gun. When they reached the living room, she showed him where the phone was. She was suddenly aware of being so tired she could barely move. And it was cold, terribly cold. The icy cold filled her lungs and brought tears to her eyes. Exhausted, she sank into a wing chair.

Officer Conway dialed and spoke into the phone, giving orders and details to someone on the other end. After a moment, he looked over at her and said gently, "Mrs. Hollister, you look awful. Is there someone you want me to call for you?"

"No," she muttered. "I just want to go to Mike's." She took a deep breath, then another one.

"A couple of officers will be here in a minute. We'll search the house and yard, make sure this guy's gone. Mrs. Hollister, don't you go and faint on me."

She opened her eyes and glared at him, making an effort to sit up straight. "I'm not going to faint. I'm just fine."

He nodded and hung up the phone. "Okay," he said gently. "If you say so." After a minute, she made it to the bathroom and vomited. Sirens announced the arrival of more police, and she sat in the wing chair and tried to stop shaking while they searched the yard and house, from cellar to attic, looking for clues to the identity of the man who'd attacked her.

"Who's been in the bathroom?" someone called out.

"I was," she answered, interrupted by another voice behind her saying, "No near neighbors, but we got a report from the next road over—Gary Getty, out watching meteor showers with his kid. Says he saw a car ten, fifteen minutes ago heading toward the highway like a bat out of hell. Could be our man."

It went on like that for an hour before the policeman in charge suggested that Conway take Shannon wherever she wanted to go for the night and get back to him in the morning. Wearily, they left the house and went out to his squad car. She got in, and they backed down the driveway. "It's the first left at the top of the hill. Plum Ridge Road. Mike's house is the third on the right, about a mile."

He nodded and turned the wheel right. They roared down the road, headlights boring into the night. Shannon gripped her hands tight in her lap to keep herself from shaking. It was all right now, she told herself. Everything was okay. It was only a matter of time before they'd catch the two men. Until then, she and Nick would stay with Mike or Angela, if Mike couldn't put them up. It'd be over soon, only a day or two at most.

"Other than the ski mask, did you notice anything else about the man?" Conway asked abruptly. "What about his build?"

"I told you, he was tall, athletic, about six feet tall. He had blue eyes," she said, looking straight ahead. "He wore the same black clothes, same ski mask. Evidently, he didn't have time to go home and change."

"Funny," Conway commented dryly. "Glad to see you still have a sense of humor."

"Let's face it, Officer. I'm glad I'm still breathing."

"Here we are," he said, turning up Mike's driveway and switching off the engine. "Wait," he went on as she put a hand on the door to get out. "Let's talk a minute. We know this guy got in through your back door, that's why you didn't notice anything wrong. He broke a window, reached in and unlocked the door. Locks like that are supposed to be secure, but any thief with an IQ slightly higher than a moron's can get in and out, which is what happened to you."

She wished he'd get to the point. "I guess so."

"Okay, so we know they robbed the Y. The cashbox was rifled, then they go after you because you can identify them."

"I can't identify them," she said quietly. "I told you that. They were both wearing ski masks and I was on the Y roof, looking in the window when the other man appeared. I never got a good look at him."

He sighed. "They must have thought you saw them, maybe when they came into the Y. Maybe they were inside earlier, casing the place, and thought you were suspicious. We may never know, and Mike can't identify them." He drew a long breath and said, "Thing is, it doesn't look like he touched anything in your house. He wasn't there to rob you, he just wanted to kill you."

"I already know that."

"We haven't had time to check everything out, but a call came in a few minutes ago. State troopers picked up two guys in a van. They found ski masks. A liquor store was hit earlier tonight by two men in ski masks."

"It could be a coincidence," she said.

"Maybe, or they could be our guys." He shrugged. "I don't want to make you any more scared than you already are, but times are violent, even in small towns like Boxford. I'd advise you to get deadbolt locks for your doors. Until this is wrapped up, you're going to be nervous, afraid—"

"Wouldn't you be?" she said, knowing her teeth were clenched.

"Right, but we can't assign someone to protect you full-time, we just don't have the manpower." He cleared his throat. "Sorry, but that's how it is. Let's hope the state troopers picked up the right guys."

"Yeah, let's hope," she said, putting a hand to her throat and touching the raw bruises.

There was an awkward pause, then he said, "If it makes you feel any better, Mrs. Hollister, I'll never forget how you looked when I got upstairs. But there's only so much we can do on something like this."

She got out with a resigned "Thanks," and walked up the path to Mike's front door. The outside light was on. The door opened, and he stood there, his body blocking the light from inside. His left shoulder was bandaged, she could see the white fabric poking above his shirt collar. Then he put his good arm around her, and it felt like coming home.

"Am I glad to see you," he said, his voice low and gentle. Windblown tree shadows danced across his face as she let her body relax against him.

Her thoughts moved away from the fringes of fear. She was safe now in the shelter of his embrace. Safe, but she was so tired. It felt wonderful to be held. Like coming home.

He gripped her to him with his one good arm. *She was so small, so fragile.* His mind went blank for a moment. All he could think about was how close he'd come to losing her. Twice in one night. It was too much to bear. She looked terrible. One cheek swollen and bruised, and her face white as a sheet. Fighting an instinct whose intensity made him break out in a sweat, he took a deep breath and said, "The police brought me home from the emergency room and told me what happened. You and Nick are staying here until those maniacs are caught."

She gave him a smile. "Thanks, but I'm a big girl. Besides, I've got a shop to run, classes to teach."

He let out a breath. "You're wonderful, but you're not Wonder Woman. Let me in your life, Shannon. Let me help."

Her wide blue eyes flicked upward to his and she admitted, "You're already in my life with both feet."

"Good," he said softly. His fingers cupped her shoulder, caressing, and she felt the brush of his lips on her hair. "Now, the kids are fine. Fast asleep. The boys set up a tent in Andy's room. I had a devil of a time talking them out of sleeping in the backyard. Chris fell asleep in a pile of comics on Andy's bed, so I just covered her up and left her there. Oh, I didn't tell them details, just said the Y had been robbed, and that you and I both got caught up in it. It'll be a two-day wonder with them, then they'll forget about it." He drew a breath and smiled into her eyes. A tingling sensation swept over her as his glance dropped lower, lingering on her mouth.

She cleared her throat. "I hope so."

"I'll show you the guest room. The bath's just down the hall." His eyes studied her with an intensity she could almost touch.

A wave of heat flowed over her from her head to her toes. An edge of sexual awareness warmed the air between them. Her eyes flickered up toward his mouth, and the answer to his unspoken question hovered in the air. She swallowed, looked away from him and said, "The guest room will be fine."

SHE KNEW she was dreaming. Her face wasn't supposed to shimmer and change in the mirror like that. Vibrating, almost melting.

She didn't know where she was, but she knew there was something familiar about the place. Pictures on the walls, old furniture. It was her antique shop. Nick was sitting next to her on a bench. Somehow they were both strapped in with seat belts and couldn't move. And there was something else, something she had to remember. It was important, but she couldn't figure out what it was.

Someone was saying, "Everything's all right." But she knew that wasn't true. Her mind told her she knew something too terrible to be put into words, something—but she couldn't remember what it was.

Her reflection in the mirror shimmered, and she tried closing her eyes because the light made her dizzy, filled her with nausea, but her eyes wouldn't close. They stayed open and she felt her hands moving without command. She looked down and in each hand was a ski mask. She watched as both hands began ripping the masks to shreds, scraps of dark material filling the air, then falling, covering herself and Nick, and the floor.

She forced herself to look up. Something drew her eyes away from her hands. There was a sound out the window to her left, and she found herself staring through the glass at him, the man with no face. All she could see was his cold blue gaze, burning like ice. Then he raised his huge hands and flexed them, pressing them against the glass. Nick was covered with ragged strips of the ski mask, and screaming. She could hear him, sense him, but she couldn't look away from the big man outside, who stared at her as if he meant to come in. She wanted to scream, too, but no sound came, and the man's face was gone, as if he'd backed into a cloud outside the window. She tried to release the last scraps of the ski masks, but they stuck to her hands. She strained, turning as far as she could past Nick, who was slumped against her, as if he'd fallen asleep. Strapped into her seat, she could barely see out the window, but she could make out a black circle on the ground. Inside it lay Mike, and over him stood the big man. Mike's face and clothes were covered with blood, and the big man was clutching an iron bar that he lifted over his head and swung downward at Mike.

As he swung, he looked once more toward Shannon with an expression of such hatred that it made her scream, scream so loud that she woke herself up. For a fraction of a second she was disoriented, not knowing where she was. But she sensed she wasn't alone. Someone was in the room with her.

"You're safe. I'm here." Mike's voice came to her from out of the dark, across the room where he'd been sitting, in a chair. Even as he spoke, his weight made the bedsprings creak and sag and she felt him slide his arm around her and haul her close. "Damn, this bandage. Gets in the way," he sighed. "It's not doing much good, might as well—"

"Don't you dare take it off," she told him, snuggling against his chest, reveling in the fact that he was alive and safe. She drew a long, shaky breath, and said, "Sorry I screamed. Bad dream."

He nodded, his face pressed against her hair, breathing in the scent of her, warm and feminine. "Go back to sleep," he said after a moment. His voice was a low whisper.

Her eyelids fluttered shut and in a few moments her breathing had softened. She was asleep.

He leaned his head back against the pillow and sighed.

Images chased through his thoughts, and he felt an answering stir in his body. Damn. He moved a little, and she stirred uneasily, then was still again. He studied the top of her head, her dark hair falling across her forehead in tousled curls. He could feel the warmth of her body beside his, her breasts against his chest, her thigh touching along the length of his leg. The impact of her in his arms, the fact that they lay in bed together like lovers. And there was nothing he could do about it.

He closed his eyes, feeling an answering desire to the warmth pressed against him. It was going to be a long, long night.

FROWNING, puzzled, Shannon awoke hours later. Sunlight slanted through the window, and something heavy lay on her arm. She stayed there a moment, remembering last night and all that had happened. Remembering where she was: Mike's guest room. She felt warm and safe. She turned her head. Mike's good arm was flung across her body protectively. Her back was curved intimately against his chest, and she felt his breath stirring her hair. A shiver of delight ran down her spine as he moved slightly, urging her closer.

Holding her breath, she risked another look. His eyes were closed, he was still asleep. His lips—were just a kiss away.

She found herself wondering what it would be like to be kissed by him, to feel his warm mouth on hers, urging hers open. A consuming, passionate kiss that made the world disappear and turned their bodies to fire.

She closed her eyes and opened them again, then carefully slid out from under his arm and out of bed, wondering at her sudden feeling of deprivation. Common sense told her this wasn't wise. He was just a friend, after all. She'd had a nightmare, and he'd stayed so she wouldn't be alone.

Then why, she asked herself as she went down the hall to the bathroom to shower and dress, was her throat dry and her heart pounding like a drum?

"EGYPTIANS TOOK the brain out through the nose. They used a special hook for it. Mummies don't have any brains," Andy asserted importantly.

Chris lowered the binoculars and looked at her brother. "That's totally bogus. If mummies have no brains, how can they figure out how to chase people?"

"Yeah, how can they do that?" Nick seconded. They were eating a knapsack breakfast consisting of chocolate bars, apples, bagels and donuts. The morning air in the sun-dappled clearing smelled sweet and fresh, and they were very hungry.

Chris grinned at Nick and helped herself to another bagel. Because she was missing her front teeth, she had to chew on the side, a difficult but necessary maneuver she hated. Like her brother and Nick, she was dressed in jeans, a woolly jacket and sneakers, and carried a shovel. Designated as lookout, her job was to scan the conservation woods with binoculars and be on the alert for suspicious movement. "Like if you see a dragon breathing fire or that mummy, or maybe even a moose," Andy had said. After all, this was Maine, and moose did turn up now and then.

"Mummies have special powers," Andy said in his usual know-it-all tone. "They don't need ordinary brains because they're *mummies,* that's why. Everybody knows that."

"So they've got mummy brains?" Nick looked at Andy who munched thoughtfully on a green apple.

"Yeah, that's right," Andy said, pushing his glasses up his nose and nodding. "It's got something to do with stuff the Egyptians wrapped the dead bodies in before putting them in the 'sarkofiguses'. I read it in a *National Geographic* I found in the attic. They put some kind of antifreeze in them, too. Like Dad puts in the car radiator."

Nick sat beside Andy and rummaged in the knapsack for another bagel. "Know somethin' weird? Mrs. Brennan said old Harry Clarke was gonna tell her a big surprise before he died. Only he didn't get a chance on account of he died first. I wonder if he saw the mummy in the woods, too?"

Andy nodded wisely. "Yeah, that makes sense. He must of seen the mummy and was gonna tell Mrs. B."

"Right, only he died first," Chris breathed, eyes wide. "What if...the mummy *killed him!* So he couldn't talk!"

Nick frowned. "Maybe we should tell your dad about this."

"Nope," Andy said firmly. "He'll just say we're imagining things."

"I didn't imagine it, there was a mummy out here the last time I was here with Mrs. Brennan," Nick insisted. "It followed us, like it was *spying* on us."

Getting to her feet, Chris lifted the binoculars and peered around at the nearest stand of trees. No mummies that she could see. Nothing but rocks and trees and that old cellar hole. She lowered the binoculars. "I still don't see why some old mummy would be out here, anyway. I mean, where's the pyramid? You've got to have pyramids to have mummies, right?"

"Well, I don't know...." Andy said, pushing his glasses up and taking a bite of his apple. "Maybe he 'scaped from a museum! Who knows? But it's our job to find him!"

Chris's green eyes widened. "Like on Saturday cartoons, where this museum truck hits a pothole and the mummy case falls out on the street!"

This was beginning to make an awful lot of sense. Nick munched on his bagel, swallowed and said, "You know, he's prob'ly mad and that's why he's got an ax like in *The Mummy's Curse.*"

"Or—" Andy stood up and pointed dramatically to the ground by the cellar hole "—there could be a pyramid buried here! Maybe that's what the mummy's protecting—the treasure of the mummy's tomb!"

Immediately, all thought of breakfast vanished as the three of them grabbed the shovels and started digging. Andy kept up a running commentary about how the conservation wood was just like The Valley of the Kings in Ancient Egypt! His green eyes took on a faraway gleam. "*The terrible mummy's curse!* Once we open the tomb, we need masks. There's this invisible killer mist that floats up and gets you!"

Chris shivered with delight and dug all the harder, but Nick had a thought. Frowning, he leaned on his shovel and said, "Okay, say the mummy comes along and finds us digging up his pyramid. We don't speak Egyptian. How're we gonna talk to him?"

"That's right," Andy said slowly. "We need an Egyptian dictionary."

"Arabic," Chris corrected. She sat down on a rock and drew a squiggly line on it with a small stone. "But they used 'hiroglifics,' like this. It's a snake, see?" She looked at her brother, who frowned back. "'Cept the mummy's not gonna wait while we draw 'hiroglifics' on the rock. He's got an ax and he's mad!"

"She's right," Nick said with a deep sigh. "Besides, what if his head's been chopped off, like in that movie? He can't read 'hiroglifics.'"

Suddenly, the faint wail of a siren floated through the woods. Andy pushed up his glasses and said, "Another fire, I bet."

Visions of another house engulfed in flames filled Nick's thoughts, and he swallowed a lump in his throat. Darn the arsonist, anyway, he thought miserably. There was a prickling feeling at the back of his neck that he ignored while he surreptitiously wiped his eyes with the coat sleeve. Finally, he turned around. A tall, blond-haired man was approaching through the woods. As he noticed Nick looking his way, the man waved and called out, "Hello there! You're the Finnegan kids and, uh, young Nick Hollister, am I right?"

Nick threw a quick look at Andy and Chris and nodded. "Yes, sir." He had a pretty good idea who the man was. The only new people to move into the neighborhood lately were the Wagoners.

"I'm living in the Clarke house on the far side of the field—name's Paul Wagoner." He solemnly shook Nick's hand, then Andy's and Chris's in turn. "Did you happen to hear that siren a minute ago?"

They nodded in unison and mumbled, "Yessir."

He frowned. "Sounds like another fire. You kids ought to get on home. As a matter of fact, I was going to stop by your dad's to see about organizing a neighborhood fire-watch."

Andy and Chris started collecting the shovels and Nick picked up the knapsack. Soon they were climbing back over the stone wall and crossing the weedy field that led to Andy's backyard. Mr. Wagoner didn't have much to say as he walked along with them, although as they passed the sign posted by the conservation parking lot, he said quietly, "You know, kids, I don't think you're allowed to dig on conservation land." Smiling kindly, he went on, "That sign says you're not supposed to take anything out or leave anything behind. Don't you think it also means you're not to disturb anything?"

Andy looked at Nick and Chris who both frowned. There was a small silence, then Nick said, "I guess so, but—"

Paul Wagoner reached down and ruffled the top of Nick's curly head. "Well, no harm done. Just remember that in future, okay?"

In the distance, sunlight sparkled on the windows of Andy's house. They walked toward it. Once in a while Nick kicked the leaves in the path and looked at Andy who shrugged and made a face behind Paul Wagoner's broad back. *Grown-ups,* the look said. *They think they know everything.*

# Chapter Seven

Shannon was already showered, dressed and down-stairs just putting the kettle on when Mike came into the kitchen. She smiled at him, running her fingers along the waistband of her jeans. The gesture held a trace of nervousness, and her voice shook a little as she said, "Good morning. Hungry?"

He nodded and got down a couple of mugs. "Waffles and coffee would do me fine. How about you?"

"Sure." She glanced out the window over the sink as he opened the refrigerator and got out milk. "Looks like you've got company. Paul Wagoner's coming up your front walk, and he's got the kids with him."

He walked by her and glanced out the window. "You're right. Wonder what he wants?"

She caught the scent of Mike's soap and after-shave. A few drops of water from his shower were caught in his dark hair, and the sun gilded his tanned skin. Her breath caught in her throat as he turned and looked at her. His gray gaze was disconcerting as it roamed over her flushed face and lower.

"Guess I'd better get the door," he said softly.

"Yes." She gave him a bright smile. "I'll get down another mug."

He nodded and opened the back door just as Paul Wagoner was about to knock. Looking disgusted, the three kids dumped the shovels by the side of the garage and came in. The next few minutes were occupied with feeding waffles to the hungry horde in the dining room. Then Shannon poured coffee into three mugs and sat down at the kitchen table.

Frowning, Paul stirred sugar into his mug. "Sorry to come by like this, but I heard the siren. Three long and two short. The fire's over on the other side of the pond, near the Girl Scout camp."

"Oh, no," Shannon whispered.

"It's unoccupied this time of year," Mike said, shrugging. "Not that it means anything to this maniac."

Paul nodded. "That's why I dropped in. We can't let it go on—barns and houses burning, set ablaze without warning. Leslie and I thought a neighborhood firewatch might work." He leaned forward, excited with his idea. "We'd keep an eye on one another's homes. Chances are we could even catch this bastard before he does any more damage."

The idea surprised Shannon, but it sounded worth a try. She looked at Mike who shrugged, then nodded. "We could take regular shifts, drive around town, report anything suspicious."

"Exactly." Paul glanced at his watch and pushed back his chair. "I'll call you later and we'll work out details. Right now I want to reach as many people on the street as I can." Thanking them for the coffee, he left just as the phone rang.

Shannon started to get up, but Mike said, "I'll get it, and took the call in the living room. A minute later, he came back, looking grim. "Police. They want us at a lineup, to see if we can pick out the two men they arrested last night."

She nodded, fighting back the sudden urge to open the back door and run outside, as far and fast as she could go.

"My housekeeper's due soon. She'll stay with the kids." He looked closely at her. "Are you all right?"

"Sure." She took a shuddering breath and tried to regain her composure. "It's still hard to believe what happened last night. Sitting here, drinking coffee, hearing the kids in the other room—" She cleared her throat. "It's difficult to think we have to go over it all again."

"Come here," he said.

"What?" she said, smiling as she walked over and he put his good arm around her. She had to tip her head back to look into his face. His slightly crooked nose and dark eyebrows, the line of his jaw. She drew a hesitant breath as his fingers caressed the back of her neck.

His eyes were serious. "Do me a favor. Don't think about anything. Just get through the next hour or so, and everything will be over, I promise."

Realistically, she knew this was impossible, but she nodded anyway. "Thanks."

"Shannon, honey," he whispered, and she felt herself begin to tremble against him.

He didn't move, and she was aware of her heart pounding in her chest. His gaze touched her face, reading her expression as her eyes shut, almost against her will. She inhaled his male scent, clean and heady. Her head was in a whirl, and somehow it seemed his face was closer. The sound of the children playing in the next room faded and disappeared. All she knew was the feel of him in her arms.

"Oh, Mike," she managed to whisper as he lowered his lips to hers. Their bodies fitted together from shoulder to thigh, pressed closely, intimately. She felt his tongue move along her lips until she opened them, then plunge inside, hotly, searchingly. Time stopped, and her entire world was his kiss, the warmth and strength of his embrace. She shuddered against him, and he lifted his head and looked into her dazed eyes.

He let out a breath and said, "I think that settles a few questions, don't you?"

She felt a flood of heat wash over her. He was watching her with a serious expression, and she was too honest to look away. "I—"

Andy came in and looked at his dad and Shannon. "Can we have seconds on waffles?"

She stepped away from Mike and he smiled and pulled her back into the curve of his arm. "Sure, I'll put 'em in the toaster." He squeezed her shoulder gently. "Shannon will pour you guys more milk." The tone of his voice was light, teasing, and she felt the intimate, sexually charged moment ease.

She poured the milk and managed to find her voice. "Do you mind if we stop by my house and pick up the mail? I've got to pay some bills."

"Good morning." The cheery voice of Mrs. Beekman, Mike's housekeeper, interrupted their discussion. Removing her coat and pulling on an apron, Mrs. Beekman bustled about, pleasant, plump and sixtyish. "Mighty nice out this time of year." Her eyes examined Shannon curiously, and Mike introduced her, explaining, "Mrs. Hollister may be staying with us for a while, until things settle down."

"Fine. I'll keep an eye on the kids till you both get back," she said, smiling. "Take your time."

"We won't be long," Mike assured her, then they left. It took less than ten minutes to reach Wild Goose Farm. As Shannon feared, her mailbox was stuffed with junk mail and bills. And a flat brown-wrapped package was hanging from the mailbox in a see-through plastic bag. Curious, Shannon removed it and turned it over, looking for the return address. Chicago. The light dawned. It was the promised photograph from Linda Clarke.

A small smile curved her lips. It seemed like years since their conversation. Mike shifted on the car seat to get a better view of the parcel.

"Who's it from?"

"An old friend. Just a picture I'm framing for her sister."

"Sounds nice," he said. A pause, then he tilted a dark eyebrow at her. "Ready for the lineup? You can open that and pay bills later."

"Right." She slid the package and the pile of bills onto the seat beside her. They could wait.

While Mike drove, she told herself she wasn't nervous. But her heart reacted like a Geiger counter as they arrived at the police station. Her lips were dry and her mouth tasted dusty. Deep breathing didn't seem to help.

Once they identified the men, it would be over. Life would return to normal peace and quiet. But as she got out of Mike's car and walked into the station, her hand was at her neck, touching the purplish welts and bruises that were still there.

WHAT THE HELL am I gonna do now? Tim Carver thought as he sat, slumped over the table in his kitchen. He was exhausted. He hadn't managed much sleep these past few nights, and his nerves were shot.

The best cure he'd found for that was a clean conscience and a pair of six-packs. Unfortunately, as things stood, he didn't possess either.

An open box of wooden matches lay on the table before him, an ashtray half-filled with charred matches nearby. Somber-eyed, hand shaky, he lit another match and held it, watching it burn.

So much destruction, he thought, a bitter smile twisting his lips. Flames leaping, devouring, consuming everything they touched. Scarlet and gold, like the tiny flame of the match that flickered and died as he shook it.

He lit another and held it with trembling fingers.

His gaze moved to the wall calendar. Six small red *x*'s dotted the past three months. Each *x* represented a fire, some barn or outbuilding that had gone up in smoke. He'd put them there, documenting the record of the Boxford arsonist. It seemed important to get it down on paper and get it right.

Sudden pain seared his fingers, and he winced and dropped the charred match into the ashtray. Mindlessly, he lit another.

He'd tried everything, even reading the Bible, something Aunt Bella swore by when she was troubled. Funny, Psalm 88 seemed to hit the nail right on the head. God knew he was crying out for help. He felt as if there were no answers, as if he were lying in the darkest pit, suffering terror and despair.

He was confused, mixed up. And frightened. He didn't know what to do next and was afraid it didn't matter one whole hell of a lot, anyway. His thoughts were panicky, difficult to control. He hadn't had a drink, but he felt dizzy, almost drunk. He was tired. So damn tired. No sleep since Sunday night. And not much before that. If he could just catch up on his sleep, he'd be able to think clearly again.

Then he could…take care of things once and for all. Grim-faced, he lit another match and watched it burn.

"DON'T LOOK at me like that. All I said was that it wasn't your fault." Mike tried to slide his arm around Shannon, but she quickened her pace and went around to the passenger side of the Bronco. His arm dropped to his side. Behind them, the door to the police station opened and closed with a bang as a man in jeans came out and walked away down the street.

Shannon got into the Bronco and sat silently as Mike got behind the wheel and started up the engine. After a full minute of fuming, she burst out, "I can't believe it! I couldn't identify any of those men. In spite of the ski masks, there must have been something distinctive about them, something that I should remember. Aftershave, a scar, maybe a watchband." She sighed. "The bigger man's hands were around my neck long enough, you'd think I'd have noticed something! But no. All I thought about was not dying. He could have had on six watches and a diamond tiara, and I wouldn't have seen a thing. Damn it! Coming down here was a complete waste of time."

"Not quite," Mike replied, pulling out into the street and heading down the hill. "They booked the two men for the liquor store holdup. They don't have an alibi for the robbery at the Y. The police think it's the same pair. The odds are slim that two sets of thieves are working in ski masks. Give it time, they'll break down and confess."

He shrugged. "They're probably hoping for a deal, a plea bargain. They face a lesser charge in the liquor store holdup. If they admit to breaking into the Y they open themselves up to charges of assault with intent to kill. They'd be put away for a very long time.'' He reached over to switch on the radio, and the weather report came on. For the next three days, it would be cloudy, with showers. After a jingle about forgetting your troubles and flying off to the Caribbean at low, low rates, a woman's voice came on, singing passionately, and Shannon frowned and flicked it off.

"If you don't mind, I'm not in the mood to listen to singers who say, 'Hey, baby.'" After a moment, she muttered, "I looked like a complete *idiot* in there. All I could say was that one man might have been bigger than the other. And, oh, yes, the tall one had blue eyes. Big deal. Half the men in America have blue eyes."

"So it takes a few days for the police to get them to confess—it's not the end of the world. Shannon, you can't do everything yourself. Give the police some time to do their job."

There was a small silence. They were on Grove Street, the Y was at the end of the block. Shannon stared at the beige and gray stone front as they drove by. "I can't help the way I feel. It's different for you. You were knocked unconscious. Nobody expects you to remember anything. But I was fully conscious and I can't give the police anything concrete to go on—" She broke off with a disgusted sigh. "I feel like a complete fool."

He threw her a supportive look. "You're just over-reacting, that's all. You're someone who can't stand it when things aren't resolved. Neatly wrapped up, no loose ends. If I had to make a guess," he added with a smile, "I'd say you like doing intricate puzzles for relaxation."

She had to laugh. "As a matter of fact, I do. How'd you guess?"

"It's not hard." He gave her a half smile. "You like being in control. That's just the way you are."

"I guess then my running and exercise classes mark me as obsessive-compulsive?" She frowned, realizing suddenly how defensive she sounded.

"No, but I wish you'd spend more time with me." He flicked another look at her, wondering how to get her to change her mind about staying at his place for a few days, then thought, What the hell, the worst she can say is no. He cleared his throat and said quietly, "While we're on the subject, why not change your mind about spending the next few days with the kids and me? You and Nick don't have to move back home right away."

She shook her head. "Thanks, but I really have to go home. I can't keep the shop closed indefinitely. Tim Carver's there in the barn anyway, so I've got protection in case the police are wrong and those two robbers are still on the loose."

"You don't know the first thing about Carver. You can't depend on him."

"His references checked out—" she began.

Mike raised his eyebrows. "What good were they last night? He wasn't there when you needed him."

"I'll ask him to stay around at night until this is cleared up. We'll be all right." She gave him a little shrug. "The police said they'd make it a point to drive past the house every few hours. Not much, but it's better than nothing. Their manpower's stretched thin as it is with all the fires."

"All the more reason to stay with me." His voice was gentler, and he smiled.

"I can't...please, Mike, try to understand."

"I'm trying," he said with a sigh. "Look, why not take it easy for a while. Have someone take over your exercise class and close up the shop for a week or two." He squeezed her hand. "You've been through a terrible ordeal these last twenty-four hours."

She sighed and rubbed a gentle thumb over his hand. "You're making me feel like Mrs. Rochester. Have you ever read *Jane Eyre*?"

"I saw the movie when I was a kid. Orson Welles before he got fat. He could have used one of your classes," he said, watching the color return to her face and noting that her voice sounded more normal, not so shaky.

"This is a small town. People talk." She shrugged. "I want to get back to a normal routine, live my own life. It's the only way I can cope."

She was frowning, and he said quietly, "Shannon, I was only trying to help."

"I know." She felt her face grow warm. He was looking at her with eyes that said he really cared, that she was more than a friend. Much more. She drew a long breath and said, "You're the nicest thing that's happened to me in a long time. No, you're the *best* thing." She smiled up at him, trying to block out the memory of last night. But it came back in the sudden, remembered smell of the damp shower room, the shadowed corner and the terrible pair of hands around her neck, squeezing, squeezing. She took a deep breath and told herself the bruises would fade soon, then it would just be a bad dream. But somehow she couldn't shake the eerie feeling of being watched, and the flickering image of a face and hands reaching through the shadows on the car window made her shudder. She moved closer to Mike.

They paused at a red light. Shannon noticed two dark men in jeans and leather jackets emerge from the hardware store across the street. The taller one wore a black baseball cap with a beer company logo on it, the other, smaller one was hatless. As the light changed, the bigger man touched his companion's shoulder, said something, and both of them looked toward Shannon as she and Mike drove on.

Frowning, she turned away from their stares and said to Mike, "Who were they?"

"The Parelli brothers. They live out near Nonie Brennan's."

Turning around, she looked out the back window. The bigger man was taking off his cap and wiping his sweaty forehead. He grinned, exposing large yellowed teeth. His brother had his hands in his pockets, and a smirk on his face. Laughing, he slapped the big man on the arm and got into a dusty blue car.

Shannon turned around and took a deep breath. "I don't like the look of them."

They hit another red light at the next intersection and Mike braked. "Real good old boys, not exactly model citizens," he agreed. "In fact, they were involved in a bad tavern brawl out on Route 6, a few years ago. Broke the place up and put a few people in the hospital."

"Didn't they go to jail?"

He shook his head. "Paid a fine, that's all. No one pressed charges. They were afraid the Parellis would come looking for revenge. They're that type. I heard Mrs. Brennan had some trouble with them."

Shannon had a sudden chilling memory of Nonie Brennan confiding that she'd turned into an old curmudgeon, something about not getting along with people. Looking at Mike, she said quietly, "What kind of trouble?"

"They cut wood, when they work at all. Mrs. Brennan caught them logging on conservation land. They had a couple of chain saws, a skidder and a truck. A pretty efficient operation, but she put a stop to it." Shannon made a small sound, and he looked at her, frowning. "What?"

"Mrs. Brennan told me about it the day she died." Unable to resist, Shannon looked back over her shoulder. The spot where the blue car had been parked was empty, but she could see it driving off in the distance. She shook her head. "They looked dangerous. I don't know how Mrs. B. found the courage to stand up to them."

Mike reached over and took her hand in his. "She had the heart of a lion, bless her." He pressed down on the accelerator as the light turned green and the car surged forward. "Not many like her left in this world."

"I know," Shannon said, her eyes serious. Had the Parelli brothers gotten even with Mrs. Brennan somehow? Were they behind all the other fires in town? Had they deliberately set fire to her house and left her there to die? An aching sense of sadness and anger passed through her.

They couldn't have done it, she thought, closing her eyes for a second and seeing in her mind the bigger Parelli, the one with the baseball cap. And his brother with the staring dark eyes. No one in his right mind would do something like that.

But what if they had? They'd stood in the street staring at Mike's car, staring at *her* until she and Mike were almost out of sight. Why? Had they recognized her? She swallowed hard. What if the police had the wrong men in custody? What if the men who had confessed to robbing the liquor store were telling the truth? What if they really had been nowhere near the Y the night she and Mike were attacked?

No, it was impossible, she thought. The police had too much evidence against the pair. Ski masks, dark clothing. They'd break down and confess eventually. Then life would get back to normal.

A chill voice in her mind whispered that this was a nightmare, only she wasn't asleep. She was wide-awake.

She pressed her palm over the aching bruises on her neck and realized they were swinging off Main Street and heading west. "Where are we going?"

"The Girl Scout camp on Westerly Road. That's what burned this morning. The whole damn place. Unoccupied, thank God." He sighed. "Something to be thankful for, anyway. I want to take a look at it."

"What good will that do?" She threw him a puzzled look.

The line of his mouth was grim and a muscle jerked along his jaw. "God knows. I thought maybe I'd see something the police missed. Something that I might have seen at Mrs. Brennan's the night her house burned."

She gazed at him, taken off guard a little by the vehemence in his voice. "But it's miles from her house, way over on the other side of town. What are you looking for?"

"You want the truth? I don't know," he muttered. "But I've got to try."

A SICK FEELING washed over him as the Bronco bumped down the rutted dirt road leading to the Girl Scout camp. The acrid smell of smoke hung heavy on the air.

A hard turn right at the bottom, and he pulled up and parked. Through the screen of trees to the left, they could see pond water glinting in the sunlight. It looked peaceful, beautiful, he thought. But looks were deceiving.

They got out of the Bronco and strode the rest of the way through the woods to the main clearing. Above their heads, the metal sign that formed the entry arch swung in the cool breeze. Its forlorn creaking underscored the lonely air of the deserted camp.

He grabbed Shannon's arm and steadied her as she stumbled slightly. "You all right?"

She nodded, looking around. Wooden sawhorses had been set up and the area was cordoned of with yellow barrier tape. "Maybe we shouldn't go in." Her footsteps froze at the sight that met their eyes. Where once bunkhouses, a cookhouse and mess hall had stood, now only blackened, fire-scarred timbers remained. "Horrible," she murmured and moved closer to him.

He lifted the tape, holding it up for her to slip beneath. "Come on, we can't do any harm. There's nothing left."

That wasn't exactly true. One structure stood undamaged—a shingled boathouse located down by the water's edge. Leaves rustled in the breeze, and Shannon started as the boathouse door swung shut, then yawned open again, creaking slightly on its hinges. She grabbed Mike's arm. "Someone's in there!"

The door moved again, and he said, "It's nothing, just the wind. Come on."

"It had better be," she whispered. "I've had all the excitement my nerves can take."

They walked around the smoking remains of the camp, finding nothing of interest: a blackened stove leaning sideways against the twisted remnants of what had once been a metal table; scorched pots in the ash-strewn ruins; a couch with only blackened springs intact; the burned rubble of the mess hall obliterated by a caved-in roof.

Mike gave the rain gutter a desultory kick and ashes floated upward. "There's nothing here now—if there ever was." Then he tensed. A faint familiar smell underlay the overpowering odor of smoke. *Gasoline.* He whirled and stared at something beneath the corner of the roof. He could just see a flash of red. "Give me a hand with this," he said quickly.

"What?" She gave him a puzzled look.

He was already lifting the curved end of the gutter, tossing it backward with a thud. "The rest of the gutter, come on." She grabbed hold and helped heave the last of it aside. Half-buried in the wreckage of the mess-hall porch . . . three red gasoline cans.

"The police probably spotted them already. It's definitely arson, all right. He must have soaked this whole area with gasoline, then lit a match. Frame buildings like these go up in a flash." Mike's jaw tightened. "This time of year the camp's deserted, so the fire took hold before anyone noticed the smoke and called it in."

"And by then the arsonist was long-gone." Shannon pressed closer to Mike, suddenly cold. "So much destruction—why? He must be insane."

"Maybe, maybe not." He shrugged. "One thing's for sure. By now he's got an appetite for it."

"What motive could anyone have to burn down the Girl Scout camp, or for that matter, any of the other buildings he's destroyed?"

"We may never know the truth. Even worse, whoever's doing it doesn't care if the surrounding woods catch fire. There hasn't been a real rain in weeks, these trees are practically tinder-dry.''

He didn't say more, and they continued walking around the wreckage of the camp in grim silence. Only the crunch of their shoes on gravel and the faint rustle of leaves disturbed the deathly quiet.

Evidence of the conflagration was everywhere. Heavy tire tracks, skid marks where fire trucks had braked. Puddles of water drying in the sun.

Shannon sat down tiredly on a large rock as Mike walked over to examine broken and burned beams lying across what once had been a building foundation. "It'll be months before they can rebuild," he said, shaking his head.

She pushed back her hair, wondering if the camp would ever be the same. Full of happy, laughing youngsters. At least no one had been hurt this time. The arsonist had already claimed one casualty. How long before there was another victim like Nonie Brennan?

A cold knot of fear settled in her stomach and she shivered a little, pulling the sleeves of her sweater down over her forearms. Something moved by the corner of her eye. A bird, she thought. Or a squirrel. But it was larger, a shadowy figure moving through the trees to the left. A man.

"Mike, *someone's coming,*" she hissed. "Over to the left...."

Mike turned just as the man emerged from the stand of trees. It was Tim Carver.

Seeing them in the clearing, he looked startled and halted, half turning as if about to flee back into the woods. Then he seemed to overcome his reluctance and came forward. "Uh, hello, Ms. Hollister. I didn't think anyone'd—uh, I was jus'—that is, I thought I'd see if there was anythin' I could do here. Like if they needed help or—"

"The fire's been out for a couple of hours," Mike broke in.

"Yeah, you're right." Tim's Adam's apple bobbed nervously as he nodded, and he shoved his hands into his jeans's pockets. "Guess I'm too late to, uh, do any good."

Mike looked into his eyes and said, "I'd say so."

"Well, what I mean is, uh, I jus' heard about the fire. I've been in Bangor all mornin'. I jus' got back."

"Bangor?" Mike raised an eyebrow.

"Yeah, the roadwork on Route 202 held me up some," Tim replied. He cleared his throat, his eyes flickering toward Shannon and back to Mike. They faced one another across the silence of the clearing.

Then Mike said, "We didn't see your truck—"

"Oh, I, uh, left it up the old loggin' road. Came in the back way." Tim gave a nervous grin. "Damn fool thing to do. That old road's hell on shocks." He grinned again and took a step backward. "Well, guess I'll, uh, be gettin' back. I'll, uh, see you later." With a slight nod, he turned and disappeared into the trees.

Mike shook his head. "That guy's an oddball."

Shannon didn't answer. For a moment, she'd glimpsed something odd in Tim's eyes. More than nervousness, she thought. It had looked like a mixture of fear and despair.

Bending down near the Bronco, Mike picked up something. "Looks like a keychain. One of the firemen must have dropped it this morning." He was right. The key chain hadn't been there long. The metal was untarnished.

Shrugging, he slipped it into his pocket.

# Chapter Eight

That night, when Shannon moved back to Wild Goose Farm with Nick, Mike went inside first and checked the house from attic to cellar to make sure it was safe. Then he let them in and told her to get dead-bolt locks for all the doors in the house and either he or Tim Carver would install them.

"Okay, I'll do it first thing tomorrow," she promised.

"Good," Mike said, nodding.

Saying he was starved, Nick ran into the kitchen and made himself a peanut butter and jelly sandwich. "I'm going to have a banana split after," he said, cramming a bite into his mouth. Then he opened the freezer door in the refrigerator and took out a half gallon of ice cream.

"Don't talk with your mouth full," she said, deftly removing the ice cream carton from his sticky fingers and putting it back into the freezer. "Wait until you finish that sandwich. And how about feeding the dog?"

"Okay." Nick put down his sandwich, and went out to the back hall where Max's food was kept. The dog trailed after him, tail wagging.

"Well?" Shannon asked, turning to Mike, who stood with his arms folded, a grim look on his face.

"You won't change your mind about staying here, no matter what I think," he said, his mouth tightening.

"The police are keeping an eye on the house. Tim's just across the driveway. I'll be fine."

His eyes scanned her face, taking in her pallor and general air of exhaustion. "Okay, you win. No more argument. Anyway, I've got to get back home, feed Andy and Chris and put them to bed. I'll talk to you tomorrow."

"Okay."

He slid his arm around her shoulders and bent his head. His lips brushed hers in a gentle caress. Then, suddenly, it wasn't gentle at all. Her body melted into his as she leaned against him and wrapped her arms around his neck.

Barely raising his head, he whispered, "Let's try that again, honey." And Nick came in and stopped in the doorway.

"Mom, where's the scissors? I gotta open a new bag of dog food."

Still dazed, Shannon motioned toward the counter by the stove. "It's in the drawer."

Mike's eyes were a deep gray as he smiled down at her. Then he squeezed her shoulder and let her go. "My timing couldn't be worse," he said huskily. "See you later, Nick," he said as he left with a wave.

The Bronco's headlights swept down the driveway and Shannon moved over by the sink where she could see part of the back hall. Nick was talking to the dog and pouring food pellets into Max's yellow plastic bowl. Shannon found the daily paper and opened it.

She sat down at the kitchen table, listening to Nick's soft conversation with the dog. Turning to the article about the Y robbery on page three, she scanned the headline: ROBBERY ATTEMPT—WOMAN'S NIGHTMARE AT LOCAL Y. There was a photograph of the building. It looked the same as it always did, although the police said the door had been forced.

So, she thought, even the headline was inaccurate. The thieves had made off with cash receipts from the front desk. The robbery had been a success, but the headline implied otherwise. She read on, hoping for something definite about the arrest of the two men. There was some, but not much. The ski masks were mentioned, the liquor store robbery earlier that night and the attacks on her and Mike in lurid if not very accurate detail. She read it as if it were something that had happened to someone else—a stranger. Left out of the article was the darkness in the locker room, her terror when she realized she was trapped there, the brutal malice in the first man's voice, Mike's desperation as he tried to get to her, the—

She closed the paper and got up to make a cup of tea. After which, she decided, she'd go take a shower. She felt tired and dirty, what with grubbing around at the fire-ravaged Girl Scout camp.

She'd just poured milk in her tea when the phone rang. she reached up for the wall-phone receiver. "Hello," she said.

It was Angela. "My God, Shannon," she cried. "I've been trying to reach you all day!"

"I've been out," she said.

"The robbery's all over TV. Are you okay?"

"Yes, I'm fine," she answered. Leaning to the right, she tried to catch a glimpse of Nick through the window over the sink. He'd gone out the back door with the dog.

"Charlie told me they'd already arrested the men," Angela said reassuringly.

"Yeah," Shannon agreed. "But they held a police lineup today, and I couldn't identify them." Her son's dark curly head was just visible. He threw a stick over the stone wall, into the woods, and the dog chased it.

"But they're in custody, right?"

Shannon sighed. "Uh-huh. Charged with a liquor store holdup. They think it's the same guys."

"It probably is, then. The article in the paper sounded pretty positive. Look, you sound tired. Maybe you should rest. I'll talk to you tomorrow."

Shannon hung up and glanced out the window again but Nick and Max had disappeared into the woods. She considered going to the back door and calling him in. Just then, the phone rang again, and she answered impatiently, "Hello?"

A woman's voice said, "Mrs. Hollister?"

"Yes." Shannon looked out the window. No sign of him, darn it.

"This is a bit embarrassing," the woman said. "I'm Mrs. Brennan's niece, Dana. We haven't met, but we have a mutual friend, Mike Finnegan."

"Why, yes," Shannon said, frowning a little.

"I hate to ask a favor, but my aunt's dog, Fred, needs a home. She's been at the vet's since before the fire, and I wondered—that is, Mike said you might be willing to—"

"Take her off your hands?"

The woman gave a small laugh. "Put like that it sounds awful, but really, I can't keep her. The alternative is the pound, and she'll probably be put to sleep—"

"No, that's all right. I'll take her," Shannon said before she could change her mind. "What kind of dog is Fred?"

"Frederica. A dachshund. As a matter of fact, I'm going to be out at my aunt's house tomorrow—I've been staying with friends since the fire—and if you could drop by, I could give you the dog then."

Shannon pushed her hair behind her ears and looked out the window again. Nick was just climbing back over the stone wall, with Max at his side.

"Fine, I'll come by around one," she said. Dana thanked her effusively and hung up with a brisk goodbye.

The back door opened and Shannon called out, "Nick?"

"Mom?" he answered, coming through the back hall into the kitchen. In just a few minutes, he had managed to cover himself with mud from head to toe. Grass and leaves stuck to his dirty sneakers. He left a trail of footprints as he headed for the refrigerator. Max followed with something in his mouth.

"What were you up to?" she asked.

"Nothing much," he said, adroitly catching a bottle of soda that fell out of the refrigerator. He closed the door, unscrewed the cap and began to gulp down the drink. Shannon watched his throat work as he swallowed.

"Did you watch TV or read the paper over at Mike's today?"

He took the bottle out of his mouth, unzipped his jacket, and, without looking at her, said, "Yeah."

"And?" she prompted.

"It made you sound like a karate expert, the way you got away from those guys." He finished his soda and held the bottle up to catch the last few drops on his tongue, then said, "I think you're one tough dude, Mom, but it's a good thing they caught them." He took a turn-around jump shot, and the empty plastic bottle landed neatly in the recycling bag near the pantry.

"How'd you like to have Mrs. Brennan's dog?" she asked, smiling. "Fred needs a home."

His grin spread from ear to ear. "Great! Fred's terrific! She can do all kinds of tricks and she likes Max, too! When can we have her?"

"Tomorrow afternoon." She took a sip of her now-cold tea and said, "It makes it easier that Fred knows both of you."

Max walked over and sniffed the recycling bag, then lost interest and went to Nick and dropped something at his feet.

Nick picked it up. "Hey, it's a wallet." Opening it, he looked inside, then tossed it on the table. "Empty. Max must have dug it up when we were in the woods. What are we having for dinner?"

"How does spaghetti sound?" she said, getting down a big stockpot and filling it with water from the tap.

"Steak sounds better," he said, yanking off his jacket and tossing it on a chair. He sat down and took off his shoes. "It's kinda muddy out back."

"So is the floor. The pan and broom's in the usual place."

"Okay, you don't have to tell me." Getting up, he opened the closet, took out the pan and broom and swept up the mud.

She turned the gas on under the stockpot and looked at him over her shoulder. His shirt collar was tucked awkwardly under on one side. Somehow, his face looked far too serious for an eight-year old. Right now, she thought, I should be saying to myself that he looks like his dad, but he doesn't. His thoughtful face didn't look like hers, either. He looked like himself. Young, solemn, and somehow terribly vulnerable. She reached out to straighten his collar.

"Mom, quit staring at me." He pulled away from her hands and put the pan and broom away. "Are you okay?" he asked with concern.

"Yes, but I'm getting very hungry. Sure spaghetti's enough? Why don't I mix up a salad and make garlic bread?" She looked on the shelf for garlic and discovered the cloves she had were dried up and useless. Well, they'd have rolls, she thought. No way was she driving downtown to get garlic, not now. Not in an unreliable car like hers. All the way downtown to the supermarket. Past the Y. This is ridiculous, she thought. She had classes to teach at the Y, of course she was going back there. She got frozen dinner rolls out of the freezer, knowing that if she gave in to her feelings, little by little, the list of places she couldn't go near would only increase. Places that scared her because of what had happened. She could not give in to her fears, she told herself firmly. She could not afford to get paranoid.

Nick was putting out plates and silverware, pushing everything else on the pine table to one side. She picked up the paper and the mail and put the package from Linda Clarke on top. She'd open it later. "I don't have garlic. Are rolls okay?"

He shrugged. "Yeah, I don't care. Guess we're not having steak."

"No, we're not." She stacked the newspaper and the mail on the counter.

"You know what really gets me?" he said, clearly annoyed. "Mom, are you listening?"

She sighed and got two plates down from the cupboard. "Yes."

"Lurene, that's Chris's name now. She told Andy and me to call her Lurene." He took a breath and added, "She thinks she knows everything. She says you can use a badminton net to catch mummies. Everyone knows that's stupid."

"Last week she said her real name was Dora," Shannon said absently, picking up the wallet the dog had brought in. It was empty, no identification inside, although there was an impression of an initial on the front. M or N.

"Flora, not Dora," Nick corrected. "And that wasn't her real name. She says her real name's Lurene now."

"I think if we ask her dad, we'll find out that her real name is Chris," Shannon said gently. "Chris just has an active imagination."

"Yeah, she's a real pain sometimes." He frowned. "Everyone knows badminton nets are too small to catch mummies. We need a volleyball net like the one in the barn. Can we use it, Mom? Please, and I'll never ask for another thing, not ever. We started digging for pyramids in the woods but didn't find any, so we're gonna dig a trap, instead. Mom, I want to start digging the trap tonight."

"Okay, you can use the net," she said, giving him a quick hug. "But not tonight. I want you inside tonight. We're celebrating."

"What?"

"We're celebrating your successful completion of a whole day without skinning your knees," she said solemnly.

"That's not funny," he said.

"I'm sorry, Nick, I know, but I'd really like to watch TV with you tonight. We can make some popcorn and put any movie you like in the VCR. You don't have to help dry the dishes. For an added inducement, I'll give you ten thousand dollars."

"Mom, you're making fun," Nick complained. "But you mean it about the movie and not drying the dishes?"

"I mean it," she said. "And tomorrow after we pick up Fred, we could ask Andy and Chris—sorry, Andy and *Lurene* and their dad over for dinner."

Nick thought about it, considered the offer with various extreme changes of expression and said, "I guess so. Andy's my best friend and if he comes over, she will, too. Sometimes she doesn't like being the only girl around. I mean, where else would she eat if her whole family's over here. Besides, you're sort of right. She's started telling stories again."

"Like what?" she said, taking the lid off the stockpot and dumping a handful of spaghetti into the boiling water.

"The men in that dark car," Nick said. He yawned and began kicking the chair rung. "Can we watch *Aliens?* You never let me watch good stuff."

"No, and what men in what dark car?" she said, turning around and frowning.

"She said there were two men in a dark car going up and down the street this afternoon. She said one man looked like a wrestler from the WWF, and the other looked like a funny guy on 'Taxi.'"

She forced herself to put the empty box of spaghetti down on the counter and say quietly, "And these men just drove up and down the street once or twice, then drove away?''

"I dunno, I didn't see 'em," Nick replied, yawning again. "Lurene said they looked like creeps."

"Did she say anything else about the car, what color it was, anything else about the men?" Shannon asked, sitting down at the table across from her son.

"I think she said it was dark blue, or black or something." He shrugged. "With a big dent in the side. I think she made it up."

"And I," Shannon said with a sigh, "think they were just lost. Now go wash your hands. Spaghetti's almost done."

He examined his hands front and back and showed them to her. "See? They don't need washing, they're only a little dirty."

She tossed a salad, threw bacon bits on top and made Nick's favorite dressing while she heated the sauce and rolls. He devoured two plates of spaghetti, three rolls and all his salad, then made a banana split to eat while they watched a movie in the VCR. Against her better judgment and hoping he wouldn't get all the jokes, Shannon agreed to *Raising Arizona*.

After the movie was over, Nick announced what he liked about the film. While she rewound the tape and put it back in the box, he said, puzzled, "How come you left all the lights on? Usually you turn out most of 'em when we watch a movie."

She shrugged and rubbed her forearms nervously. "No reason, I guess. I just felt like having them on."

"Oh," he said, accepting without question that his mom acted a little weird now and then. "I'm going upstairs to bed."

She hurried after him. "Wait, let me, uh, come up with you. Your bed might need changing."

It didn't but there was no way she could tell him that she couldn't let him go upstairs alone. She had to check and make sure his room was empty, that there wasn't another surprise lurking there.

He pushed open his door and switched on the light. Max jumped up on the bed and put his nose on his black paws, clearly set for the night. Nick yawned, pulled off his shirt and padded off down the hall toward the bathroom. When he shut the door and she heard water running, she searched the room, every corner of it. No one was there, of course. Then, feeling foolish, she turned down his coverlet.

He came back, and she kissed his cheek. "Good night, sweet dreams."

"G'night, Mom." He slipped into bed and turned over.

She went down the hall to her bedroom, looked out the window and noted with relief that Tim Carver's truck was parked by the barn. Just the sight of it made her feel better. He might be an oddball, but he was tall, strong and male.

She yawned, feeling totally drained. The sheets felt cool against her skin. She turned over in bed and closed her eyes. Worry made her tense, and she didn't think she'd fall asleep right away in spite of being dead-tired. Nerves, she thought, heaving a deep breath. She heard the soothing sound of rain falling through the trees, then the hoot of an owl. Her eyes closed, and she slept.

ACROSS THE DRIVEWAY in his apartment in the barn, Tim Carver was sitting staring at his TV. Flickering images on the screen came and went, but his gaze remained vacant. He was deep in thought. A series of nightmarish images flickered through his mind. Fire burning in a hearth, then devouring a nearby curtain, leaping up the wall and spanning the ceiling. With an explosive *whomp,* the ceiling blew and fire was everywhere.

He blinked, and for an instant had the crazy notion the fire had been on television. But no, on the screen before him, a man and a blond woman were making out on a beach. And that shiver crawling down his spine was just the residual vibration of fear and shame that filled his thoughts.

Sooner or later, there'd be another fire, he knew it as sure as he knew the morning sun would come up. It was necessary.

His mouth twisted, and he popped a beer and drained it. He looked terrible. His face was milk-white, greasy with sweat, and his eyes were bloodshot. *Why did he have to set the fires?* he thought. *Why?*

# Chapter Nine

She felt awful. Still tired, Shannon crawled out of bed at six-thirty. She made tea and drank it, looking across the driveway at the barn. Tim's truck was still there. It was a comforting sight. She had orange juice and changed into a pair of faded old jeans and a sweat-shirt, suitable for repapering the upstairs hall. Coming back downstairs to the kitchen, she was tempted to have more orange juice, but there wasn't much left and Nick liked it in the morning.

She'd glanced in as she passed his doorway, but he was still asleep, Max at his feet. Well, he had plenty of time yet before he had to get ready for school.

She washed her glass and put it on the draining board to dry. The sun was just coming up, golden light streaming through the trees. Morning mist rose from the puddles in the driveway. It was going to be a good day, she told herself. A day to get a lot done in. Before she thought about what she was doing, she leaned over and switched on the little black-and-white TV on the kitchen counter.

The news was on. Threats of a nationwide rail strike, then local news. A bad accident on Route 6, two peo-ple dead. Drunk driving suspected. Then a commercial, and she almost missed it because she'd reached out to snap the TV off. The robbery at the Y. Her name wasn't mentioned this time, nor Mike's. A taped scene of the two men being arraigned at the courthouse. Heads down, they shuffled into the courtroom, hands handcuffed behind their backs. The judge looked over a bunch of papers and their lawyer requested that bail be lowered. This was denied with a bang of the gavel. Fifty thousand dollars apiece. The judge was clearly annoyed at the epidemic of fires and robberies in the area. He was making an example of these two.

"So they're safely locked up," came a voice behind her, and Shannon drew a startled breath, her heart in her throat.

Tim Carver stood by the back door. "Heard what happened to you the other night. It sounded real bad. You were lucky. People today, they don't care who gets hurt."

She shrugged. "Actually, I wasn't hurt. But the man who was picking me up was stabbed in the shoulder."

"Right, Mike Finnegan. I saw it on the news. He's gonna be okay. Guess he had a close call." Tim shook his head. "It's not over yet, not by a long shot."

"Why not?" she asked, frowning. "Oh, come on in. Have you had breakfast?" Saying he'd already eaten, thanks, he sat down at the table and said maybe he could use another cup of coffee. The water was still hot, so she made instant and poured him a mugful, pushing milk and sugar across the table. "What do you mean, 'it's not over'?"

He paused, sipped some coffee and put down the mug. "I seen it happen. Some guy gets arrested and tried for something bad. Say he shot somebody. Say it was murder. Well, it don't matter if the whole state of

Maine testifies that they saw him pull the trigger, there's still a chance he'll be back on the street. Maybe bail'll be reduced. Maybe someone'll make a mistake, and they walk away clean from the trial. Or they hire a smart lawyer who makes a deal and they do easy time. Then they're out in three, four years. You'll still be around then, see what I mean?"

Frowning, she turned off the TV and sat down at the table. "Sure, I see what you mean...."

A flash of fear and anger touched her. When was she ever going to feel safe again? "I can't believe this is happening," she said with a cold shudder, her voice flat and angry.

"Maybe it'll work out." Tim gave her an apologetic smile. "Hey, I didn't mean to upset you."

"You didn't," she lied.

He rose. "Guess I'd better be gettin' to work. Barn roof's all but done. I got a coupla framin' jobs the other side of town."

"I'm buying stronger locks for the doors today," she told him, getting to her feet and going with him to the back door. "I'd appreciate it if you'd—"

"Install 'em? No problem."

"And Tim, could you stay in nights for a while?"

"Sure. What with everything going on, uh, I mean the fires and all, uh, I'm gettin' kinda scared, myself."

And Shannon thought, he did look a little frightened, but he also looked determined and capable.

"Will you tell me somethin'?" he said, his voice suddenly gentle. "How come you're not scared?"

"I am," she said. "Terrified. I have nightmares about it. But they'll catch whoever's setting those fires, and the men who robbed the Y are locked up. I have to believe they'll be put away for a long time."

"Listen, you want a gun?" he whispered, as if someone might be eavesdropping.

"No, thanks," she said. "I can take care of myself."

He backed away with a wave of the hand and disappeared into the barn. A minute later, he emerged with the ladder on his shoulder. A short time afterward, he was back on the roof, hammering.

For the next hour, Shannon concentrated on getting Nick up and dressed and ready for the school bus. When it had trundled downhill and around the bend in the road, she went back inside the house and took a portable radio upstairs.

She half listened to a discussion of troubles in the Middle East. Two or three times, she considered switching to soothing music, but gradually found herself caught up in what was being said.

The bell in the shop rang, and she went downstairs. A man and his wife looking for a small pine cupboard. Luckily, she had two very nice pieces, and in half an hour had sold one. They arranged to come back with a van and pick it up later, and left.

Putting their check into the desk drawer, she went back upstairs to the wallpaper mess. Almost done. Funny, she thought. The right-hand wall had some weird bumpy surfaces. She ran her hand over the worst of them, frowning. It almost looked like a straight edge under the paper. All the way to the floor. She was trying to imagine what that meant, when she heard a sharp whistle, and looked down to see Mike at the foot of the stairs. "Hi," he said, smiling and looking as if the past few nights hadn't happened. "Glad to see you're working hard." He held up a large paper bag. "Locks. I stopped at the hardware store."

"Oh, thanks. I planned to get them later."

He rummaged in the bag, then held one up for her to see. "This okay for the back door? I'll put it in."

She applied herself to scraping the wall for ten minutes, then went downstairs to see how Mike was coming with the back-door lock. It was already in, shiny, new and formidable. He showed her how it worked and put the new keys on the kitchen table.

"Put one on your key ring and don't forget to show Nick how it works when he gets home." Mike looked down at her and smiled. "It's probably just as well you're replacing the locks. The one on this door must have come on the Ark."

"Not quite as old as the house," she admitted. "But close. Want a beer?"

His smile widened. "Yeah, that would hit the spot."

She got a beer from the refrigerator, handed it to him and he popped the cap, watching her as he did. Finally, uncomfortable, she said, "What's wrong?"

He took a sip, smiled and said, "I got a call from Dana Jennings this morning. Mrs. Brennan's niece. She said you were taking Fred off her hands."

"That's right." She got a beer for herself, popped it open and shrugged. "It's either me or the pound, so Fred doesn't have much choice."

He grinned and finished his beer. "I heard our friends from the Y didn't make bail. On the car radio, coming over. Does that mean you won't need my strong shoulder to lean on?"

A little preoccupied because she was wondering if Fred had been fixed, and if not, how to fit that into a monthly budget, she said, "Not necessarily," and told him about the wall upstairs. "It's definitely peculiar, but...you'll have to see it." Putting down her beer, she took his hand and pulled him upstairs to show him the odd contours of the right-hand wall. "What do you think?"

They were next to the door leading to the attic stairs. Mike gave the wall a long, reflective look. "This is just about where the house does that funny jog. The outside proportions don't match this." He tapped the wall with the scraper handle, looking for studs. "Could be someone blocked off a small storage area, then papered it over." He looked down at her. "It wouldn't take more than removing a few feet of old plaster and lath. No valuable Porter murals in evidence, so what do you say? Want to give it a try? I'll even help clean up the mess." She nodded, and he handed her a screwdriver and told her to tap the wall about three feet to the left. "We don't want to take down more than necessary, so take it slow and easy. Remember, the less we knock down, the less we have to put back."

Soon, billowing clouds of dust from falling plaster filled the hallway as he broke through the lath. "How can you see what you're doing?" She coughed, wiping her streaming eyes and tugging open a nearby window.

Mike was bent over, peering into the gaping hole he'd knocked in the wall. He withdrew his head and said, "You're right, it's dark as hell. Can't see a thing."

"Wait a minute, I'll get a flashlight," she said.

By the time she'd gone downstairs and returned with it, he'd enlarged the hole. She pulled the stepladder farther from the pile of debris and said, "We can get a saw from Tim Carver. He's home."

Mike stared at her. "What's all this 'home' talk? He's only a temporary tenant, right? You're not thinking of letting him stay here indefinitely...? " His voice trailed off as he saw the indecision on her face.

"It was just an expression." His attitude annoyed her. What business was it of his who stayed there? "We never put a time limit on how long he can stay. It's really between him and me." Her voice held a thread of temper.

"Someone's burning down half the town, and if Carver left, you'd rent that apartment to the first person who showed up, wouldn't you." It wasn't a question.

"If he had references, sure."

"Fine." He turned and banged away at the wall again. More plaster fell and dust filled the air. A cold draft came in the open window clearing the air, but Shannon still found herself coughing. He wore a set expression and continued enlarging the hole although it was already big enough to allow him a good look inside.

So what if he's mad, she thought, leaning back against the other wall. Just because she'd let him kiss her didn't give him carte blanche to run her life. She took a deep breath, coughed and decided she didn't need to feel guilty about renting to Tim Carver. She had a perfect right to rent her barn to anyone she chose.

He knocked down another foot of plaster and lath before he was satisfied. Then he looked in the hole and shone the flashlight around. "It's a room. Messy as hell." His voice was muffled. "There's a window, no, two of them in adjacent walls. They're both boarded up." Pulling his head out, he gave her the flashlight. "Take a look for yourself."

The small room was dark and stuffy, curiously still. Dust lay everywhere. She moved the beam of light from side to side. Boxes, piles of old papers, newspapers, unbelievable clutter. A table with a cracked leg leaned drunkenly against the near wall. A pair of broken-down chairs. A bird cage. She wondered why all this hadn't been stored in the attic. If this room had been turned into a storage closet, perhaps it had served the same purpose.

"You ought to get a cat up here for a while. Mice have had a field day in there." Mike's voice came closer, and he put his arm around her shoulders and leaned inside. "Smells terrible."

She trembled, aware his hand was tightening around her. And oh, if felt so good to be held by him. Warm, loving, safe. Pushing the flashlight into his hand, she stepped back, took a deep breath and said, "I'll get a broom and clean up this mess." She looked around at the piles of wallpaper and plaster. Anywhere but at his laughing eyes. In another minute, she'd forget all about the broom and walk right into his arms.

"Good idea," he said. "Then we'll have room to drag more stuff out into the hall." He was whistling when she came back with the broom and a large garbage pail. Setting it down, she began sweeping. Already he'd removed two boxes of papers. She stopped sweeping and poked around in one of the boxes while he dumped an armload of lath and plaster into the pail.

"This is fascinating," she said as she scanned one yellowed sheet of paper. "Listen to this. It's a reward poster, dated October 21, 1835. Two-hundred dollars for the return of a runaway slave. 'Thomas Scott of Maryland will pay $100 and all reasonable expenses if his runaway slave, one Frank Mullen, about twenty-one years old, five foot ten or eleven, is brought home to the subscriber, living in the city of Baltimore. Mullen's hair is close-cropped. He has a mild countenance, is polite when spoken to and very genteel in his person. As he has absconded without any provocation, it is presumed his destination is Canada.' "

Wide-eyed, she stared at Mike who dropped the lath and came over to read the poster. "My word!" he breathed, taking it from her hand. "What else is in that box?"

She sorted through it and found old receipts, broken dishes and an iron key, a good five inches long. Holding it up, she mused, "Wonder what this opened?"

"From the look of the poster, maybe a set of leg irons."

"Be serious," she said, putting the key back into the box.

"I am." He picked up the key. "Boxford was a stop on the Underground Railroad. This house could have sheltered runaway slaves heading north for freedom."

She stared at Mike, stunned. This house or perhaps others in town, stations on the Underground Railroad!

He turned the poster over. There was writing in faded brown ink on the back. "Listen to this," he said. "'P.S. I will give the above reward of $200 only if Mullen is returned in good health. One caution, if it is deemed necessary to shoot at this runaway, use bird shot so as not to damage. Oct. 25, 1835, Thos. C. Scott.' "

Near the bottom of the back of the poster in faded black ink, someone had scrawled a crude drawing of a flower and what looked like a lizard.

"They marked safe houses with cryptic signs," Mike said thoughtfully. "I wonder—"

"But why bother with cryptic signs and secrecy up here in Maine? We're a long way from the slave states."

"As I remember, there was a Fugitive Slave Law of 1850, giving slaveholders the right to organize a posse anywhere in the U.S. to recapture a runaway slave. Courts and police had to help them.''

"My God," she breathed.

"Runaways weren't safe anywhere," Mike said, his voice grim. "People who helped them faced criminal prosecution and heavy fines, plus the prospect of being sued by the slave owner for loss of property." Shaking his head, he turned the poster over again. "The poor devil."

"I wonder if Frank Mullen was ever caught?" she said quietly. "I hope not."

He looked up at the sloping ceiling with its jogs and angles. "If the house could speak, maybe we'd know for sure."

Gazing down the hall at whitewashed beams, splayed gunstock posts, notches, cracks, beaded door frames, original hardware—Shannon felt a strong sense of comfort. For a long time, this house had provided shelter and warmth, and if Frank Mullen had come to the door for help, somehow she knew he'd received it.

Mike smiled at her and went back to sweeping up fallen plaster. After cleaning up most of the mess, they took the loaded garbage pail out to the barn. A hay-stuffed scarecrow with a pitchfork in one hand leaned against the side of the weathered barn. Mike tilted its baseball cap a bit more rakishly. "What's this for?"

She shrugged. "Local color for my antique shop. It helps bring in business."

"Really?" He glanced toward the sign near the end of the driveway. "Wouldn't it be easier to see if you positioned it down near the road?"

She gave another shrug. "I like the way it looks by the barn."

The driveway near the barn was deserted, and there was no sign of hammering on the roof. Tim Carver had disappeared again. "Where's Carver?" Mike asked quietly.

"How should I know?" she said, hunching her shoulders. "He's got a few other jobs, but he'll be back."

From the set expression on Mike's face, that's just what he was afraid of. "Can't figure that guy out," he muttered. "Well, never mind. Look, I'm heading over to Mrs. Brennan's place. Dana's asked me to draw up some plans to rebuild the burned wing. As long as you're picking up Fred anyway, why not come along?"

*HORRIBLE,* Shannon thought, as they pulled up Mrs. Brennan's driveway and she got her first look at the house since the night of the fire. Most of it was still intact. The damage had been confined to the back wing, which yawned open to the sky, blackened and empty, like a bombed-out crater. "My God," she whispered. "I hope she didn't suffer."

They got out of the Bronco and walked up toward the house. The lawn spread out from a side terrace to a stone wall beyond which they could see a well-kept perennial border. Beyond that lay a rose garden. The winter burlap covers had been removed from the bushes and mulch had been cleared away. Mrs. Brennan had been getting ready for spring.

She sighed and Mike put his arm around her. Just then, a car roared up, and they turned around. A small blond woman got out, waving. She glanced at Mike and then Shannon and said cordially, "Hi, I'm Dana Jennings."

Mike smiled and introduced Shannon. "I thought we'd kill two birds with one stone. Shannon's come by to pick up Fred, and you can show me exactly what changes you want in the reconstruction."

Dana nodded and led the way up to the house. Shannon dropped behind a little as they walked around to the back. Dana Jennings looked cool and sophisticated. Her hair was coiled smoothly atop her head. She wore black linen trousers and a cream silk blouse with a cashmere sweater tied carelessly around her shoulders. Her pristine appearance made Shannon feel rather untidy and grubby. Well, jeans and a sweater were what she'd put on this morning. She was stuck with them.

Every now and then, she caught snatches of Dana and Mike's conversation as they went through the house. According to Dana, the whole place was in a state of disaster; never mind the fire damage, there didn't seem to be a window frame that wasn't rotted or a floor that didn't sag. The walls need painting, and she thought perhaps a conservatory would make a nice addition. And French doors leading to the terrace.

They reached the kitchen, which had about half the number of cabinets Dana deemed necessary. "You're not living here while it's being rebuilt, are you?" Mike asked her.

"No, I've still got my place in Portland until the end of the month, but I'm spending most of this week in Boxford with friends." She shrugged. "I've been toying with the idea of moving out of Portland for some time, so now that Aunt Nonie is dead, I've decided to move here permanently. I'd like to be in by the middle of April."

Mike looked skeptical. "That doesn't give us much time."

"Oh, I don't care. I'll offer the builders a ten percent bonus if they meet my deadline."

Hmm, she's got money to throw around, Mike thought, wondering if her inheritance was a factor.

When they had finished their tour of the house, Dana led them out on the terrace and they all sat down on the stone wall. "Have a drink?" she asked sociably. "I've got a bottle of Chablis in a cooler in my car." They declined and she sighed. "My life's been a mess for months, ever since I filed for divorce from my husband." She looked at Mike. "You must have seen the private detective he put on my tail. Big man, cold blue eyes. He's been following me for weeks." Gesturing toward the road, she went on, "Look down there if you don't believe me. That dark blue car, that's him."

Shannon stared down the driveway. Sure enough, through the bushes she could see a car parked by the shoulder of the road. Beside her, Mike rose to his feet. "Do you want me to tell him to get lost?"

"Why bother?" Dana laughed sourly. "He'll just turn up again like a bad penny." She got to her feet and smiled at Shannon. "Well, I suppose you'd like to see Fred. She's in a cage in the car. I'll give you the cage, as well. I won't be needing it."

She led the way over to her car and opened the back door. A small wire dog crate lay on the seat. It contained a mahogany-colored dachshund who'd obviously given up hope of being let out soon. Her mournful eyes looked through the bars, and her tail didn't move.

Dana frowned and fiddled with the catch on the cage. "Damn thing, honestly! This dog's more trouble than she's worth—"

"Here, let me." Pushing her hands away from the cage, Mike had it open in no time, and Shannon gathered the little dog up in her arms, noticing Fred's tail was wagging a mile a minute.

She endured a furious licking on the chin and patted Fred's smooth head. "She's adorable. My son, Nick, will love her."

"Well, to each his own I always say," Dana murmured as she turned to Mike. "Listen, I'd like to go over a few more ideas for the back wing, but I don't have time right now. Why don't I give you a call later, maybe we can get together for dinner?"

Glancing at Shannon, he nodded. "If not tonight, then we'll make it some other night. I might be tied up with a neighborhood fire-watch, though—"

Dana shrugged. "I know what you mean. It's just one thing after another. I just came back from Portland today, a meeting with Aunt Nonie's lawyer." Her face clouded over. "Would you believe it, I lost a damn hubcap on Route 202 where they're fixing that bridge! It'll cost close to four hundred dollars to replace four of them, and they don't sell just one."

"They get you coming and going," Mike said, nodding.

Shannon shifted Fred into a more comfortable position in her arms. She was like a wriggly hot dog, every inch of her squirming every which way at once.

*Route 202, Portland.* Where had she heard that recently? Oh, yes, Shannon thought. Tim said he'd been there, and that the roadwork hadn't held him up much. Well, Dana had confirmed that roadwork was taking place on the highway. So he was telling the truth of his whereabouts—at least about that.

MIKE WAS RIGHT about the probability of his being busy with the neighborhood fire-watch. Paul Wagoner flagged them down as they were driving back from Mrs. Brennan's and said it was on for tonight. He'd take the shift from eight to ten if Mike would patrol the neighborhood until dark. Another neighbor would cover from ten till midnight.

"The volunteer fire-watch makes me feel safer," Shannon said as Paul drove off down the street.

"We're taking some action, anyway," Mike agreed pulling into her driveway. She got out of the Bronco, and he left, saying he'd bring the kids over when he was done with his shift.

The back door was slightly ajar and she turned to call Mike back, but it was too late. He'd already driven away. Well, maybe she'd forgotten to close it tightly. Sometimes the latch didn't catch. Feeling like a fool, she went inside, her heart knocking in her throat. Everything looked normal, nothing out of place. She put Fred down and ran water in the dog dish.

Someone rapped on the door, and she all but jumped out of her skin. "Oh, it's you," she gasped as she saw Tim.

Fred started barking and woke Max, who trotted in from the front hall. His tail wagged furiously at the sight of the little dachshund. She smiled. What a relief that was. The dogs were going to get along famously.

Tim glanced at Fred and said, "German dog, right?"

"Yes," she said, wondering what he'd stopped by for.

"Stubborn little cusses, but cute." He scratched the back of his head. "Listen, Ms. Hollister, reason I stopped by, I noticed your door was unlatched earlier. Uh, I thought I'd come in and take a look around for you. Everything was okay. I, uh, just wanted you to know I'd done that. Uh, come in and checked upstairs, and all.''

She nodded. "Thanks, the door swells if it's humid and doesn't quite catch."

"The phone in the apartment has been on the fritz off and on today. It's workin' now, but you might want to check yours." He opened the door and paused. "Oh, I'll be goin' out for a while, but I'll be back later on."

"Okay, thanks again." She picked up the receiver and dialed the police station. When they answered, she asked to speak to Officer Conway. There was such a long pause that she thought the line had gone dead, but he finally came on.

"Officer Conway."

"It's Shannon Hollister," she said. "I just wanted to make sure you'll be keeping a watch on my house."

"That's right. An officer will drive by every hour or so."

"Good, I—" she began, but he'd already hung up, "appreciate that", she finished to a dead line. Talk about being all business, she thought wryly. Oh, well, she had dinner to fix. Chicken oriental, she thought, getting out chicken breasts and setting the table. A quick check in the refrigerator, and she discovered she was out of milk. Glancing at the clock, she decided there was just time to run down to the store for a half gallon.

She locked the door and hurried to the car, her mind churning as she sorted through everything she still had to do for dinner. Noodles and rolls could be heated when she got back, and for dessert they'd have short-cake. She had strawberries in the freezer.

Night was just settling in, with streaks of clouds scudding across the sky. A cold wind rattled the bare tree branches, and she pulled her jacket around her.

Cold as death, she thought suddenly, then chided herself for getting morbid, and pressed down on the accelerator. Praying it would start and wishing she'd remembered to take it to the garage for a tune-up, she turned the key in the ignition. The engine turned over once and died. Oh, God, no, she thought, biting her lower lip and trying again. Come on, this is no time for games!

# *Chapter Ten*

"Damn it, start!" she burst out, infuriated. As if startled into action, the engine backfired once, then rumbled beneath the hood. She grinned, patted the wheel and backed down the driveway. Of course, there were still the brakes to worry about. The grin faded from her lips as she tried them gingerly. A bit spongy, but they'd be all right for this short trip.

The interior of her car was damp and cold. She switched the heater on after she'd driven a few miles, and it warmed up slowly. A glance at the temperature gauge reassured her that it wasn't overheating—as it was known to do. The arrow was safely in the blue.

When she made the turn on to Route 110, she discovered traffic was surprisingly heavy and slowed down. A many-legged insect flew into the windshield and died. She tried to ignore it without much success. Maybe the radio. She reached over and turned it on. A Celtics' basketball game. They were playing the Lakers. Half time, and the Celtics were losing. She sighed and turned it off.

She slowed further as she turned and drove down a street lined with summer cottages closed for the winter. Ghostly mist blew in from the sea, and she had the sudden feeling of being all alone in the world. She switched on her high beams and felt better.

Another turn and Shannon hit Mountainville Street and the little market on the corner. She pulled off the street into the side parking lot and hurried to the door. Then, over her shoulder, she saw a truck pull into the lot. It was the same make as Tim Carver's. She pushed through the plate-glass door into the blast of warmth. Inside, she turned to look out the window at the truck, which was slowly searching for a parking spot. She couldn't tell how many people were in it. It was on the far side of the lot which was ill-lit. The truck stopped and turned off its lights. Feeling like a fool, she stood and watched to see if Tim Carver got out.

"Can I help you, ma'am?" a voice said behind her.

"Just a second," she said, without turning toward the voice. "I just want to catch my breath."

"Okay, but I'm stocking the shelves. When you've got the things you want, give me a yell," the man said, moving away.

She nodded and stood there a few minutes more, thinking it was perfectly natural for Tim to be stopping here, too. He'd said he was going out. Maybe he was just picking up some things for himself or a date. *Then why didn't he get out of the truck and come in?*

Another second, then the passenger's door opened, and a young woman got out. She ran across the lot, her jeans tight, her breasts bouncing against her heavy wool sweater. As she came through the glass door, she was panting, her long brown hair swirling around her face.

"Damn, it's cold!" The woman threw her hair back, and Shannon noticed she wasn't so young, after all. There were fine lines around her eyes, but she had a nice smile.

Shannon walked to the back of the store and picked up two half gallons of milk. Then she joined the brown-haired woman at the register as she was scratching the surface of a lottery ticket with a quarter. "Nuts, a loser," the woman said, tossing the ticket in the trash. The plate-glass door was still swinging shut as she dashed back toward the truck. Shannon watched as the woman hurried across the lot and opened the door. The truck's interior light came on, and in the flash of time it took the woman to get in and close the door, Shannon could see a pair of dice dangled from the mirror and the door was dented. And the man behind the wheel was not Tim.

The clerk rang up the milk. "That all?"

"Yes," she said, handing him money, then glancing back at the truck. Headlights sprang on, and it moved gently back into the stream of traffic.

She put the change into her purse and picked up the two half gallons of milk in both arms. Awkward, she thought. But she could manage it. She felt the cold air burn all the way to the bottom of her lungs as she took her first breath, stepping outside the store. Then she glanced all around the parking lot, telling herself she was being an idiot. She had to shake the sense that she was being followed. The men who attacked her were in jail. She ought to feel safe. She shouldn't be going into a panic every time she went out at night.

Besides, the coast was clear now. Her car was the only vehicle in the lot. And she'd left the headlights on.... She dashed across the lot, her feet scraping the gritty paving.

"How about a break?" she said, putting her key into the ignition and speaking to the car, fate and any gods or goddesses that might be listening. She turned the key, heard the sick grinding of a tired battery, and then the catching of the engine. It turned over and she sat feeding it the gas gently, thankful she had a small car.

THE MAN with ice-blue eyes sat in the dark car, parked down the street from the market. He'd been following Shannon Hollister and had nearly lost her a couple of times, but not quite. He had almost pulled into the market parking lot, but something had warned him. He wasn't exactly sure why he'd decided to park a block away, but he was glad he had. When he switched off the lights, he'd been able to see Shannon standing inside the store by the door, looking out at the parking lot. A truck had just driven in, and she was staring hard at it. She couldn't have seen him, he thought. Maybe she was just being more careful since the night at the Y. He should have killed her then, he thought angrily.

If that damn Mike Finnegan hadn't shown up.

He tapped his fingers impatiently on the steering wheel. Damn, she was still looking out at the parking lot with those damn blue eyes of hers. Blue with black specks around the iris. Magic, burning, staring at him in his dreams while he choked the life out of her. Breath hissing between his teeth, he gripped the steering wheel so hard his knuckles turned white. She was still looking out the store window. Staring at the truck.

He swore softly. No one was getting out of the truck. Dammit. He checked his watch. He didn't have all night. His tapping increased, then slowed as a woman in tight jeans suddenly opened the truck door and ran into the store. He grinned as Shannon turned and disappeared behind a stack of canned goods. All right, he thought. It was only a matter of time now, and then she would lose the last of her nine lives.

A BLOCK AWAY, Tim Carver slipped one hand under his sweatshirt and gripped his aching stomach. An ulcer, more n' likely, he thought. He all but doubled over behind the wheel of his truck. After a moment, the pain eased some, and he straighted up. Now it was just a dull burning in his stomach. He drove down Main Street, looking for a particular business establishment. Past Grove Street, the Y, the hardware store. Two blocks on, a traffic light turned yellow, so he braked.

OH GOD, she thought, glancing at the glowing clock on the car dashboard. She was really late. Mike and the kids were probably already sitting in the driveway, unable to get into the house because the locks were changed, and all the keys but one were safely stowed away in her purse.

She pulled out of the parking lot, her mind totally occupied with getting dinner on the table and feeding Mike and the kids. She'd forgotten all about the truck and never once thought to glance in the rearview mirror to see if she was being followed. Chewing on her bottom lip, she thought about passing the car ahead of her. Too much traffic, she'd never make it. She sighed and wondered about taking a back road home, a shortcut. But the shortcut was narrow and bumpy, too. If she met a car coming the other way, one of them would have to pull over and wait. It just wasn't safe.

She stayed on the main road, then made a left turn at the next corner and then another left, and went on until she hit Meadow Street. She turned right and speeded up. Almost home. Her neck felt tight and tense. She rubbed it, planning, thinking, juggling ideas. Wondering if she'd been right to ignore Mike's advice and move back home with Nick so soon after the robbery. Guilt, she thought. Enough of that. Coming up to the next intersection, just as the light turned green, she noticed a truck a few cars ahead. The truck looked like Tim Carver's. Oh, no, not again. Every damn truck she saw looked like his.

Telling herself she was being a complete idiot, she nevertheless kept her eye on the truck as it pulled away. A half a block on, its right-turn signal clicked on, and the truck pulled in and parked in front of a dry cleaners and a corner bar.

She stared as she went past. No dent, so it wasn't the one she'd seen at the store. But a man was getting out. *Tim.* And behind him in the background, she saw the sign for Lucky Dry Cleaners. The logo was a jaunty green four-leaf clover.

It was late, the cleaners was closed. So what was he doing there at that hour?

He could have any number of reasons, she told herself. A girlfriend in one of the nearby apartments. Or maybe he'd just been looking for a parking spot. There was a phone booth on the corner. Maybe he wanted to call someone.

Any number of innocent reasons, she told herself again. Besides, he'd told her he was going out for a while. Maybe he was playing poker with a couple of his buddies. Or dropping in at that bar on the corner for a drink.

BY THE TIME she got home and parked by the barn, she'd convinced herself she was jumping at shadows. She was relieved that Mike and the kids weren't waiting. Getting out of the car she went up to the back door, forcing herself to walk slowly. Once inside, she locked the door securely and turned to accept the reassuring normalcy of her cluttered kitchen and the sight of Fred and Max lying under the table, their heads on their respective noses.

A little while later, she began making dinner. She set the table with her favorite Mexican ceramic plates.

She let the dogs out before feeding them, then called them in a few minutes later. Fred came right away, eager to eat, but Max was nowhere to be found.

By now it was pitch-black out. She switched on the porch light and called Max again. Lights were on in the apartment and Tim's truck was back. Funny, she hadn't seen him pull in. But she'd been busy getting dinner on the table, she thought. And hadn't noticed his headlights come up the driveway.

She went to the drawer and got a flashlight, made sure it worked and went outside to look for Max. Pushing aside the lilac bushes that grew thick by the corner of the barn, "Max!" she called. Nothing. She whistled. Nothing. Damn him! He liked to hide once in a while when he had more important things to do than come when she called. Raccoon or skunk business, no doubt.

She worked her way through the hedge by the stone wall, along the weedy flower bed, and across the back lawn. "Max, come here, boy!" No answering bark, and no jingle of his collar tags. The flashlight beam picked out the back porch, which, she noticed with a sigh, needed painting.

"Max!" At the side of the barn, she turned and looked back the way she'd come. Black as the inside of a tomb. "Max!" She continued on the brick path past the daylilies and the bench Nick had knocked together out of an old board and two tree stumps. "Here, boy...come on, Max," she cried, looking around.

Nothing. Only the vague elongated shape of the grape arbor. Now it looked almost like a ghostly tunnel, she thought. Looming out of the night mist, its black mouth yawning wide.

She turned away, knowing she ought to search the grape arbor—what if Max had dug up a bone or worse. The papers were full of the rabies danger. A few wild raccoons had been infected with the virus. Max had had his shots, but if he came across a rabid raccoon, he could still get a painful bite.

Get a grip, she told herself. It's just the grape arbor. No big deal, for heaven's sake. Twenty-five feet of arbor built of logs and covered with grapevines, clematis and climbing roses. A short walk through it with the flashlight, and at least she'd put to rest the fear that Max was somewhere inside it, eating something she'd rather not think about.

She took a deep breath and walked toward the arbor. To the left, a stand of blackberry bushes she'd been meaning to trim. As she passed, a thorn caught her sweater, and she stopped to pull it free. Suddenly, she raised her head, feeling she was being watched. She looked toward the arbor. A few loose vines stirred in the wind, making a whispering noise. Other than that, everything was still. Shannon, sometimes you act like a silly fool, she told herself. Who would be watching?

She stopped at the entrance to the arbor and peered into the darkness. The flashlight flickered and dimmed in her hand. She shook it, and it settled into a yellowish glow. Great, the batteries were going. "Who's there?" she called. The loose vines rustled eerily again, then she thought she heard a faint whimpering sound, like an animal in pain. "Max?" No answer. She hesitated, listening as the whimper came again. Deep inside the impenetrable blackness. About twenty-five feet away. Directly in front of her.

She took a step forward, and the flashlight went out. Damn. It was brand-new. The batteries couldn't be more than two months old. Nick had probably been playing with it. Flashlights and kids. Damn. Shaking it produced a feeble glow that wouldn't last more than a few minutes. She took a deep breath. "Max, come here, boy!" Nothing. And the whimpering sounds had stopped. Well, the wind had died and it could have been the sound of vines scraping on the arbor. She felt slightly foolish, standing in the dark yelling for her dog who was probably at the back door, scratching to be let in. As she stood there, debating with herself, the flashlight went out altogether. That did it.

Thunder rumbled as she whirled and headed back up the path, feeling as if eyes were watching her from the shadows. By the time she passed the bench, she was almost running. She was breathing fast and shallow, unable to stop her legs from shaking. The house loomed just ahead, past the lilacs at the corner of the barn. She broke into a dead run and stumbled as she rounded the corner, half falling to her knees. Heart pounding, she reached out to stop herself and touched the brim of a cap, smooth cloth, scratchy hay. *The scarecrow.* She got up and ran, panting, by now terrified half out of her wits.

Vaguely, she heard something fall behind her. The pitchfork. Then a strong pair of arms grabbed her shoulders. "Hey, what's wrong?" Mike's voice came out of the darkness. He was holding her, keeping her from falling flat on her face.

"I was looking for Max," she gasped, heart pounding. "I thought I heard something out by the arbor."

"It wasn't Max?" he asked.

She struggled upright. "No, I'd have heard his collar tags. It whimpered—it could be a sick raccoon."

She could vaguely see him nod his head. "Okay, want me to take a look?"

"Please, only you'll need another flashlight. This one's dead." She looked around. "Where are the kids?"

"In the house. Nick found the key under the rock." He gave her shoulder a warm squeeze. "I'll get my flashlight." She nodded, and he disappeared for a moment. She heard the crunch of his footsteps on the gravel driveway. The Bronco's interior light came on momentarily, then went out again as the door slammed and he returned. He flicked on the light. "A rechargeable. Expensive, but worth it in the long run."

"I've been meaning to get one. Batteries die just when you need them." She was talking too much and too fast, in an attempt to cover her lingering sense of unease. She moved then, just ahead of him, turning to face the corner of the barn where the scarecrow stood. Mike took a step behind her, shining the flashlight ahead of them. The face of the scarecrow sprang out of the darkness. Painted with broad strokes, eyes, nose, mouth and chin. A happy smile. Below the head and rakish cap, it was nattily attired in a green-checked shirt and overalls. But Shannon noticed something new had been added since she'd seen it last. *Someone had plunged a knife into the scarecrow's chest.*

Shannon felt as if the bottom had dropped out of her stomach. Mike gripped her shoulder and pulled her back against him. "God, look at that!"

When her stomach crawled back to its familiar niche, she said grimly, "I *am* looking at it."

"It's a knife."

"Obviously," she snapped. Her voice was shaking, her arms and legs were shaking. She felt as if she was on the verge of hysteria.

"You didn't put it there as some sort of display for your antique shop, did you?"

*"No, I didn't!"* She drew a gulping, heaving breath as light from the apartment door spilled across the driveway.

"Ms. Hollister, is that you?" Tim Carver strode toward them, then halted as he took in their grim expressions and the knife buried in the scarecrow's chest.

"Holy jeez," he breathed and reached for the knife.

"Leave it," Mike ordered. "I'll call the police."

Shannon looked at Tim. "Did you do this?"

"No, ma'am. I've been in the barn, heatin' up supper, hot dogs and beans. I, uh, ain't been feelin' too good."

She nodded. "Okay, Tim, we'll take care of it."

They walked to the back door. Lights slanted from the kitchen windows, warm and welcoming, and there lay Max on the back step, wagging his tail. Thunder rumbled again, and it began to rain heavily, drumming on the porch roof. She let the dog in the house and sank into the nearest chair.

Tim hovered by the back door. "Uh, if you don't need me, guess I'll be gettin' back to my supper."

Mike nodded. "The police may want a word with you later."

"Sure, I'll be in the barn." Glancing at the new door lock, Tim added, "Better use this till they get here. That knife is some kinda sick joke."

"Mom, what's going on?" Nick was standing in the hall doorway, eyeing them warily. Shannon managed a small grin.

"Nothing, just some vandalism."

He came into the kitchen, followed by Andy and Chris who looked around and said, "We're hungry. Are we gonna eat soon?"

"Soon," Mike said, sighing. "Why don't you kids go watch TV for a while?"

"But Tim said there was a knife in the scarecrow, Mom." Nick's voice was tense and his eyes wide.

"Don't worry about it. Somebody played a sick joke and it backfired," Mike said, herding all three of them back into the living room. Shannon heard his voice sounding calm and normal, as if nothing had happened.

"You kids sit tight for a minute, and we'll get supper on the table. It's in the oven, smell it? I'll bet it's chicken!"

She went to the sink and splashed water on her face. Glancing up, she caught sight of her reflection in the black glass. Huge, shimmering blue eyes, pale face. And she'd pushed her hands through her hair so many times it was practically standing on end. As she stared at the glass, an inexplicable chill ran over her. What if the man with the knife was still out there, watching? Fear shot through her like a bolt of lightning.

She turned, her movement jerky as a puppet, staring at the door, knowing even as she did that it was locked. No one could get in.

But the top half was glass. Easily smashed with a rock. Then an arm could slip through, flip the lock, and the door would open. Perspiration filmed her forehead and she felt sick. *Stop it!* She made herself take the chicken out of the oven, and ladled fragrant sauce on top. Then the vegetables and noodles. She switched the kettle on for tea and got milk from the refrigerator as the kettle whistled. Steam fogged the window over the sink, covering it as effectively as a curtain. She made tea and even managed to choke some down although tension clogged her throat.

Why was this happening to her? Who would plunge a knife into a scarecrow? A sick prankster? She propped her elbows on the table, burying her face in her hands. She could scarcely bear to recall her terror those last few minutes when she'd run from the grape arbor. That awful feeling that someone had followed her. The sight of that knife buried in the green-checked cotton shirt, its handle gleaming in the light. Shannon felt sick to her stomach.

# *Chapter Eleven*

While the children ate in the dining room, Mike called
the police. After explaining about the knife found stuck
in the scarecrow, he listened a few seconds, then said,
"How should I know what the *motive* is? Obviously,
the guy's a sicko. Mmm, yeah, uh-huh, don't worry,
we'll be here." He hung up.

"I don't call wanting to scare me to death 'no motive,'" Shannon told him. "The guy did a good job of
it, too."

Mike came over and sat beside her. "They're sending a car over, but don't expect much."

"Why?"

He sighed. "They're busy with a bad accident on the
highway. A seven-car pileup, with a mercy helicopter
flight to Bangor."

"Great."

He gave her a quick look. Her voice was grim, and
her expression dejected. "Honey, they said there'd been
a spate of vandalism lately. Mailboxes smashed, cars
with slashed tires and broken windshields. This could be
just another sick joke."

She nodded, staring out the window at the corner of the barn. "Well, I'd rather believe it was a mindless act of vandalism. In a way, it would be a relief."

"I tell you what. How about I make popcorn? The kids can watch TV." He cleared his throat. "If it's okay, I'd like to stay here tonight. I don't want to leave you alone."

She nodded, almost sick with relief. "That's fine."

"Good." He grinned. "I wasn't taking no for an answer, anyway."

As she got up and went to the pantry for the popcorn, he put his arm around her shoulders and kissed her. An ache of protectiveness tightened his chest. Like her, he wanted to believe it had been an act of mindless vandalism, but what if they were wrong?

IN THE DINING ROOM, Andy was laying out their battle plan. "No kidding, I saw it, a big knife! It's gotta be the mummy, for sure!"

Chris frowned. "We didn't see him. Besides, I thought he had an ax."

Her brother waved that away as a mere technicality. "Well, maybe a knife's all he could find. The thing is, we'd better dig that mummy trap."

With a big sigh, Nick pointed out that they'd already started doing just that. "Okay, so we were looking for his treasure. Either way, a hole in the ground's a pit or a trap. And we would've found the pyramid if Mr. Wagoner hadn't come along."

"Yeah," Chris remarked thoughtfully. "It's all his fault we haven't caught the mummy yet."

"Yeah," Andy agreed. His green eyes narrowed behind his glasses. "What a bummer. We could've got him by now! Our names would've been in the papers and TV! We prob'ly would've missed school to be on TV!" Frowning at this lost opportunity, he gave a thoughtful nod and said, "In my experience, that's what those news guys do. Take you out of school to interview you. That's because they have to ask you lots of important questions."

Nick chewed a mouthful of strawberry shortcake and said, "So what we gotta do is head for the woods and dig when old Mr. Wagoner isn't around to mess things up."

The dining room went dead quiet. Chris was eating the last of her shortcake. She rolled a strawberry around in her mouth before chewing it. "After school tomorrow."

"Why wait till then? What's wrong with right now?" Nick asked, leaning down to scratch Max's ears. Fred was underneath the table, too, eating noodles beneath Chris's chair. The dachshund's fur was dry, but not Max's. His fur was damp, and his paws were muddy. Especially his front paws, Nick noticed. Wow, he thought. Max had been digging somewhere. What a great dog he was! A world-class digger, all right!

A soft plop, and Max dropped something on the floor. Nick bent down and picked it up. Hmm, it was the wallet he'd found yesterday. He must have got it off the little table in the kitchen.

Andy adjusted his glasses and peered at what his friend was holding. "What's that?"

"Just a dumb old wallet Max found out in the woods someplace," Nick told him.

"Has it got any money in it?" Chris asked, her eyes wide.

"Nope, it's empty. Mom and me already looked."

"Maybe you missed something. Lemme see it," Andy demanded.

Nick shrugged and handed it over. "You're not gonna find anything. I told you, we already checked. It's empty."

"Right," Andy said with a patronizing little laugh. He examined the wallet with care. "That's why *I'm* the president of the Martian Spaceship Society. I was elected because I'm *smart*. I always double-check stuff."

"Ha!" Nick snorted. "We never had any elections! You named yourself president at that meeting you called when I had chicken pox and Chris had to go to the dentist."

"So you weren't there, so what?" Andy said, digging into the wallet's depths, looking for a secret compartment. "If you would've been at the fort, the vote still would've been anonymous, I bet."

"'Unanimous,'" Chris corrected. "And it wouldn't have been because *I* would've voted for *myself!*"

"You're not supposed to vote for yourself," Andy said indignantly.

"Who says?" Chris fixed him with a fiery green stare. "You can vote for anyone you like."

"It's not right," Andy muttered. "The whole point of elections is to vote for the right person. Somebody smart and older. Not some little kid in first grade."

Chris went rather pink. "Well, just because you're in fourth grade doesn't mean you're smarter. Anyways, you're a real bad speller."

"Spelling isn't everything," Andy said with an airy shrug. "Besides, you're secretary-treasurer of the Martian Spaceship Society. That's an important position. You can be president after Nick has a turn at it."

Chris made a face as if to say, "fat chance," but contented herself with eating another bite of shortcake and cream.

Looking pointedly at the wallet, Nick said, "Well, was I right or not?"

"Right about what?" Andy said, pushing his glasses up.

"The wallet, dummy! It's empty, right?"

"Well—" Andy shrugged and pointed at the place on the wallet where the initial had worn away. "It used to have a letter here. Looks like an *M*."

Chris nodded and said, her mouth full of dessert, "*M* for mummy."

Andy looked startled, then grinned. "Yeah, it's gotta be the mummy's wallet!"

"Yeah, only someone stole all the money," Nick breathed, his mind busy with all sorts of intriguing scenarios. They could catch the thief, then the mummy would be grateful. They might even get a reward! Maybe the mummy would give them part of his treasure, once they dug it up, of course.

"What if...Mr. Wagoner stole the money, and that's why he kicked us out of the woods," Andy murmured. "Sure, he prob'ly had a fight with the mummy, stole his wallet and wants the glory of catching him for himself!"

Nick thought about that. It sounded plausible. Mr. Wagoner had acted as though they were a bunch of little kids who didn't know anything and had no rights. Sure, Mr. Wagoner prob'ly had his eye on digging up the mummy's treasure and stealing that, too! What a rat! No wonder the mummy got mad and went around sticking knives in scarecrows. He prob'ly thought it was Mr. Wagoner.

Looking smug, Andy pronounced importantly, "This calls for action!"

Nick frowned. "I already said why don't we dig the trap tonight."

"Good idea," Andy allowed. "We can use my dad's flashlight. It's in the Bronco, and it's real bright."

"I bet Dad won't let us," Chris said, yawning.

"Neither will my mom," Nick agreed with a long-suffering shrug.

Andy looked around the table. "So? What they don't know won't hurt them, right?"

Nick smiled. "Right."

Just then, Mike appeared in the doorway. "How's it going? You guys want seconds on shortcake?"

"How ARE the kids doing?" Shannon asked a little while later when Mike came back to the kitchen. There was a small silence as she finished scrubbing the baking pan and rinsed it before he answered.

"I guess they're okay. Funny, they didn't want seconds. They couldn't wait to go up to Nick's room and play Nintendo." He shrugged. "Well, they also said they were having a secret meeting of the Martian Spaceship Society and didn't want to be disturbed."

"That's good," she said. "Then they won't be around when the police get here."

Sliding his arms around Shannon's waist from behind, he kissed her neck. "Mmm, you taste good."

Her shoulders slumped as she leaned back against him. "Oh, Mike, I'm so tired of all this. The robbery, the fires, now the knife in the scarecrow. *When is it going to stop?*"

Her voice was strained, and he let go of her waist and slid his hands up her arms, holding them in a tight grip.

"I don't know, honey. But I'm going to make damn sure nothing happens to you or the kids. You can count on that!"

She tilted her head back and looked up at him, silently assessing his words. She was twenty-seven years old, with one bad marriage behind her and enough fear and terror these past few days to make her doubt her sanity. He leaned down and kissed her. When he raised his head, he smiled. "Trust me?"

"Yes," she breathed, shifting in his arms to face him. "Mike, why don't we try that kiss again?"

His eyebrows rose a little. "You think we need more practice?"

She nodded. "A whole lot more."

He drew a ragged breath at the look in her eyes, then lowered his head. Gently at first, then harder, persuasive, possessive. Saying without words that he loved her, that she was his now.

When they both came up for air, they leaned against each other, her cheek on his shoulder, his arms around her tight. Caressing her back with slow, gentle movements of his hands.

Suddenly, his hands stilled, and she felt him stiffen. Turning her head, she looked to the left. Lights flickered across the driveway, coming up to the house. "Maybe it's the police," Mike said. "No, it's your carpenter pal, Carver."

The slam of the pickup door was clearly audible in the house. They watched as Tim Carver hurried inside the barn. "Wonder where he's been just now. I didn't see the truck leave—" Mike leaned closer to the window and peered out. "He couldn't have been gone long, but he's dirty as hell, and his shirt's torn. Sure looked upset about something. He almost tore the door right off his truck.''

Shannon looked past Mike's shoulder. The barn was just visible. A light sprang on inside the apartment, then Tim's shadowy figure moved across the room and disappeared. ''That's funny. He said he'd be in all night.'' She heaved a sigh and added, ''But he wasn't feeling well. Maybe he went out for medicine.''

Mike shrugged and opened the back door. ''Here come the police.'' The gray-and-blue squad car pulled up and Officer Conway got out. He looked drawn and tired.

Mike and Shannon joined him by the squad car. ''It's over there, by the barn,'' she said, pointing.

The policeman walked over to the hay-stuffed figure and examined it in silence. Then he put gloves on and pulled the knife from the scarecrow's chest in one swift motion.

Shannon had to turn away. Just the sight of it made her feel sick. Laying a hand on her arm, Mike said quietly, ''Come on, let's go back inside.''

Ten minutes later, Officer Conway came in. He was still holding the knife. ''Does it look like one of yours?''

''No,'' she said, shaking her head. The handle was wood, the blade long and shiny. And sharp.

He put it on the kitchen table. ''You've got a tenant across the driveway there. Maybe it's his.''

''I don't think so.'' She shook her head again.

''Well, I looked around outside. Whoever is responsible is long-gone by this time. Rain's washed away any footprints, naturally.'' He shrugged. ''I'll take this along, test it for fingerprints, but we probably won't find any.'' At her questioning look he added, ''With all the TV they watch, even kids know about how not to leave incriminating fingerprints these days."

She stood there, stunned. "What you're saying is you don't think you'll find the culprit."

He nodded. "Unless we get a lucky break."

Mike let out a long breath. That shiny glint in her wide blue eyes looked suspiciously like tears. He saw her blink furiously, then tilt her chin. Quickly, he said, "You mean an eyewitness who might have seen someone near the barn earlier tonight?"

"About as likely as finding a needle in a haystack," Officer Conway said quietly. He took out his notepad and flipped a page. "Why don't you tell me exactly what happened?"

"What good's that going to do?" she demanded. "You just said you need an eyewitness."

Conway nodded. "That's right."

Mike said, "We found it together. I'd just driven up and got the kids in the house when I heard Shannon come running around the back of the house. I went to meet her—"

"Yes," she broke in, nodding. "I fell by the corner of the barn, and when I got up, Mike grabbed me."

"That's right," he commented. "She was looking for her dog and thought she heard an animal whining by the grape arbor in the backyard."

Shannon flashed him a look of gratitude. "My flashlight had died, and I—" She paused, then sighing, she went on, "The truth is, I got sort of frightened and ran back to the house. That's when I fell and Mike found me. He got his flashlight, and when we started back around the barn, there was the scarecrow with the knife in it."

Officer Conway looked up. "Where was your tenant while this was going on?"

"In the barn apartment, making his supper," she said.

"Maybe I'll just have a word with him," Officer Conway said, shutting his pad and putting it into his pocket. He picked up the knife. "Something wild's going on in town. Besides the fires and that robbery at the Y you were involved in, we've had a great deal of malicious mischief, slashed tires, windshields broken. This could be just part of the pattern."

"What about strangers in town?" Mike asked.

"We have the usual good old boys who get drunk and violent on a regular basis, but we don't get many strangers," the policeman said with a shrug.

"What about the private detective who's been following Dana Jennings around for the past few weeks?" Mike asked.

"The P.I.'s name is Ted Murray. He operates out of Boston, which means Mrs. Jenning's husband is paying top dollar. Mr. Murray's already dropped by the station to introduce himself. He let us know he was in town and why."

Shannon gave Mike a despairing look and he slid an arm around her. "Murray wouldn't be mixed up in something like this, anyway," he told her.

"Not unless he's crazy," Conway muttered.

Mike felt a surge of annoyance at the policeman's tone. This wasn't a childish prank. This had been frightening, vicious.

"What about the Parelli brothers?" Shannon said grimly.

"Unlikely," Conway said with a shake of his head. "They're probably drunk in some bar with a dozen witnesses who'll say they've been there all night."

"Couldn't you drive by their house and at least question them?" Her voice rose in disbelief.

"Give us some credit, Mrs. Hollister. They live with their father. He's in his eighties and has a history of heart problems. We can't just ring his bell and say, 'Don't get upset, but your sons may be harassing some woman, stabbing her scarecrow.' We want to protect citizens, not give them coronaries."

"But—"

"We'll keep an eye on them," Conway said.

"Great, that makes me feel so much better." She glared at him, and he waved an impatient hand.

"Look, we can't run around arresting people. So far you've given us a knife and a scarecrow, but nothing to connect the Parellis with them."

"The last I heard malicious mischief's a crime," she retorted.

He yawned and stretched. "You didn't see them in the vicinity of your house tonight, did you?"

"Well, no," she said, frowning. "But it was dark, they could have been out there by the barn. That's my point."

"I know what your point is," Conway said tiredly. "But you have no case. You've got to establish motive and opportunity. We don't even know for sure if they were here."

"But they're about the same size as the men who robbed the Y. You could—"

He opened the back door. "We've been over this before. Those two are already in custody. The state cops picked 'em up the night of the robbery." He shrugged.

"Look, I've had a hell of a day—no, make that three days, plus the damn fire this morning. Although, thank God, no one was hurt this time."

"The Parellis—" she began, and Mike's arm tightened around her.

"Mrs. Hollister," Conway interrupted, "I promise not to show up at your exercise classes and tell everyone how to do jumping jacks. How about your not trying to tell me how to protect the public and catch criminals?"

"Fine," she said sarcastically. "You're not really going to do anything." The police didn't take her story seriously. No, she was just a hysterical woman who had to be humored.

"Do me a favor," Officer Conway buttoned the pocket flap over his notebook. "Close your doors and windows and lock 'em up tight. We'll fingerprint the knife and see if we can run down the owner. In the meantime, practice a little common sense. Don't go out alone after dark."

"That makes sense," Mike said quietly, looking down at Shannon. He could feel her sigh of resignation.

"Would it make you feel better if I said that Moose Parelli—the big one—is probably heading for Florida soon? Running out on support and alimony payments. His ex-wife's got a restraining order and she's called the station half a dozen times with complaints. By next weekend, he'll be gone, I guarantee it. That type always cuts and runs." Conway shrugged. "Probably he'll take brother Hank with him for the ride."

"And what do I do in the meantime?" she asked, so angry she hardly knew what she was saying. The policeman stood there, not three feet away, his eyes flat and expressionless. He didn't answer. He doesn't really give a damn what happens, she thought bitterly.

Fuming, she turned without another word and began finishing up the dinner dishes.

Mike took in the stiff set of her spine and the flush of color in her cheeks. This wasn't the time to thrash things out. Quietly, he let the policeman out.

She heard their murmured conversation at the door above the clatter of the plates she was rinsing. Then the click as Mike closed the door and came toward her. The moment was suddenly awkward.

"You could have gone easier on him," Mike said, touching her shoulder. "He was just trying to do his job."

"I don't care," she snapped. "He's already said they won't find anything, he's got a list of excuses a mile long. 'It's raining, it's dark, none of your neighbors saw anything.'"

He turned her around, and she wiped her eyes with the back of her wet hands. "Come on," he coaxed. "If it makes you feel better, I'll talk to this private detective and find out if he was near the house tonight. Who knows, maybe he was driving by and saw something. But—" he said, glancing out the window at the barn "—we should have a word with Carver about his whereabouts. He's here one minute, gone the next, like a damn jack-in-the-box. Not exactly reliable. He has a few questions to answer, and there's no time like the present."

He walked over and opened the back door while Shannon hurriedly dried her hands on the dish towel and cried, "Wait for me. I'm coming too."

MIKE POUNDED on the apartment door without ceremony. "Carver, I want to talk to you. Open up!"

Shannon ran up in time to see the curtain at the window pushed to one side and Tim's face peer out. "Who's there?" he yelled.

"Mike Finnegan and Mrs. Hollister," Mike said. "Open the door!"

Slowly the door opened and Tim stared at them. "What do you want?"

Mike said, "Mind if we come in?" and Tim backed away, looking at them suspiciously. He'd showered and changed. His shirt was faded, but clean. So were his jeans. His hair was dark with water and flat against his scalp. His eyelids fluttered nervously and he didn't seem to know what to do with his hands. Finally, he shoved them into his jeans pockets.

"Whaddaya want? I told the cop all I know, which is nothin'. Ain't you through botherin' me?"

"Not yet," Mike said grimly. "Where did you go earlier?"

"Hey, I don't have to answer no questions, I didn't do nothin'," Tim said belligerently.

They stood just inside the doorway. In the short time since he'd moved in, Tim had pinned up half a dozen nude centerfolds and a calendar on the wall. As an attempt to cheer the place up, Shannon thought, it was a dismal failure.

"Where did you go a while ago?" Mike's voice was flat and hard.

"Man, that ain't no business of yours." Tim cleared his throat, swallowing nervously, then backed away and leaned against the wall. "So, um, you can turn around and get t'hell outta here. I don't have to tell you nothin'."

"You promised to stick around," Shannon inter-rupted. "You said you were cooking your supper, then you left. Tim, what happened tonight scared me. I have to count on your being here if I need you."

"Come on, Carver, where'd you go?" Mike de-manded.

Tim threw him a baleful glare and said, "I got stom-ach pains, an ulcer maybe. I already been to the doc-tor, so I called him and he said he'd phone in a prescription." He shrugged. "I went down to pick it up. It wasn't ready, so I gotta go back to the drugstore. I was, uh, just gonna leave when you banged on the door."

"Your clothes were torn earlier," Mike said flatly, aware that Carver was nervous to the point of bab-bling. Maybe he was sick, he looked like hell. But somehow Mike knew he wasn't telling the whole truth about his whereabouts.

"So what. I tripped." Tim grinned and threw his head back, and Mike noticed a faint swelling by his right eye.

"Been in a fight recently?" he asked.

Tim's grin faded and he shrugged. "Yeah, I ran into a buddy of mine and we, uh, had an argument. It wasn't nothin', jus' a friendly disagreement. Look, I gotta go. Drugstore closes soon, and I need my medicine."

Shannon looked as if she had a few more questions to ask, but Mike bundled her out the door. "We won't keep you, then. Sorry you don't feel well." Pulling her along with him, he strode across the driveway and went into the house.

"Great!" she snapped as he peered out the window. "What good did that accomplish? I wanted to get the name of that 'buddy' of his. What if it was Moose Parelli? I saw Tim's truck downtown earlier tonight. Maybe he was dropping into some bar for a drink. What if he and the Parellis are up to something? What if they're setting the fires?''

"We'll find out soon enough," Mike muttered.

"What if the knife was meant for Tim?" Shannon said thoughtfully. "A warning to keep his mouth shut?"

"There he goes," Mike said, watching the truck headlights recede down the driveway. He opened the back door. "Come on."

"Where?"

"The barn. We're going to search it top to bottom."

THE DOOR to the barn was locked but Shannon had a spare key. The apartment inside was hot and messy. The air was stale and reeked of too many french fries, onions and hamburgers. And beer. No wonder he's got an ulcer, Mike thought. The place could have used a good airing out.

Tim's clothes were scattered everywhere, magazines and newspapers, too. He'd cut articles out of the papers. Bits of clippings lay all over the floor by the table.

Mike went into the kitchen while Shannon examined the desk drawers. "Son of a gun," he muttered, looking around in disgust. The refrigerator held apples, eggs, a half gallon of milk, butter and two six-packs of beer. The kitchen table was covered with dirty dishes, including remnants of Tim's last meal—hot dogs and beans.

There was a half-empty bottle of bourbon, three cans of beer and a trash can filled with empties. Mike was hurrying, trying to get a picture of the man, and the picture was uneven. A slob, but a pretty good carpenter, according to Shannon.

The bedroom didn't hold many secrets. A tiny chest of drawers held a few shirts and socks; two drawers were empty, and a pair of slacks and a jacket were in the small closet. All the pockets were empty. He ran his hand under the mattress and he looked under the cushions on the old sofa. Nothing. He picked up a crumpled paper near the table and opened it. A map of town. He folded it and tucked it inside his pocket and stood surveying the place for a second.

Shannon was flipping through a wall calendar.

"Did you turn up anything?" he asked.

She shook her head, then said, "I don't know. Come look at this."

The calendar, a promotional giveaway from a local dry cleaner, had a generic photo of a Maine town on the front. Trees, white-spired church, small brick schoolhouse. Not a single bare thigh in sight, and it looked a bit incongruous positioned among all those naked pinups. But there were several small red *x*s scrawled on it. Five of them spread over the last few months.

He leaned closer to get a better look. One for the day Mrs. Brennan's house burned, several marked before then, and one hastily scrawled on today's date. Coincidence? Or was Tim keeping track of the arsonist's fires? Trying to figure out a pattern, when each fire was set and where?

"And look at this," Shannon said, glancing at the table near the sofa. An ashtray, filled with charred matches.

Mike whistled soundlessly. "Doesn't look good."

"None of it looks good," she retorted. "The calendar, his mysterious comings and goings, the way he acts—tense and jumpy."

Mike put his arms around her and kissed her cheek. It was cold. She was shivering, and he held her tight. "Hey, it's okay. I'm here, and I'm not going anywhere."

"Tell me it's a bad dream, all of it," she whispered.

"I'd give anything if I could, you know that."

She buried her head in his chest, then, after a heartbeat, looked up into his eyes. "Mike, I can't explain it, but I have this weird feeling. Terrible danger all around us. Not just the fires, something else—I'm really scared."

## Chapter Twelve

"So where do we dig first?" Chris asked. Nick aimed the beam of the flashlight between two trees near the cellar hole.

Andy shrugged and looked around. "The other day we dug over there," he said, gesturing with his shovel across the clearing. "I bet the pyramid's right there, if we'd have kept digging, we'd have found it."

"Maybe it's not there," Nick said, slouching on the stone wall while Andy dug.

"Hah! Bet it is, and we're wasting our time over here."

"Maybe not."

A few minutes later, Andy looked up and scowled. "Hey! How come you're not digging?"

"I brought Max along, and he's a world-class digger," Nick said modestly. "He's gonna dig for me."

"Is that so?" Andy pushed his glasses up his nose.

"Yeah, I thought I'd just hold the light and you guys and Max could dig."

Chris contradicted him instantly. "Like fudge, we will! If you don't dig, neither am I. Besides, secretary-treasurers don't have to dig if they don't want to."

Andy dug a shovelful of earth and cast it aside without saying anything. Out of the corner of his eye he could see Max digging like mad over by the cellar hole. "Where'd you get ol' Max, anyway?" he asked.

"A pet shop in Bangor. Me and Mom," Nick said, smiling. "We just got in the car one day and went and bought him. He was just a puppy, of course, so we didn't need much for him. No big collar or leash. We just told him who we were, that she was Mom and I was Nick, and he smelled us and then began to wag his whole rear end."

Chris took out some bubble gum and put it in her mouth and chewed. "So what happened when you got him home?"

"We had to take him all around the yard and let him pee now and then and smell the trees," Nick told her. "He had to do that, you know, to find out where he lived. Then we had to introduce him to friends, like here's Chris and here's Andy. You can't just put him with a whole lotta people and expect him to know who's a friend and who's a robber guy."

She nodded and blew a bubble. "What about Fred? She's a girl, and she'd prob'ly make a good guard dog. She barks real loud. Are you gonna do that with her? Take her around and let her pee on trees and stuff?"

"Prob'ly not. Max'll tell her what's what. She's real smart, too."

"Know what I heard?" Chris said with a superior look at her brother. "I heard girl dogs are better at guarding and stuff than boy dogs. They take their responsibilities seriouser. And you don't have to have a great big black dog like on TV, you know, with big teeth and fangs. Even a small girl dog can be a good guard dog."

"For cryin' out loud!" Andy snapped, throwing down his shovel. "What difference does it make? You told us that a hundred times already. Who cares if girl dogs are better than boy dogs?"

Chris ignored her brother and turned to Nick. "She's real pretty, too. I like her."

"Who cares if she's pretty? I'm the only one doing any work here," Andy muttered, picking up his shovel and attacking a shadowy cranny by the stone wall. Dirt and leaves flew.

"Okay," Nick said, getting up and grabbing a shovel. He looked around. The ground sloped here by the stone wall, hardly noticeable among the brambles and low sumac. To the left, the trees were all about thirty feet tall or taller, stretching to the black night sky. But on the right, by the wall, the trees had mostly been cleared away. For some reason, he found himself looking at the cellar hole with a sense of unease. Just dirt and leaves. No grass grew here, no vines or weeds. It was eerie, like everything was dead.

Max must have thought it a good place to dig because he'd dug down so far he almost disappeared. Only the top of his tail waved above the hole.

"Max is so smart," Nick said, "that you can hide things, and he'll go find 'em and bring 'em to you."

After another moment, Max climbed out and sat beside the hole, looking at it with satisfaction. Andy watched him closely, but the dog didn't move. He just sat there with his tongue hanging out. He'd had it with digging, evidently.

Nick and Andy both walked over and knelt down to look in the hole. Chris joined them and looked in, too. Something was sticking out of the dirt at the bottom of the hole. It looked like a handbag.

The flashlight shed enough light for them to see that it was empty.

Chris blew a bubble and popped it. "I'm tired. Let's go back to Nick's and dig some more tomorrow."

Yawning widely, Nick tossed the handbag back in the hole and stood up. "Yeah, mummies don't have one of these, anyway. It's just some old stuff somebody threw out a long time ago."

"Come on, you guys, let's go." Andy grabbed the flashlight and led the way back through the woods.

TIM CARVER HAD his truck moving down Mill Hollow Road at a steady clip, five miles above the speed limit. He didn't dare go faster, his tires were bad, and the road was still rain-slick. He had just enough time to get to the drugstore before it closed. A siren in the distance, across town, he thought. A medical emergency? Or another fire?

His fear breathed close behind him, making the hairs at the back of his neck stand up. *Pyromaniac.* That's what the newspaper had dubbed the arsonist. They said he got a kick out of watching buildings burn. Which meant cops would be checking the crowd at the next fire. Just his luck.

He turned on the radio, humming along with Willie Nelson about all the girls he'd known, swung down Main and parked by the drugstore. The druggist had Tim's prescription packaged and ready to go. He paid and left.

HALF AN HOUR LATER, he was on Corbin Street watching a warehouse engulfed in flames. Upholstery and yard goods. It had gone up like a torch. Ordinarily, so close to town, the fire department would have got a handle on things and put it out without too much damage. But the wind had kicked up somethin' fierce, he thought, watching flames shoot out the warehouse windows. The whole place was a mass of fire. Acrid smoke choked the air, billowing from the warehouse in thick black clouds. He coughed and covered his mouth with a handkerchief. Corbin Street had been roped off, but he'd found a way through the crowd and now stood on the corner, his eyes darting everywhere. Watching, staring, waiting.

The fire department was out in full force, straining with the heavy hoses, snaking them across the street, playing streams of water on the blaze. But they didn't have a snowball's chance in hell of puttin' this one out, he thought.

A man standing next to him shook his head. "Terrible thing." Tim glanced at him. Not a local, the accent was different, and his voice was strained.

Reddish glow from the flames across the street lit his features. Smooth-faced, with queer light-blue eyes, so light they almost looked colorless. A big man, at least six-two, he wore a dark blue Windbreaker and khaki slacks.

The man looked at Tim. "You like fires?" he said.

Tim swallowed hard and shook his head. *"Hell, no."* A little shrill. He tried again. "You'd be crazy to like somethin' like this."

The man nodded. "They say this is the seventh fire in three months."

He felt his muscles tighten at the stranger's tone. Sly, as if he knew something about the fires. Carefully, Tim shoved his hands into his pockets and just as carefully, he avoided the other man's eyes. "Could be coincidence. Old buildings, faulty wiring, kids foolin' around."

"Let's not waste any more time, Tim—"

"How'd you know my name?" He gave the man a suspicious look.

"I asked around."

"Why? Whaddaya want?" he said coldly.

The man smiled and said, "I'm interested in the fires. In who's setting them. I think you know who that person is."

"You're full of crap. I don't know nothin'!"

"Look, I'll be straight with you. I'm a P.I. Ted Murray. I was hired on another matter, but the fires are related. Mrs. Brennan's house—" Murray raised an eyebrow.

"You ain't gonna pin that on me," Tim blurted out. "I didn't set that fire. I didn't set any of the fires." Then he turned and shoved his way through the crowd. He was more than nervous, he was scared out of his wits. The man on the sidewalk—Murray—was he coming after him? What the hell did he want? Money? Would he go to the cops?

His muscles bunched up with tension and cold as he crossed in front of the vacant lot where he'd parked the truck. Only a few more yards to go now to reach safety. He'd drive home, lock the door and take the phone off the hook. He risked a quick look behind him and didn't see anything suspicious. A dark car turning a corner, but no one on foot. Everyone was two streets over, gawking at the warehouse fire.

Yeah, he was safe, all right. He'd go home, down a six-pack and watch TV until he couldn't stay awake anymore. But he was afraid to sleep, afraid he'd wake up screaming again, caught in the same nightmare he'd been having for weeks. Fire. Blazing all around him, and he couldn't get out. This time he knew he'd be consumed by the flames. Burned alive. He dreaded sleep, but he needed it desperately.

He got into his truck and revved up the engine. He pulled out and drove off, hard and fast, north on Highland Avenue, then west on Main, putting the truck up to forty miles an hour by the time he reached the edge of town. Faster now, hitting fifty, engine laboring, windows and loose dashboard knobs rattling. At the bottom of the hill, the traffic light was red. He didn't brake. He pressed the horn in warning and raced across the intersection. He slammed across the crosswalk by the Catholic church, a slight rise that catapulted him into the air for a fraction of a second, making him thump his head on the roof in spite of his seat belt. The truck came back to the pavement with a bang, a chorus of rattles and clanks and a sharp bark of tortured rubber. It began to shift left, its rear end sliding around with a blood-curdling screech, smoke curling up from the protesting tires. For a terrifying instant, he thought he'd lost control, but then abruptly the wheel was his again, and he was more than halfway up the next hill without realizing how he'd got there.

His speed was down to forty, and he got it back up to fifty. Headlights in the rearview mirror, but way back. Some dude headin' out of town. He settled back and relaxed some behind the wheel. Not far to go now. If he wrapped the truck around a tree or rolled it over and killed himself, what good would that do.

He was still going much too fast and wide on what few turns there were, swinging out across the crown of the road into the other lane, saying a prayer of thanks that there was no oncoming traffic. All he wanted was

to get home to his apartment and lock the damn door
behind him. He'd lay low for a while, till this whole
goddamn mess blew over. Yeah, that's what he'd do—
hide out until the hue and cry about fires died down.
Maybe that P.I., Murray, knew Tim's name, but he
didn't know where he lived.

He had a hunch that if Murray found that out, life
would be a living hell.

As he swung the truck up the driveway, Tim felt more
awake than he had in hours. He'd reached a state of
grainy-eyed alertness that came from having been up for
a day and a half. Suddenly, his body and mind were
clear and firm, purposeful. He stopped yawning as he
got out of the truck and went into the barn. He even
began to feel optimistic. He'd outwitted that damn P.I.
He'd outwitted everyone.

A FEW MINUTES after Tim had slammed and locked his
apartment door, a car pulled up and parked in the
driveway. Paul Wagoner got out, looked around curiously for a second, then rapped on Shannon's back
door. Leslie Wagoner got out of the car and hurried up
the path. "I decided to come with you. It's cold in the
car."

"Suit yourself," he said rapping on the door again.

As the door opened, light sprang on above it, illuminating the two of them. Shannon saw who it was and
called over her shoulder. "Mike, it's the Wagoners."
Turning back, she said, "Come on in, we just came in
ourselves."

Leslie rubbed her arms. She wore a brown suede
pantsuit with a chunky gold necklace and matching
bracelet. Her cheeks were flushed pink, and her brown

eyes sparkled. "Ooh, it's getting cold out there! Wind's picked up in the past hour."

Mike came in and nodded hello. "Close to freezing tonight. Bad night for a fire. Let's hope our friend the arsonist doesn't get the urge. He could do a lot of damage." Turning to Shannon, he added, "The kids are fine. They're upstairs, watching TV."

"I'm sorry," she explained. "We came in a few minutes ago, and I had this weird feeling. I can't explain it, and I know it sounds silly, but Mike went to make sure—"

"And they're there, all three of 'em. For once, they're not up to any mischief," he said.

"Well," Paul said. "There is bad news. Another fire. It was on the radio coming over. A warehouse on the other side of town."

Leslie shuddered. "It's horrible! When is it going to stop?"

"The only one with the answer to that," Paul suggested, "is the nut setting the damn fires."

"I don't care," Leslie snapped. "I just want them to stop! How are we supposed to sleep nights, wondering if we'll all be burned in our beds like—"

"Like Mrs. Brennan," Paul said.

"Mrs. Brennan was a lovely person. I was just saying how awful it was that her house burned—"

"Talking about it isn't going to bring her back," Paul interrupted.

"You're right," she retorted. "But sometimes talking helps."

Paul gave a small shrug. "I'm sorry if I seemed offhand about Mrs. Brennan's death. I certainly don't mean to sound as if I don't care."

"I'll just put water on for coffee," Shannon began, and Nick came into the kitchen with Max at his heels.

"Can we have more popcorn, Mom? Maybe some ice cream, too?" He yawned and patted Max. "You shoulda seen Max, Mom. He's one world-class digger. Found a pocketbook in the woods."

"When was this?" Shannon asked suspiciously.

Nick's face assumed a bland expression. "Uh, a while ago. It's no big deal. How about the popcorn?"

She sighed. That innocent look of his was a dead giveaway. He'd been up to something. Well, she'd get to the bottom of it later, she decided, and went to the pantry. "Okay, I'll pop it in the microwave."

"Reason we came by," Paul said to Mike, "we were driving by earlier today and noticed the police car in your driveway. Is everything all right?"

"Just a small problem with vandals," Mike said quietly. "You'd think it was Halloween."

"Our mailbox was bashed in tonight," Paul said, nodding. "If I ever catch the kids who did it—"

Leslie gave him a look. "Admit it, darling. You wouldn't do anything. As an attack dog, you're all bark and no bite."

"Oh yeah?" He kissed her on the ear. "Enough about my faults. You're giving our friends the wrong idea about me."

"Let's sit down to some coffee now," Shannon suggested. They all settled in the kitchen talking while Shannon made some popcorn for Nick. He shoveled some into his mouth, announced it tasted okay and that he'd take it upstairs to the other members of The Martian Spaceship Society.

A little while later, everyone said their good-byes and Shannon collapsed into Mike's arms. "It was nice of Leslie and Paul to stop by, but I'm exhausted."

"Well I have plenty of energy," Mike said, as he took Shannon into his arms. They came together in a movement as spontaneous as the wind, clinging to each other, their bodies fitting curve to curve like a hand in a glove.

Then the telephone rang. Shannon blinked as Mike raised his head. "I'll get it," she whispered, groping for the phone. He grinned while she tried to regain her composure. "Hello?"

A man's deep voice said in her ear, "Mrs. Hollister?"

"Yes, that's right. Who is this, please?"

"You don't know me, but my name is Murray. Ted Murray. I'm a private investigator. I was at the warehouse fire tonight and thought you should know a few things." Murray drew a breath and seemed to hesitate, then said, "There's no easy way to put it. You've got a tenant, Tim Carver, right?"

"Yes, if it's any business of yours," she snapped.

Mike frowned. "Who is that?"

She covered the receiver with the palm of her hand. "Ted Murray, the private investigator."

"What the hell does he want?" Mike reached for the phone and she pulled it away.

"I can handle this. I'm not a baby."

He raked his hair back with a frustrated hand. "I never said you were. Let me talk to the guy."

"No!" She uncovered the receiver and said crisply, "What was that about my tenant?"

"Just a friendly warning," Murray said. "I saw him at the warehouse fire tonight. He acted damned odd, staring as if he was mesmerized. When I tried to talk to him, he jumped like a scared rabbit and took off in his truck like the hounds of hell were after him." Murray sighed. "If I were you, I'd be damn careful around a guy like that. And I'd make sure I kept matches out of his way."

A thought that had already occurred to her more than once. "Thanks, I appreciate your concern."

"Well, I heard from the cops that he was renting an apartment from you, and I thought you should know what he's been up to."

She frowned. "He was here for a while tonight, but he did leave. Listen, we had something ... unpleasant happen here a short while ago. Did you happen to drive by my place and see anything ... odd?"

"Sorry, I've been downtown all evening. And like I said, I got to the fire right after it started. Tim was already there."

Shannon swallowed. Her throat felt dry. "What did he say when you talked to him?"

"He denied knowing anything about the fires." Murray's voice grew grim. "I think he was lying."

He hung up, and Shannon stood there listening to the dial tone. As she replaced the receiver, Mike said, "What did he say?"

She told him, and he shook his head grimly. "We'd better tell the police about the matches and calendar we found. Something else," he added. "It's a damn good thing I'm staying here tonight."

She cleared her throat. "It's getting late. I'll get the kids to bed. You can call the police."

"Okay." He punched in the number as she went upstairs and got the three children ready for bed. Teeth were brushed, pajamas donned, then they were bundled into three sleeping bags on the floor in Nick's room. "The Martian Spaceship Society is camping out," he informed her importantly.

"Just so you go to sleep."

"Okay, but we need marshmallows and a camp-fire," he complained.

"No campfire, and no marshmallows, either." She kissed them all and turned the light off. "Now go to sleep. I'll see you in the morning."

She closed the door in time to see Mike coming up-stairs. "What did the police say?" she asked.

He looked grim. "They already have their eye on him. Murray told them he'd been seen acting oddly at the fire tonight. They said they'd talk to Tim in the morning about the calendar and the matches."

"Well, that's progress at least."

He shrugged. "Maybe." Glancing toward Nick's room, he went on, "Are they okay?"

"In sleeping bags, dead to the world."

He smiled and opened the door and went in to kiss them good-night. Shannon waited and showed him where the guest room was, then went to her own room, fighting a ridiculous feeling of loneliness. Silly, she scolded herself. She took a shower and pulled on an oversize navy-blue nightshirt. Barefoot, she padded to the dressing table to brush her thick, curly hair.

She gazed at her unhappy reflection in the mirror, her wide eyes telling her the truth. She loved him. Head over heels, that dizzying feeling of champagne bubbles in her veins. That wonderful feeling of lightness, as if any minute she'd float right up off the floor. But—there he was, down the hall and he might as well have been half a continent away for all the interest he'd shown since they'd come upstairs.

Her hand holding the hairbrush stilled at a soft knock on the door. She opened it. Mike stood there.

His eyes roamed her face and the V-shaped neckline of her nightshirt underneath which her heart was beating a furious tattoo. Soft cotton, the nightshirt slipped sideways, and one shoulder was exposed. She yanked it back up and tried to look unconcerned. "Yes?"

"There aren't any sheets."

Her mouth an O of surprise, she took a tentative step toward the door. "I'm sorry," she said, realizing suddenly that Mike was effectively blocking the doorway. He didn't move.

"I really don't care about sheets," he said huskily. His gaze drifted from her eyes to her parted lips, down over the swell of her breasts and back up again. "Shannon?"

It was only a step into his arms, but it felt like a lifetime before he pulled her close. She slid her arms around his neck, curling her fingers in his hair.

Groaning, he kissed the side of her neck, then lower to her collarbone and the soft skin of her shoulder. Her eyes closed with delight, and she murmured, "Oh, Mike."

Then his lips were on hers, hard and satisfying, urging them apart, drawing the very breath from her lungs.

It felt so good, so right. Her last rational thought before he pushed her down on the bed. She melted against him as his arms caressed her shoulders, moving over her feminine curves, pushing the nightshirt aside to touch the soft skin of her thighs.

He pressed against her. He was hard, aroused, and there was no turning back. Not that she wanted to, anyway. No, she was his. They'd been working up to this moment for a long time. Against his mouth, she whispered, "One of us has too many clothes on."

He grinned and began to unbutton his shirt. Impatient, she reached up to help, her fingers slipping the buttons loose, then pulling the shirt from his jeans. She drew a shaky breath at the sight of his broad, muscled chest, the dark silky hair and bronzed skin.

She fumbled with his belt, and he helped her unbuckle it, his eyes never leaving her flushed face. Then he slid the jeans off and settled back on the bed. Kissing the hollow at the base of her throat, sliding lower, drawing the nightshirt off, exposing her soft breasts. Kissing, teasing her already aroused nipples. Circling them with his tongue, biting gently.

She arched her back with need, and he sent shudders through her body with more intimate caresses, kissing, stroking, murmuring her name. Agonizing sensuality exploded as she moved beneath him. "Please—"

He kissed her breasts, cupping them in his long fingers, tracing her nipples with his tongue. She slid her leg between his, feeling his maleness rub against her thigh. Moving slightly so it touched the damp velvet skin below.

He went rigid, staring down at her with passion-filled eyes. "You're so beautiful, Shannon. I've wanted to do this for so long."

Sliding his body completely over hers now, he entered her, at the same time kissing her mouth hotly. And the world exploded. Stars burst behind her eyes, squeezed shut, moving, rocking rhythmically beneath him. He thrust deep within her, the elemental, passionate rhythm of love.

He whispered her name, pushing down into the very center of her being, holding her close. Her hands were tangled in his hair as her eyes drifted closed and she shuddered with passion, moving in hot surrender.

When he collapsed beside her, she laid her head on his chest and listened to the hammering of his heartbeat. Smiling, she whispered, "Good thing I forgot the sheets."

Gently, he stroked her shoulder and the lovely line of her breast. Cupping, kneading tenderly. He traced a fingertip down her hip, and said huskily, "You didn't. I lied."

She laughed. "You rat."

His eyebrow quirked. "What else was I to do? You walked off and left me standing in the hall. I figured I was getting the cold shoulder."

"I was just—shy," she admitted.

An insufferably smug smile curved his wide mouth. "That's what I thought."

She rubbed her cheek against his chest and felt the rumble of his laughter. He bent and kissed her forehead, and she lifted her face to his. "Mike, I'm not shy anymore." Her fringed blue eyes were dark with passion and need. He drew a deep breath and kissed her with the urgency of a man dying of thirst.

## Chapter Thirteen

Mike made the decision to pay a visit to the Parelli brothers almost without thinking. The next morning at seven, he slid out of bed, careful not to wake Shannon, showered, dressed and knocked on Nick's door. He could hear a computer beeping and knew the kids were already up. He pushed the door open and stuck his head in. "Hey, I've got to run an errand for an hour. Come on downstairs and have breakfast."

Nick turned off the computer and said, "Waffles."

Andy said, "Pancakes."

Mike looked around. No sign of Chris. "Where's Chris?"

"She's already downstairs, watching cartoons," Nick told him.

As he turned around, he saw Shannon coming down the hall. She was already dressed. "I've got an idea," she said firmly. "It's the Parellis. I can't get them off my mind. I don't care—if the police won't do anything, *I will*. I'll go out to the house, myself." Mike drew a sharp breath, and she went on, her voice tense, "I know what you're going to say, and I don't care."

"I planned to pay them a visit this morning," he said with a sigh, realizing there was no point trying to persuade her to stay out of things. "Give me time to go get my housekeeper. She can keep an eye on the kids while we're gone."

She smiled. "You've got a deal. Just give me half an hour, and—" she reached up and kissed him "—thanks."

He went out to the Bronco and got in. Then he sat for a moment, thinking. Why were women so damn much trouble! The more he thought about it the less he liked the idea of taking Shannon with him. But it was too late now. Eventually, he started the engine and drove over to his house. Mrs. Beekman had just arrived. It was her day to clean. He explained his predicament, and she agreed to come back to Shannon's to watch the children.

Mrs. Beekman smiled. "No problem, I'll make banana bread. The boys will love it, and Chris can chop nuts and lick the bowl." She followed him in her car, and a few minutes later they turned up Shannon's driveway.

"Give me a few minutes to show Mrs. Beekman where things are in the kitchen, and I'll be right out," Shannon said, already getting out a mixing bowl and a bunch of bananas.

He went outside and got back in the Bronco. For an instant, he considered not going to see the Parellis. The police had said the father was old and in poor health. But Mike knew he and Shannon would go in the end. They had to, not only for her sake, but to resolve any doubts of his own.

After five minutes of sitting in the Bronco with the window partly down and the sound of birds in the nearby trees, he was aware that Shannon was coming out of the house.

She grinned as she slid into the Bronco's bucket seat. "Okay, pardner. Let's go."

"I've got to be nuts," he muttered, looking over his shoulder as he backed the car out.

"I'm tougher than I look. Really." She frowned and yanked the rosy-red sweater she wore down over the waistband of her jeans.

"Let's hope so," he said under his breath as he drove off down the street. "Just let me handle things when we get there. I'll do the talking for both of us."

She cast him a worried glance and fastened her seat belt. "What are you going to say?"

"Don't worry, I'll think of something," Mike said grimly. He had questions that he'd make damn sure were answered.

He had a sketchy idea of where the Parellis lived. If they ran into difficulty finding the place, he could ask directions. Someone was sure to know. Shannon lapsed into silence as he drove west and turned on to Metta-commett Path. It was hilly, and the trees grew almost down to lichen-covered stone walls along the roadside. High above the road, arching branches shut out the sun. Depressing and dark, he thought, frowning. There was a dank smell in the air, as if not enough sunlight ever reached down through the trees. Not many people lived out here; there were just a few scattered homes. He slowed, passing a tired-looking cottage with a front porch up on brick pilings. The name on the mailbox was Spencer. They drove on. Three houses and a quarter mile farther west, they noticed a small two-story house whose peeling red paint had faded to a dull maroon.

The mailbox was rusted and tilted on its post, but the name was still legible. Parelli.

The house was a modest frame building with a sagging front porch and a detached flat-roofed garage. As Mike got out of the Bronco, he crushed some of the weeds that sprouted between the stone-paved driveway beneath his feet. He shut the car door and said to Shannon, "You stay here."

"Not on your life," she said, quickly getting out and following him up the path to the front door.

Great, he thought, just great. He heaved an annoyed sigh and looked around the weedy front yard.

No sign of a dark car anywhere, but a rusted orange van was parked in front of the garage, and beside it a pickup truck was sitting on cinder blocks.

As he raised his fist to knock, the screen door opened and a thin, sixtyish woman in a housedress and apron appeared. Her expression wasn't promising.

"You want something?" she asked crisply. Her manner indicated bill collectors were unwelcome. Her eyes narrowed shrewdly as she sized them up.

"In a way," Mike said, smiling. "I was looking for Moose or Hank."

"They're not here," the woman said, starting to close the door.

"Wait, er, are you a relative?" he asked.

"Maybe, maybe not. Depends," she said, still examining him with an unblinking expression. Her lips tightened as she flicked a glance past him at Shannon. Then an old man appeared and stood behind the woman.

"What'd they want, Ella?" the old man grunted. He was small, wearing thick glasses. His sparse white hair was wispy, and snowy strands of tufted hair grew from his ears. He wore a clean, worn green shirt and baggy trousers held up by suspenders.

She turned and said irritably, "That's what we was just gettin' to when you had to go and interrupt us."

The old man had a cookie in his hand. He gave Ella a look as if he thought she was an idiot and then peered at Mike. "Ain't I seen you before?"

Mike introduced himself and Shannon, explaining that he wanted to see Moose and Hank because he owed them some money. "I bought two cords of wood a month ago. They delivered it and didn't leave a bill."

"Well, heck, c'mon in," the old man said. "Ella, the man owes the boys some honest money. Never thought I'd see the day."

She pursed her lips and looked from Shannon to Mike without speaking, then shrugged. "I guess it's all right. That's my father. He's not the easiest person to get on with, but he's not senile." She led the way into the house and said, "Well, you can settle up with him about the money you owe. I got washin' to do."

She disappeared into the kitchen through an archway. The old man settled himself into a chair and stretched out his slippered feet. Peering at Shannon through his thick glasses, he said irritably, "Always goin' on about somethin', Ella is. Nosiest woman on God's green earth, just like her mama was." He coughed and said to Mike, "You said somethin' about money?"

"Yes." Mike reached into his back pocket and pulled out his wallet. He withdrew two hundred dollars and placed it on a nearby table. "That's for the two cords of wood." he looked around. "Where are the boys by the way? I'd like to thank them for the prompt delivery."

"They ain't here," the old man said, shaking his head.

"Oh, will they be back soon?" Shannon said, the tone of her voice expressing polite interest.

"I didn't say they would, didn't say they wouldn't." The old man smiled slyly. "They said somethin' about goin' to Florida. Or it mighta been California. Someplace warm. My hearing's almost as bad as my seeing. When the day comes I can't taste food, I'm goin' to shoot myself."

"Pa," the woman said from the kitchen. "You're not goin' to shoot yourself. Don't go tellin' strangers you're goin' to shoot yourself. You don't even have a gun."

"You can go to Bill's Sport Shop downtown and buy a gun," the old man said.

"They wouldn't sell one to the likes of you, Pa," Ella said, coming into the room and wiping her hands on her apron.

"Moose and Hank," Mike said patiently. "When did they leave?"

The old man reached for another cookie and took a bite, his face anticipating a bitter taste. Apparently, the cookie wasn't bitter. He took another bite. "I dunno, this mornin' or it coulda been yesterday. I said I'd like to go someplace warm for the winter and they laughed and said 'What good would it do you, Pop? You're an old man.' Think they's so dang smart all the time, tellin' me what I already know. Next they'll be tellin' me it snows in winter."

"Pop, you're ramblin' again. Be polite to the folks. They came all this way to give you some money," Ella said with a tired sigh. She nodded at her father and said to Shannon, "He gets like that sometimes. Don't pay him no mind."

The old man looked down at the cookie and seemed to be thinking of something far away.

"Will they be gone long?" Mike asked Ella.

She shrugged. "Who knows? Not long enough. I hate to say it, seein' they're my own kin, but the truth is, they're nothin' but scum. If they don't come back, it'll be too soon."

Mike took Shannon by the arm and went back out to the porch. Ella followed them and closed the sagging screen door. "I'll forward the money to Florida once they send an address."

"Why don't you keep it?" Mike said quietly, looking through the screen at the old man who was prying raisins out of a cookie in his hand.

Ella shrugged. "Maybe I will. Pop doesn't have much, just his pension. I come by and see him a couple times a week, bring a few groceries, make him a hot meal. Yeah, the money sure would come in handy. He's not goin' to last out the year."

"That's too bad," Shannon said quietly. "I'm sorry."

"No need to be. He's lived out his time and then some." She gave them a mirthless smile and said, "Well, if that's all—"

Nodding good-bye, they walked out to the Bronco. The sun was higher in the sky over the frame house, and it felt warmer. Mike breathed deeply only when he and Shannon got in and closed the car door. As they backed out and drove away, he saw Ella standing on the porch, her eyes watching them.

Shannon didn't say much as he threaded the Bronco through the narrow back roads, but her expression seemed lighter. He shot her a glance as they hit the highway and headed downtown.

"Well, what do you think?" he finally said. "They're gone for sure. The police will talk to Tim Carver. You're out of danger."

She pushed her hair back and gave him a small smile. "I suppose so. Yes, you're right. The Parellis are on their way to sunny Florida. And we'll find out about Tim, one way or another." Then flushing, she looked out the window. "Mike, you didn't have to give that woman all that money. Two hundred dollars...I'll pay you back."

"They looked like they needed it," he said with a shrug. "Forget it. It's a small price to pay for peace of mind." She was playing nervously with the lock button on the car window. "Look," he added quietly, "I'd give every cent I own if it meant your safety. Don't you know that by now?"

She nodded and sat close to him, leaning her head on his shoulder. He felt her sigh after a moment, then she said, "We should be celebrating, but I'm too wrung out to feel anything but tired."

They drove downtown. The streets were filling up with morning traffic. Two blocks ahead, he saw the twirling Shell sign and remembered he needed gas. The tank was only a quarter full. He pulled up to a self-serve pump, filled the tank, checked the oil and paid too much for a bag of balloons for Chris and a couple of equally overpriced comics he wasn't even sure Andy would like. The lurid covers featured grotesque monsters and a great deal of blood. Nick deserved something, too, he thought, looking around. Suddenly, he noticed just the thing. A full set of vampire teeth encased in a plastic bag.

"They look like a perfect fit," Shannon said, looking over his shoulder. She held up a bottle of fruit juice. "I got thirsty waiting in the car."

At the cash register he picked up a dozen muffins, as well. Then he paid for everything and they went out to the Bronco and got in. Hell, he thought, I feel as if we've just come back from a nightmare and we're bringing presents.

For the rest of the trip home Shannon sat close, and he breathed in the fresh scent of her. Shampoo and some kind of flowery soap, he thought with an inner smile. He felt his spirits lifting. They'd checked out the Parellis, and learned that they'd left town indefinitely, perhaps even permanently.

Shannon was relieved, he knew. He might not be able to convince her the Parelli brothers hadn't been mixed up with Tim or the scarecrow incident last night, but at least they wouldn't be around to bother her in the future. And that was something.

"MIKE, what do I do if the Parelli brothers come back?" she said suddenly.

"Simple. Pack up and move in with me."

There was a small silence, and Shannon felt Mike's fingers lace through hers. She found their warmth and firmness comforting, but she couldn't look at him. "I can't do that, you know why." She shifted a little away from him on the car seat, then said, "At least not now."

"Why the hell not?" His hand tightened on hers. "Shannon, what we had last night was real. Look at me."

There was another awkward pause. Why hadn't she told him the whole truth? she asked herself. She'd never told anyone before.

With a feeling of disgust, she remembered the way she'd been before her divorce, and without consciously willing it, heard her voice describing her lack of self-esteem, her inability to make even simple decisions without constant soul-searching.

"Tom grew moody and bad-tempered. All he did was complain about our life together. He had to dominate everything, and somehow—maybe it was instinctive self-preservation—I began to withdraw from him emotionally. We didn't have anything in common anymore. He didn't want to be tied down. He didn't like our friends, our life-style." She shrugged. "And he didn't like me."

"Why on earth did you marry him?" Mike interrupted.

"I've asked myself that over and over. I suppose youth and inexperience had a lot to do with it. I was stupid, I'd never been anywhere or done anything but go to school and college. Anyway, it was a mistake. The only good thing to come out of it was Nick." She smiled. "And I wouldn't give him up for the world."

"You don't have to talk about it if you don't want to," he said, gripping her hand.

"No, I want to tell you. It helps explain why I need to stay in my own house." Drawing a ragged breath, she said, "Tom picked Christmas Day to tell me he was leaving us. His idea of a gift, I suppose. Anyway, it took me a long time to get back on my feet emotionally. I feel as if I've taken a journey of a thousand miles." She took another breath and went on, "I know I can't go back to the person I used to be."

"For heaven's sake, Shannon, that's the last thing I'd want." He paused. "Will you tell me something, honestly?"

She raised her eyebrows quizzically. "I'll try. What?"

"Are you afraid of me—that I'll try to dominate your life the way your ex-husband did?"

"No, but you don't understand. In a way I've become focused on being in control and running my life the way I want to, without asking for anyone else's permission. Before the divorce, I never had that luxury, and now I have to learn to relax and let go."

He looked down at her, his eyes grim. "But you love me?"

She gazed back, a world of love and need in her eyes. "Yes, of course I do. I just need time."

DAMMIT, he thought as they arrived home ten minutes later. All Shannon needed was time, and all he needed was her. All the time.

Still holding Shannon's hand, he went into the house, looked in the kitchen and said "hi" to Mrs. Beekman who was just taking sugar cookies out of the oven. The banana bread lay on the counter, cooling.

"I thought the three children might like some sugar cookies, too," Mrs. Beekman explained. "Though that sweet tooth of theirs doesn't need any further encouragement."

"You spoil them," he told her with a grin.

Chris walked up, clutching a bunch of crayons tied together with a red rubber band, and her Barbie doll. She noticed the paper bag he held and demanded to know what was inside.

"Yours," he said, pulling out her bag of balloons. Immediately, her face lit up and he said, "No water bombs."

"Okay," she promised. "But I owe Andy and Nick one. They hit me last time we had balloons, and I didn't get them back."

Mike had no trouble remembering the last time he'd been foolish enough to bring home a package of balloons. The front hall had been soaked, anyone walking past the stairs presented the perfect target. "What are you smiling about?" Shannon said as the phone rang. It was Paul Wagoner. He asked for Mike.

"Glad I caught you," he said when she put Mike on. "I tried your house and no one answered, so I thought I'd try this number. Remember the work you were doing for Leslie's Uncle Harry before he died—the paneling in the library? The wall with the French doors?"

"Sure," Mike said.

"Well, we'd like you to do the other wall by the fireplace. Could you come by and take a look at it?"

"I suppose," Mike answered, picturing how the Wagoners' library would look with so much woodwork. It was a shame a previous owner had removed half the paneling, but he knew sources where he could locate a reasonable facsimile.

"Good, how about this afternoon?" Paul said. "And we're giving a dinner party this coming week. Wednesday, about seven-thirty. Bring Shannon if you'd like. Okay?"

"Sure, that would be fine," Mike said, a little surprised at the invitation. Although friendly, they hadn't been very social since old Harry Clarke's death and Leslie's subsequent inheritance. He hung up and went and asked Shannon if she was busy Wednesday night. She was in the kitchen with Mrs. Beekman, poring over a cookbook.

"Lunch?" She looked up and grinned at him. "Chicken soup or a Spanish omelet?"

"Before we talk about lunch, I want to know if you're free on Wednesday night. Paul called and invited us to a dinner party."

"Sounds good to me," Shannon said.

"In answer to your question, an omelet sounds good...but I'll cook," he said solemnly. Mrs. Beekman shook her head and Shannon laughed. "Looks like I'm surrounded by a bunch of doubting Thomases. I'll just prove you wrong."

While Shannon loaded the dishwasher, Mike went back to the living room to call the kids. "Omelet party, who wants mushrooms and who wants spinach?"

"That's gross," Chris giggled.

An hour later, they were finished with lunch and Mike left for his appointment at the Wagoners.

"Wonderful, you're here," Leslie cried as she let him in. "The work you did for Uncle Harry is perfect. We wanted to get the room finished before putting the place on the market." She led the way back to the library, still talking about how authentic the paneling had turned out.

They passed the front staircase and he stopped to admire the wonderful mural of a waterfall cascading down the wall. "That's a Rufus Porter, one of the last few left in New England," Mike remarked. "He painted another upstairs."

"Oh, yes," Leslie said, smiling. "A line of soldiers in funny hats carrying bayonets."

"The Portland Light Infantry," Mike told her. "Porter served with them as a musician in 1814. Played the flute."

Leslie shook her head. "My, I didn't know the murals were all that important."

"They are, and they'll add to the value of the house, too," Mike went on. "Your uncle said that when he inherited the place, it was a shambles. The roof was falling in, the floors sagging, the foundation cracked. He spent a great deal of time and money renovating it and making it as authentic as he could. A real labor of love."

"Well," Leslie said glancing around the front hallway, "it's not my cup of tea. I prefer a more modern home."

Mike smiled. "You should have seen it years ago. There was a henhouse where the kitchen is now, and a grain room and a cider mill connected to the wagon house—and all connected to the main house."

She shuddered.

"The woodshed is the columned breezeway out back, the cider mill became the garage."

"Don't say another word," she protested with a laugh. "I have nightmares as it is, wondering what's behind every cupboard door. Besides cobwebs, that is!"

Paul Wagoner waved at the far end of the hall. "Mike, glad you made it. Come on in. I had an idea for the paneling on this wall. It's suffered some water damage, needs a bit of repair."

Mike knelt down by the marred paneling and ran his fingers along the joints. "Mmm, it's water damage, all right. Wonder how it happened." Getting to his feet, he looked up and down the library wall. "Hard to tell where the water came from. Must have happened years ago."

"The land out back gets pretty wet when it rains heavily. We seem to have an underground spring somewhere." Paul wandered over to the French doors and looked out with a frown. After a moment, he turned back toward Mike and said, "We'd like to get the house ready for sale within a week or two. How soon can you replace that damaged paneling?"

"Well, I'll have to see," Mike temporized, examining the wall and thinking. The paneling was of oak and extended from floor to ceiling. Fanciful creatures and foliage had been carved in the wood, bands of them horizontally along the ceiling as well as the chair rail. He ran a thoughtful finger along the curving tail of a beautifully carved lizard. "Interesting work. Looks almost Dutch."

Paul came over and bent down to look. "Hmm, I wouldn't know. You're the expert."

"It would be interesting to know where the paneling actually came from," Mike told him. "Harry never mentioned it, but it might be somewhere in his papers. Perhaps Leslie or the lawyers have them somewhere. Harry said he'd kept a detailed accounting of all the renovating he'd done, so it would be easier for his heirs if they had to repair something."

Paul shrugged. "The lawyers didn't say anything about any journal, but it could be with his papers at the bank. He had a safe-deposit box."

Still marveling at the wonderful paneling, Mike glanced toward a pair of nearby windows. The library had folding interior shutters, security against Indian attack long ago. But his sharp eyes spotted something odd. On one side of each casement about halfway up were two plugged holes about a half inch in diameter and two and a half inches apart. The other side had a single hole. He grinned, realizing at once what the mysterious plugged holes were.

He showed them to Paul and explained. "A year or two ago, I was working on an old house in Bath. It had the same holes along the casements. The owner came up with the answer. His wife dug up a large staple in the garden. It had five-inch legs. At first, I thought it was a barn-door hinge, then later, I was examining the windows, and knew at once what it was. Just like this." Mike gestured at the library window. "Long ago, the staples held a wooden security bar across the shutter. The one-legged staple was open at the top so the bar could be lowered and lifted, rather than slid." He shrugged. "There are probably staples buried in your backyard, as well. This is proof there were bars across the shutters at one time."

Leslie came in with a tray of coffee. "Isn't that interesting. Well, if you're through poking around that old wall for a minute, come have coffee. I made scones, and there's some of Uncle Harry's favorite raspberry jam."

Mike sat in a nearby wing chair and sipped coffee. The old house was really a masterpiece of restoration. Harry Clarke hadn't spared a penny when it came to making the place look as it had in the eighteenth century.

"The cellar's just a hodgepodge of old doors and boards. I don't know why Harry never got it cleaned up. He was so particular about the rest of the house," Paul said, choosing a scone and lathering it with jam. He took a bite and smiled with appreciation at his wife. "Delicious, dear. Mike, have a scone. Leslie's a terrific cook."

She passed the plate to Mike. "Don't praise me to the skies. Wednesday night, I'll probably burn dinner to a crisp. You're coming, aren't you, Mike?"

He nodded. "Certainly, I wouldn't miss it."

Leslie stirred her coffee. "I hope you're bringing Shannon." She tilted her head at Mike and raised a slim eyebrow.

"Yes," he said, smiling.

"In fact," Leslie went on, "she brought us that wonderful old portrait on the wall by the window. The girl in the red dress, a birthday gift from my sister!"

Glancing at it with interest, Mike said, "It's lovely."

"We didn't know where to hang it," Paul explained with a shake of his head. "That spot's only temporary. We've moved the painting half a dozen times. There used to be a mirror there. I finally took it down and put it upstairs." He took another scone and then stared at Mike, stunned. "I just remembered! Wasn't Shannon involved in that robbery at the Y the other night? Terrible thing!"

"Oh, no," Leslie cried, concern in her wide eyes. "I didn't hear about it. I never listen to the news, too depressing. What happened?"

So Mike gave a shortened version of the terrifying episode. Shannon's screams, the absolute blackness of the upper track. Running footsteps, then a figure lunging out of nowhere with a knife. "I wasn't much good to her," he admitted with a grimace. "I got there in time to get knocked out and stabbed. She really saved herself."

A gray-striped cat stalked across the floor and out into the hall as the grandfather clock chimed the quarter hour, and Paul said grimly, "A *horrible* business, you both might have been killed. I've said, haven't I, Leslie? This country's going to hell in a hand basket, and no one seems to give a damn. Disgusting, you're not safe anywhere these days, not even in Boxford."

Leslie shook her head. "I can't believe it." She drew a breath and said, "Did they catch the men who—"

"The state troopers picked them up later. They'd hit the liquor store as well as the Y." Mike shrugged. "They're in jail, couldn't come up with bail."

"I hate to say it, but in a way I'm glad Paul and I are leaving," Leslie said suddenly. "Boxford's changed from the days when Linda and I used to spend school vacations with Uncle Harry. Now half the town's on fire, and hoodlums are running wild." She sipped her coffee and set the cup down so hard the spoon clattered in its saucer. "Sorry," she said ruefully. Her mahogany-colored hair swung around her smooth face as she frowned. "One thing I meant to tell Shannon last night and didn't. That tenant of hers, the carpenter—I wouldn't trust him. Yesterday, I saw him kicking her son's dog. The little black one. I was driving by, and there he was, kicking that poor little dog. I got so mad!" She shrugged. "Maybe it's a sign of the times, like the rest of the violence in town. It's sad, though, when I remember what it used to be like when we were kids."

"Did you spend all your summers here with Harry?" Mike asked curiously.

"No, let's see, two summers, I think, and one winter. I was nine and didn't make any friends at school that year. It was awful, I was so lonely." Leslie gave a little shrug. "Linda was at the age where she wouldn't have anything to do with a kid sister."

The clock chimed again, and Paul rose. "Your stories are boring Mike, darling."

Mike shook his head. "No, really."

"You should have said something," Leslie said, frowning. "I never know when to shut up."

It was time to go. Mike said he'd see what he could do about restoring the damaged paneling quickly. A few minutes later, he walked across the graveled driveway to the Bronco. Harry Clarke's cat watched from a second-floor window.

## Chapter Fourteen

The man with cold blue eyes didn't like dogs and he had a special reason for disliking this dog. It was a digger.

He opened his refrigerator, found the package of meat on the shelf beside the cartons of cottage cheese and fruit salad and took it out. Unwrapping it, he dumped it in a bowl. Beside the bowl stood a small blue can with white lettering on the label. Rat poison.

He had several more pressing things to do, but upon reflection had decided, first things first. He had to get rid of the damn dog.

The hamburger meat lay fresh and bright red in the bowl. It cost $2.68 per pound, no more than ten percent fat. Wasted on the dog, he thought. He pried up the lid of the rat poison with a beer-can opener and sniffed the contents judiciously. Funny, musty smell. Here it was, mass-produced for only $5.99. A surefire method to get rid of rats. The smell of death in his cheery kitchen.

The portable radio on the counter to his right played country-and-western music. Barbara Mandrell or Dolly Parton crying about losing a guy to her best friend. It was loud and squawky, and he didn't like it.

He reached over and turned it down as a voice said behind him, "How's it coming?"

"Ready in a minute," he said. "I'll leave it where the dog will find it, and then that particular problem will be out of the way. Permanently." His strong fingers kneaded pellets of death through the hamburger meat. They felt cool and smooth against his hands.

Images remained in the man's mind. Shannon Hollister, arching beneath his hands like a dancer, her mouth gaping, neck tendons tight under his fingers. Her damned eyes staring.

He wiped the perspiration from his forehead. Sunlight dappled the counter as he finished preparing the bait. Plastic wrap would do. He'd open it, spread it out in a spot where he knew the dog would find it.

"MAX?" Shannon called again and again. No sign of the dog anywhere. It wasn't like him. He was always underfoot at this time of night. "Max, supper—" She opened the apartment door and looked around. Dust motes swarmed in the thin shaft of sunlight. Beyond, the interior of the barn lay in absolute darkness. He wasn't there.

The door creaked as Mike pushed it wide. "Maybe he's in the apartment with Carver." She nodded and they went up to his door and knocked. She stood for a second, then called the dog's name again, louder this time. Tim Carver opened the door with a frown. "Whassa matter?" His eyes were bleary, and there was a smell of beer around him. Behind him they could see his TV. A basketball game was on. Judging from the pile of empties by the couch, he'd been home for a while.

"Have you seen Max?" Shannon said.

"Nah." Carver coughed and shook his head. "I ain't seen him since this mornin', sorry. Hey, by the way, the police dragged me downtown and grilled me about the fires. Thought you'd like to know, I got an alibi for most of 'em. So that lets me out."

"Good," she told him. "I'm glad to hear it." She turned and walked away, and Carver shut the door.

"He's a big help," Mike muttered as they went around to the back of the house.

"At least we know he's not the arsonist," she replied. "What do you think the calendar meant? And the burnt matches?"

"He's probably been trying to figure out who's responsible for the fires," Mike said, shrugging. "But he sure acted guilty."

By the edge of the brick terrace stood a large rosebush. The canes were just leafing out, little sprigs of bright green. Through the green she could see something black on the ground. She ran, her heart banging against her side, knowing that if anything had happened to the dog, it would break Nick's heart. Please, don't let it be Max. She grabbed the thorny canes as she knelt down. Blood scored her palm but she didn't feel it.

It was Max.

He lay on his side, still breathing. His tail thumped feebly as she touched his head. There was a strong smell of vomit. His eyes were vacant, and a thread of spittle drooled from the corner of his muzzle.

"Looks like he threw up whatever it was he ate. That's a good sign. Here, let me," Mike said quietly. He picked the dog up in his arms and she followed him back to the Bronco. "You use the vet out on Lancaster

Road?'' She nodded. "Get the hatch open and I'll slide him in.''

They reached the vet's in ten minutes. He examined Max and said, "I'd say he got into some kind of poison. It would help if we knew what it was. Anything caustic lying around, weed killer, that sort of thing?''

"No," Shannon said. "I keep all that locked up.''

"Well, I'll rehydrate him and see what I can do.''

An assistant gathered Max's limp body and bore it away to the back room. The vet looked at Shannon's worried expression and said, "We'll save him. He's a lucky dog, he did a pretty good job of getting the poison out of his system. Call me in the morning.''

They told the three kids that Max had gotten into something that had made him sick. They'd taken him straight to the vet's, so chances were, he'd be all right.

Nick stiffened, staring at his mother. Then his face crumpled and he began to cry. She slid an arm around his shoulders and said, "Honey, it's okay. Dr. Easley knows what he's talking about. He thinks Max'll be all right.''

"But he doesn't know for sure." Nick's face was streaked with tears, and he started hiccuping. Andy looked pale and frightened, and Chris's lower lip was quivering.

"What if he dies?" Chris said, tears welling in her big green eyes.

"Yeah, vets don't know everything," Andy said in a small voice.

"No," she said to them, smoothing Nick's curly hair back from his forehead. "But Dr. Easley's pretty smart, and he thinks Max will pull through.''

"When will we know for sure? Tomorrow? Maybe if we went over and saw him tonight, he'd feel better." Nick drew a ragged breath. "Can we, Mom, please?"

"No, he needs rest and quiet. We'll call in the morning." She hugged him for a long time, and gradually, Nick seemed to understand that Max was in good hands, that everything that could be done was being done for him.

But she noticed the little dachshund, Fred, stayed close by Nick's side, and every now and then, he scratched her head. Even Fred was subdued, as if she knew what had happened to Max.

They ate the informal supper Mrs. Beekman had prepared before she'd left. A hearty crab dish and a ring of rice and vegetables. Mike noticed Shannon didn't take a serving from the crab dish, but filled her plate with vegetables.

"Is this a vegetarian statement?" he asked, pouring milk for the kids.

"No," she said with an embarrassed shrug. "I'm allergic to seafood."

He was stunned. "I never thought—it's something my late wife, Helen, always made. The kids like it, Mrs. Beekman makes it a lot, and I never thought—"

"It smells delicious," she said, smiling. "Don't worry, I'll fill up on rice and carrots."

He passed her the basket of rolls. "Here, carbohydrates are good for you, too. I'm really sorry, Shannon. I'll do better next time."

After they washed up the supper dishes and the three kids were busy playing Nintendo, Shannon collapsed on the sofa next to Mike and arranged her head comfortably on his shoulder.

"Well, do you think you could stand this on a regular basis?" he said. "If I promised not to mess up like tonight?"

"I'll give it serious consideration," she said, turning her mouth up for his kiss.

THE THREE CHILDREN had their own idea of after-dinner conversation. Andy had plenty to say about who could have poisoned Max. After giving lip service to the theory that, in his words, "the evildoer must be brought to justice," he enlarged on his main theme, the thrust of which was that it was a serious mistake for any-one—especially dog poisoners—to mess with The Martian Spaceship Society.

He pushed his spectacles up on his nose and said, "We gotta question everybody who might've done it."

"What if it was the arsonist?" Nick's blue eyes narrowed in thought. "How're we gonna know who he is?"

"Simple," Chris said. "We go door-to-door and ask questions. Then we figure out who's lying and who's not." She patted Fred who was curled up in her lap. "If one of us keeps the person busy at the door, the rest of us can look in garages for stuff like kerosene or poison."

"Good idea," Nick said.

Andy looked at his fellow members of the spaceship society. "But what excuse do we use when we knock on the door? We can't just walk up and say, 'Hi, did you poison Nick's dog, and by the way, are you the guy settin' all the stupid fires?'"

"Easy," Chris said, coming up with the answer as she usually did. "We pretend to sell candy. People fall for that stuff all the time."

EARLY THE NEXT MORNING, Shannon phoned the vet's office and learned that Max had pulled through and might even come home in another day or two. She woke Nick, who grinned with relief and said he knew Max would be okay, he was one tough dog. They were still discussing what kind of poison Max could have gotten into, when Nick grabbed a banana and said he had to go. "A big meeting of The Martian Spaceship Society. Important things to do," he added. The door banged behind him, and he jumped on his bike and was on his way.

By noon, The Martian Spaceship Society had canvased three streets and talked to twenty-nine people. They'd taken orders for more than a dozen boxes of homemade chocolates, which they planned to persuade Mrs. Beekman to make. The eventual disposition of monies collected was still up for discussion, with Andy vehement that it should go to some charity. "Like for homeless dogs and cats," he said.

"The Humane Society," Chris said.

"Yeah, the Human Society," he agreed.

"Humane," she corrected.

"That's what I said." Andy pushed his glasses up on his nose and glared at her.

Nick frowned. "So how many cans of poison stuff did we see? Weed killers and rat poison."

Andy had a pad with a list of homeowners whose garages had been open and fairly accessible to snooping. The trouble was almost every garage had contained some gardening chemical in one guise or another. It was hard to rule anyone out.

There were only a few houses left on the street, among them, Mrs. Montgomery's. She was a large fat woman with glasses and a bulbous nose. "I don't like her," Chris muttered as they went up the front walk to her house. "She's mean, always yelling at her cat. Sometimes she goes away on vacation and leaves him home alone. I've seen him in the window, crying. He looks like he's hungry."

"Maybe he's just glad she's not around," Nick suggested.

"Yeah, he could be meowing for joy," Andy said.

"Don't be so stupid," she hissed.

Ignoring his sister, Andy rang the doorbell.

The door rattled, and then opened. Mrs. Montgomery's suspicious brown eyes stared down at them. "What do you want?"

"My little sister's selling chocolates for charity," Andy said with a smile. Mrs. Montgomery didn't smile back.

"I'm on a diet," she snapped.

"We have both kinds," Chris announced. "Diet chocolates *and* ones that taste good and make you fat." She held up a small brown paper bag. "We have some samples, if you'd like to try one."

Mrs. Montgomery's eyes brightened. "That would be very nice! I don't mind if I do."

With the fat woman's attention firmly fixed on the bag of chocolates in her hands, Andy and Nick sidled away behind the bushes by the garage. "Do you think Chris can keep her busy while we search it?" Nick whispered anxiously. The garage door yawned wide, but the interior was a cluttered mess. Cartons and old furniture stored, higgledy-piggledy, all over the place. But there, on a shelf on the far side near a window, stood several pesticide containers.

Nick read off the names. "'Bug-Be-Gone, Weed-Away, Rat Motel.' What's a rat motel?"

Andy adjusted his glasses and took a long look. "Who cares what it is, use your head! It's gotta be poison. People don't send rats someplace nice, like a vacation. Hey," he said triumphantly, "there's an empty space between these two cans. Look at the clean place in the dust. *Another can used to be here!* Prob'ly some kind of poison. This is where she stores stuff like that."

"Do you think Mrs. Montgomery poisoned Max with it and used up the whole can?"

"Nope. He would've been dead if she'd used it all." Andy looked around thoughtfully. "The door's open, anyone could've come in and stole it."

"I dunno," Nick said stubbornly. "It's her garage, she knew where the poison was. Maybe she doesn't like Max. Maybe he saw her setting some fires, and she got scared."

"No way," Andy snorted. "She couldn't have got away if Max chased her, she's gotta weigh five hundred pounds."

They were standing just inside the garage. Nick turned and glanced at the side window. Andy's eyes followed his, just in time to catch a glimpse of the face pressed to the glass.

"Chris," Andy muttered. "She's supposed to be keeping Mrs. Montgomery busy. What's she doing here?"

"Let's find out," Nick said. He ran around the garage, with Andy close behind. "What happened?"

"What do you think? She ate the whole bag, that's what," Chris snapped. "And she ordered five more pounds." She glanced toward the garage. "Did you find any poison?"

"We found some that was missing," Nick told her as they got on their bikes and rode home. "Looks like an important clue!"

They were in high spirits by the time they raided the kitchen for a snack to take to the woods near the cellar hole. Things were falling into place. It was only a matter of time now before they'd nab Max's poisoner and bring him to justice.

"Wanna know what I think?" Andy said suddenly. He leaned back against a tree and chomped the last of Mrs. Beekman's sugar cookies. Nick didn't want to know what Andy thought, but knew an avalanche of information was forthcoming, anyway; so he sighed and let him talk without interruption.

"Even if Mrs. Montgomery didn't do it, I'll bet it was the arsonist that poisoned Max," Andy said hoarsely. "What if he was gonna set fire to your house, and Max started barking so the arsonist had to get him outta the way? Prob'ly he tried to stab Max first, only he missed and got the scarecrow, so he had to poison him."

That at least made sense. Nick nodded, then frowned. "But why would the arsonist want to set fire to my house? We didn't do anything to him."

There was a glum silence. Then Andy snapped his fingers. "I got it! You were real friendly with Mrs. Brennan. She died in that fire, and the arsonist prob'ly thinks you know who he is." Andy's thin face, surmounted by a mop of carroty hair, was alight. He could put two and two together and get four.

"That's crazy. I don't know anything about the old arsonist."

"Sure, but *he* doesn't know that!" A gleam came to Andy's large green eyes, then faded. "Too bad we can't set a trap like the one we're making for the mummy.

Which, now that I think of it, could be some kinda vampire-mummy, like in comic books, on account of he stalks around at night. We could leave hay around and keep an eye out for anyone with matches and a can of kerosene. Heck, I guess it's too dangerous. Your mom prob'ly wouldn't go for it. Anyways, good thing Max's okay.''

''Yeah, good thing,'' Nick said thoughtfully. He peered through the binoculars. He could see that Chris had reached the last house on their side of the woods.

Andy started digging the vampire-mummy trap. They'd brought shovels and a volleyball net and planned to dig the pit near the cellar hole—where there weren't so many rocks. This time the mummy wouldn't escape! ''What's Chris doing?'' he asked after he'd dug a sizable hole.

''Gimme a minute.'' Nick refocused and took a look. ''Mrs. Wagoner's opening the door and letting her in the house.'' He swatted a mosquito and started digging, too. A bright green fly buzzed near. He watched it for a minute, frowning. Mrs. B. had said you didn't see them often.

He staggered around the far side of Andy's hole. Rain had softened the ground, but there were brambles and weeds with thick roots to dig up. Once, as he stopped for breath, he found himself staring at the spot where Max had dug the other night. The slight depression not ten feet away, just inside the old cellar hole. He took another breath, the shovel motionless in his hands. He'd just remembered something else Mrs. B. had said about green flies. You only saw them near something...dead.

Some old squirrel, maybe. Or even a moose. It could have died right there and been covered with leaves until all you could see was the depression.

Andy grabbed the binoculars. "Hey, here comes Chris. She keeps looking over her shoulder."

Minutes later, Chris climbed over the stone wall. "Guess what! The Wagoners are giving a big party tonight, and they're moving next week. And that's not all!"

"Oh, yeah? What else did you find out?" Andy asked.

"Well, she's a *vampire!* She started putting on lipstick, and I didn't see any reflection in the mirror."

"Really?" Nick's jaw dropped, and Andy gulped.

"I been watching their house anyway," Chris went on. "Vampires sleep all day and fly around at night. I never see them while the sun's up, honest! And their lights are on all night. Ha! Maybe you only thought you saw a mummy that day in the woods with Mrs. B. Maybe it was Mrs. Wagoner the vampire. I looked for old bandages, which would prove they were mummies for sure, but I didn't see any lying around."

Nick's eyes narrowed. "He didn't want us out here in the woods, remember?"

Andy went back to digging, and suddenly his shovel struck something wooden with a hollow thunk. "Hey!" he cried. *"I found the mummy's treasure!"*

All three kids began digging like mad, but what they uncovered finally wasn't a treasure chest. It was a small door sunk into the side of the slope. With a little more effort, they pried it open. Behind it lay mossy stone steps leading down into the earth. *A tunnel!* It smelled dank and musty. Tangled roots barred the opening.

"Well," Andy said, looking from Nick to his sister. "Who wants to go first?"

Nobody volunteered.

Finally, Nick spoke up. "Just to the bottom step, because we don't have a flashlight, and I'm not going anyplace I can't see." Visions of vampire witches floated in his head. Demons, mummies, every awful monster he'd ever read about seemed to await him just beyond that last step in the pitch-black dark.

Chris held the door and said, "Mrs. Wagoner's cat's prob'ly her familiar. He's got double paws. That's a sure sign of witchcraft. She must've cursed him."

That did it. Nick climbed back up and shoved the door closed. "We need a flashlight. I'm not going back in there until we get one."

BACK AT THE HOUSE, Shannon was taking the scarecrow down. She couldn't bear to look at it anymore. Just as she dropped the pliers and swore, Mike drove up and got out of the Bronco. "What's up?"

"I bolted the damn neck to the barn with a clamp, and now it's stuck."

"Let me give you a hand." He emptied his pockets, looking for his jackknife. "You need a screwdriver. I think I've got something that'll do." He sorted through the contents of his pockets. Handkerchief, pencil, key chain, jackknife— Shannon frowned. "Where did you get that?"

"What?" He glanced up, puzzled.

"This." She turned the key chain over. A four-leaf clover with the logo for Lucky Dry Cleaners.

"At the Girl Scout camp, remember? It was lying on the ground."

She nodded. "The other night I saw Tim parking in front of Lucky Dry Cleaners. It was closed. I thought he was going to the bar next door, but what if—" Her eyes darkened. "I just remembered, Tim told me his uncle owned the cleaners."

Mike frowned. "The calendar in his apartment's got the same logo on it, and I found the key chain hours after the fire. Could be whoever set the fire dropped it."

"Or Tim could be blackmailing him." She glanced at the barn. Nothing stirred. The windows were dark and still.

Mike looked grim. "That's a dirty word, blackmail. The only way to find out for sure is to confront Tim with it."

Shannon made a wordless sound of protest. "Couldn't we—" But she was too late, Mike was already banging on the door. After a moment, it opened, and Tim stood there, looking hung over. Mike held up the key chain, and Tim's face darkened.

"How'd you find . . . I mean, where'd you get that?"

"At one of the fires. You know who's setting them, don't you?" Mike said, his jaw tightening.

Tim swallowed and opened his mouth, but nothing came out. He tried again. "I, uh, I tried to stop him, but he said he wouldn't hurt nobody. He needed the money."

"Who?" Mike said, his voice hard.

"My Uncle Don, he owns Lucky Dry Cleaners, only he . . . plays the horses and he lost a bundle." Tim shrugged helplessly. "He had a coupla bank notes he couldn't meet and thought he'd burn down the place and collect the insurance. Nobody'd know the difference if there'd already been a bunch of random fires, nobody hurt, of course. His shop'd be just another fire."

"So he's the one who's been setting the fires," Shannon whispered, horrified.

"Right," Tim admitted. "I been goin' nuts wonderin' what to do. I tried talkin' to him after Mrs. Brennan died, but he swore he didn't set that one." His throat worked as he swallowed hard. "Thing is, the fires are my fault. If I hadn't showed him the newspaper story about some guy in Colorado doin' the same thing, Uncle Don would never have gotten the idea. I tried to talk him out of it, and he said to keep my mouth shut. Only I got scared after Mrs. Brennan died. We got into a fight the other night. He punched me out pretty good."

Mike gestured to the Bronco. "Come on, I'll go with you to the police, but you have to tell them everything."

"Yeah, I guess so." Tim heaved a tired sigh and went with them to the car. As Shannon got in and closed the door, he spoke from the back seat. "The worst of it is my Aunt Bella—she doesn't know, this is gonna kill her."

# Chapter Fifteen

"Thanks, the town will breathe easier," Officer Conway said, shaking Mike's hand as they left Tim at the station. They'd been there for over an hour while Tim told all he knew about the fires.

A squad car peeled out and took off down the hill toward Lucky Dry Cleaners. Mike and Shannon got into the Bronco, and she looked at him. "Will Tim be all right?"

Mike nodded. "He came in voluntarily. The police know they don't have a case without his testimony."

Shannon's mind reeled as she considered the pain Tim's uncle had caused. For what? *Insurance money.*

Mike glanced at his watch. After five. It was getting late, and they were expected at the Wagoners' dinner party shortly. Mrs. Beekman was baby-sitting. There was just time for one more errand before they went home to dress.

He pulled up at the library. "We'll only be a minute," he said. The first person they ran into when they went inside was the well-corseted figure of Viola Tibbs, head librarian.

"Of course we have the town history," she trilled when Mike asked where it was. "We keep it locked up."

She removed it from its glass case and said, "Closing time's in half an hour."

Mike flipped through the red leather-bound volume while Shannon sank into a nearby chair. "What are we looking for?"

"I'll know when I see it," he muttered, scanning pages of old photographs. "Bingo," he said suddenly. He jotted down a line or two on a piece of paper, then snapped the book shut. "Okay, let's go."

"That's all we came in for?" Shannon's face registered astonishment.

"You'll see." Mike winked mysteriously as he gave the book to Miss Tibbs and they left the library.

An hour later, on the way to the Wagoners', Shannon was dressed in black and pearls and still no closer to learning why they'd stopped at the library. Finally, as they pulled up to the Wagoners', he said, "Remember the runaway slave poster we found in the boarded-up room? Frank Mullen?"

"Sure," she said, frowning.

He showed it to her. "I brought it along tonight for a good reason. Remember the cryptic signs they used to help runaways to safety? A black band painted on a chimney meant it was a safe house, part of the Underground Railroad. An old photo of Harry Clarke's house in the town history showed a black band on one of his chimneys. There's something else. Harry said he had a big secret he planned to reveal to the historical commission. He died before he could." Mike shrugged. "I bet there's a tunnel beneath the house, part of the Underground Railroad. It comes out in the library. That flower and lizard on the back of the poster? I saw the same design on the library paneling."

"My God," Shannon said, stunned. A tunnel, part of the Underground Railroad—she wondered if Frank Mullen had ventured down that tunnel on his way to freedom.

"I'M STARVING," Shannon muttered as they walked up the front steps and rang the bell. "I hope this isn't just a wine-and-cheese wingding."

The door opened, and Leslie, tall and resplendent in a red dress with black batwing sleeves, welcomed them with open arms. Her glorious mane of russet hair was held back with a tortoiseshell clip, and she wore a heavy gold chain around her slim neck. "Wonderful to see you," she said in a low, husky voice. "You probably know everyone else here. Circulate. Supper will be ready soon, so help yourselves to something to drink in the meantime." She took Shannon's coat and hung it in the hall closet. "I thought hot buttered rum would be fun for tonight, but if you're feeling sensible, there's also gin and whiskey."

Mike moved off toward the library, and Shannon mingled among the other guests in the two large connecting sitting rooms. Admiring the furniture, nodding every now and then to a familiar face like Viola Tibbs, who had found time to change into a purple caftan before the party.

From the second sitting room, Shannon wedged her way through a knot of people standing at the door to the library. Dana Jennings was deep in conversation with a man. She caught Dana's eye and smiled. Paul Wagoner and Mike were standing by the fireplace wall, talking. Mike had the slave poster in his hand. He turned it over and pointed at the drawing on the back. "The lizard with the curly tail is really a griffin, like the one in the paneling. I looked in the town history down at the library and learned that old Ephraim Clarke was an ardent abolitionist back in the 1830s. The end chimney of this house was originally painted white with a black stripe around it. Part of a secret code of that time. It alerted those in the know that this house was part of the Underground Railroad."

Shannon listened with one ear, her eyes wandering to the paneling on the fireplace wall. Mike showed Paul the panel with the water damage. Then he tapped the panel in several places. "Sounds hollow." He tried twisting the carved flowers, then by chance tried the griffin. A loud creak, and the panel swung open with a gust of cold, damp air. Sagging cobwebs billowed out and they could see stone steps that led downward into absolute darkness.

"What the hell—" Paul stared for a moment, then stuck his head gingerly in the opening.

"Your own private stop on the Underground Railroad," Mike explained. "According to town history, this tunnel was built originally as a kind of back door. The account's sketchy, but it's there. Protection from Indian raids. It leads under the fields behind the house into the woods."

Pulling his head out, Paul brushed a cobweb off his shoulder and stared at him. "You can't be serious."

"Perfectly serious." Mike smiled. "This house is a historical gem." Oohing and ahing, everyone in the room surged forward wanting a peek inside the tunnel, but Mike closed the panel up tight. "After all this time, it's not safe. The historical commission will have to check it out."

After that, dinner was almost an anticlimax. Curried lamb, new potatoes with peas and mint, a wild mushroom tart and salad. A soufflé rounded out the meal. Shannon got up from the table, feeling as if she'd never need to eat again.

A trip to the bathroom seemed in order. Leslie waved a hand in the direction of the stairs. "Down the hall, first door on the right."

Shannon went upstairs past a series of framed eighteenth century samplers. The last one at the top of the stairs had been stitched by Phylinda Hubbard, aged ten, in 1795.

Smiling, Shannon opened the bathroom door. Gleaming silver and pink. It was still reasonably neat despite all the dinner guests who had been in and out.

Glancing in the mirror over the sink was a mistake. She smoothed her dark hair, which in damp weather had a regrettable habit of standing up like spikes. Her black dress looked vaguely funereal. Frowning, she washed her hands and laid the towel over the bar. A rough patch on the towel bar tore her fingernail. She looked in her purse, but no emery boards anywhere. She opened the medicine cabinet on the off-chance Leslie would have some. Let's see, bottom shelf: mouthwash, toothpaste. Second shelf: contact lens rinse, vitamins and a colorful array of nail polish. Mauve, cherry-red, peach.

Sighing, she craned her neck and examined the top shelf. Aha, one lonely emery board. She used it to good effect and replaced it on the shelf.

Downstairs, Shannon found Mike standing beside Viola Tibbs, looking a little uncomfortable as she waved a finger at him. "You naughty man, not telling me what you were up to with the town history! Just think, forgotten all these years! How lucky that you noticed that panel!"

Mike shoved his hand into a pants pocket. "It's my job to notice things like that."

Viola Tibbs shook her head. "You're wasted on architectural restoration. That sardonic, sexy look, and those fantastic black eyebrows! I direct theatrical productions for the Boxford Playhouse. We could use you this summer, now don't you forget!" And Viola, leaving Mike with his black eyebrows raised, floated off in the direction of the front sitting room.

"I think it's definitely time to leave," he muttered.

Shannon swiveled around, trying to catch their hostess's eye. There she was, over by the fireplace. Shannon whispered that they were leaving, and her lustrous green eyes widened in dismay. "Do you have to go?" Shannon explained about baby-sitters and late hours, and Leslie nodded, understanding, and went off to fetch their coats.

In the Bronco a few minutes later, Shannon yawned, and Mike said, "What did you think of old Harry Clarke's house? Quite a place, isn't it?"

She yawned. "Lovely, but it's like a museum. I'm not sure I'd like to live like that. It seemed almost lifeless. All that front hall needed was a velvet rope. It didn't feel like a home." She glanced at Mike's face. He nodded agreement, and she found herself examining him critically. He looked tired, as if he hadn't had enough sleep lately. His face seemed leaner and drawn. *I'm about in the same shape,* she added to herself. *Tired, edgy and too pressured these past few weeks.* "We need a day off," she announced. "Either that or a sunlamp."

"How about a week or two in the Bahamas?" he said with a sideways smile.

"Sounds wonderful, but not likely."

He gave her another smile. "We'll have to see about that."

"WHERE ARE the kids? I thought we were going out for pizza," Mike said, puzzled. It was the day after the Wagoners' party, and he'd worked hard all day on the plans for Mrs. Brennan's house.

Shannon looked up. "They've been in and out all day. They'll turn up soon." She dug into the pile of accumulated bills. Gas, telephone, mortgage. She groaned and pushed them aside in favor of the package from Linda Clarke which she'd forgotten about.

She tore the wrapping off, thinking simultaneously that she had a nice pewter frame that would do. The photograph lay in her hands. A color snapshot of the two girls sitting on a fence. At a guess, they were fourteen and twelve. "Cute kids," Mike said.

"Uh-huh," Shannon answered absently, while she stared at the photograph. Linda was tall and lanky, though still flat-chested at fourteen. She was turned a little toward her sister, who faced the camera.

Green-eyed Leslie, laughing. The scar along her jawline clearly visible. Shannon remembered Linda telling her about the scar. "Mom was drunk. She ran into a brick wall, smashed up the car. Leslie was hurt the worst. She went right through the windshield. Glass slashed her jaw. She's still got that scar, faded now. Mom didn't get a scratch."

In the photograph, Leslie wore a gold locket around her neck. Shannon took a closer look. The locket was a dead ringer for the one Mrs. Brennan had found in the woods and asked her to return to Leslie. It had an *L* engraved on it. Sure enough, the L could be seen in the locket in the photograph.

But Leslie had said Paul had given her that locket. Obviously, that wasn't true. She'd met and married Paul years after college. So why had she told the lie?

Mike pulled out a chair and sat down. "Do you want me to call and order pizza, or what?"

"Sure, whatever you like." She scarcely heard him. She was trying to figure out why Leslie's bizarre little lie was so disturbing.

Thinking of how Leslie had held up the locket and said to Paul, "Remember this?" And the light from a table lamp falling on her face, revealing her lovely, unblemished skin and the smooth line of her jaw.

No scar.

Perhaps she'd had plastic surgery. Doctors could work wonders these days. Shannon frowned. Hadn't Leslie's eyes been brown that first night? At the party she'd had lustrous green eyes, just like her eyes in the photograph. But there was contact lens solution in the medicine cabinet.

She shook her head. If Leslie wanted to wear brown contact lenses and have cosmetic surgery, so what.

She fitted the photograph inside the pewter frame. A quick polish and it was all set. Mike wrapped it while she called Leslie to ask if she could drop it off.

The line buzzed ominously when she dialed, and she hardly heard Leslie's voice when she answered. "How nice!" she said. "We'd love to see it. Come by and have a drink. We're eating late tonight. Paul's been moving furniture to the barn for the sale."

Leaving Mike in charge, and with clear orders to call the local sub shop for two large pizzas with the works, Shannon dashed to her car. It was almost seven, and the sky was dark with storm clouds. Breeze-blown rain spattered her windshield. The car started with a little coaxing, and she made another mental note to get a battery and a tune-up.

Not much traffic, and she made good time. A few minutes later, she arrived at the Wagoners', pulled into the driveway and switched off the engine, remembering to turn the lights off. She dashed for the house with the photograph tucked under her arm.

They'd turned on the light by the front door, and Leslie welcomed her with delight. "Come in," she said, smiling. "You don't know how I've been waiting for that picture!" Her eyes flickered over the package Shannon carried. "Such memories, summers in Maine, the ocean—Linda always put sand crabs down the back of my bathing suit!"

Paul came out of the living room as Leslie closed the door and took Shannon's damp coat. He had a drink in his hand. "Hi," he said, smiling. "That the picture Linda sent?"

"It came in the mail the other day," Shannon said.

Leslie hung her coat in the hall closet. "Spring's so late this year. Paul's been trying to put in tulips, and every day, more rain!"

A little puzzled, Shannon glanced at Leslie's mobile face. It was the wrong time of year to plant tulips. Her eyes flickered from Leslie's to the photograph she was unwrapping. There was no scar on Leslie's jaw. Her eyes were brown tonight. A deep chocolate brown. *Leslie hadn't bothered to put in her contacts. The green contacts!*

Paul looked at the photograph, then he looked at Shannon and he saw the knowledge in her eyes. With a little smile, he walked over and locked the front door.

The click of the lock sounded like a gunshot.

She backed up a step, still not altogether sure what was going on. Her sixth sense was telling her to *run, run,* but there was nowhere *to* run because Leslie had moved to block the back hallway. Leslie was eyeing her with such malice it was hard to breathe.

"What's...going on?" Shannon said hoarsely. She looked at Paul, and her blood froze. Paul tilted his head, still smiling. Light from the brass chandelier overhead hit his face and his *light blue eyes. Dear God, it was him!* The man who had terrorized her in the locker room at the Y, the man in Nick's bedroom with his hands reaching around her neck, squeezing, squeezing the life out of her!

Oh God, she mouthed silently. Oh God, no! She resisted the urge, the screaming urge to dash past him somehow, to make it to the front door. But she knew she'd never get it unlocked in time. His expression dared her to try it. His ice-blue eyes seemed fastened to hers with an invisible thread. Hideous eyes, so frighteningly close and deep and empty. The eyes of a killer. She backed up another step and hit the hall table. Numb, disbelieving, she shook her head. "You'll never get away with it. They know I'm here."

Suddenly, he had a gun in his hand. "Now, slowly. Walk into the library and sit down."

One hesitant step and her legs almost buckled. She grabbed the edge of a table and held on. Thunderous heartbeats shook her chest and shoulders so hard she could barely move her legs at all.

He slowly crossed the few yards that separated them. His eyes were brimming with cold, cold anger. She took another hesitant step, her legs shaking. But she didn't fall. She had more strength than she thought.

"Hurry up," he said. "You've caused us quite a lot of trouble! You and those *damn* kids!"

His hard voice was unmistakable. Why hadn't she recognized it before now? She managed to step backward down the hall to the library, but overwhelming fear gripped her like a pair of giant hands, closing over her ribs and pushing the air from her lungs.

Leslie came into the room. She kept looking at her watch. "We don't have a lot of time. Get rid of her now."

Then the phone rang. It rang again stridently, echoing through the house.

Leslie turned toward the phone on the table. Paul grabbed her arm. "Let the damn thing ring!"

WHY DIDN'T ANYONE at the Wagoner house answer the phone? Mike checked the kitchen clock again. The second hand crawled toward a minute and a half. He let it ring six times before giving up.

Three small faces watched him from across the table. They were eating pizza. "Where's my mom?" Nick asked, reaching for another slice.

"She went to the Wagoners', but they don't answer," Mike said, picking up the phone and dialing again. This time he let it ring eight times before hanging up. He looked at the kitchen clock, expecting fifteen minutes to have passed. It was ten to eight. "She might have car problems. They're probably trying to get it started for her."

Chris said around a mouthful of pizza, "They're vampires. We found their escape tunnel in the woods."

"*What?*" Mike turned and frowned at her. "Where in the woods?"

"By the old cellar hole," Andy explained, pushing his glasses up. "Where the tunnel comes out, there's sort of a door. We found it yesterday. We've been digging all the old roots out of the entrance."

Mike raked his hair back. "You kids stay away from that tunnel. It's not safe!"

A burst of rain and wind rattled the window, and Andy frowned. "It looked okay. We were just exploring."

Glancing at the clock, Mike saw that it was after eight. Damn, Shannon should have been back by now. Or called if she needed help. Had to be that damn car of hers. Why the hell hadn't he told her to take the Bronco?

"Shannon's car probably broke down," he said to the three kids. "I'm going out to look for her. Will you be all right for about half an hour? We'll be right back."

"Sure." Andy opened the second box of pizza and selected a big piece.

"Mrs. Wagoner's eyes change color. They turn red in the sun," Chris said solemnly. "She's a witch-vampire."

"Please, no more nonsense," Mike said tiredly.

"She has a special witch name, 'Iris.' Mr. Wagoner called her that and looked real mad that I heard him."

"What?" Mike turned, frowning. For some reason, his mouth felt dry and his heart had started pounding.

"She's weird," Andy said. "But don't worry, we made a great trap in the woods, with saplings and a volleyball net."

"Find my mom," Nick said. He didn't look frightened, but he hadn't eaten much.

"She'll be home soon," Mike said, hoping it was true.

GETTING TO the Wagoners' took less than ten minutes. Mike slowed in front of the house. Shannon's car was still in the driveway, but a man was at the wheel, trying to start it. Paul Wagoner got out, slammed the door and, head down against the rain, ran back to the house.

So Shannon was still inside.

Why hadn't they picked up the phone? There were other questions he wanted answered. Why had Paul called Leslie 'Iris'? Shannon insisted Leslie's eyes were odd, that they looked brown the first time she saw her. He'd shrugged it off as contacts. But what if her real eye color was brown, and she wore green contacts to look like Leslie. *What if her real name was Iris?*

He got out, tense and furious. Shannon had walked into a very ugly situation, and he'd let her do it.

He looked in the front window. The room was empty. Quietly, he worked his way around the side of the house. The library. Shannon was sitting in a chair, looking frightened and pale. Paul waved a gun at her. "Get up, bitch. You're going down that tunnel!" Behind him, Iris, or whoever the hell she was, twisted the carved griffin, opening the panel and Paul said, "Scream if you like, I'll just shoot you here."

Suddenly, Mike realized exactly where they were going. Heart hammering furiously, he raced back to the car for a flashlight, then, at a dead run, set off for the woods and the tunnel entrance. Near the old cellar hole. He knew where that was.

"THIS IS all your fault, damn you," Leslie snarled. "If you'd dug the grave deep enough, we wouldn't be in this mess!"

"For God's sake, Iris," Paul shouted, "I did the best I could."

*Iris*, Shannon thought, staring at them. Who was this woman? Where was the real Leslie?

"Every time I came near the damn grave, old lady Brennan was snooping around with that kid." Paul jerked the gun at Shannon. "The old bag wouldn't stop poking her nose around in the woods. Said Harry left her permission in the will to dig anywhere she damn well pleased. Arrowheads and junk. She was going to dig in the cellar hole, dammit!" His mouth twisted in a grin. "I had to kill her, she would have found the graves. I hit her on the head, then set her house on fire. The cigarettes were a nice touch." He paced around, a bundle of nervous energy. "Damn dog dug up Leslie's wallet. He ran off with it before I could catch him."

Shannon drew a shaky breath. "I don't understand how you got away with impersonating Leslie—you must be mad!"

He smiled. "No, it was simple. The night Leslie and I moved in, Iris's husband, Roger, showed up dragging her with him, furious. He'd found out about our affair, and well, we had it out. All four of us. Leslie was livid, said she'd divorce me. I wouldn't get one red cent of her inheritance."

"Roger hit me," Iris said, shrugging. "So I picked up a poker and—"

"Killed him, so we had to kill Leslie, too," Paul finished. He tilted an eyebrow. "What else could we do? Roger dead, and Leslie in hysterics. She insisted she was going to the police, then a lawyer. She was going to cut me off without a penny."

Shannon stared at him. "How did you think you'd get away with it? Someone who knew Iris would have seen her and known she wasn't your wife."

"We were lucky. Old Harry Clarke was the only one in town who really knew Leslie and he was dead. She'd already signed all the necessary inheritance documents by mail while we were in Detroit. Her sister, Linda, was in Florida and hadn't seen her in ages." Paul shrugged. "We'd put the house on the market, sell the antiques and fly to Europe. A couple of weeks at most. Iris could pose as Leslie for that long." He grinned at Shannon. "You were a dead woman from the moment you said that Linda was mailing you that photograph. After I failed at the Y, I followed you for days, even threw a knife at you—only I got your damn scarecrow. But—" his grin widened "—they say third time lucky." He jerked the gun at the tunnel entrance. "Get in there."

Her heart in her mouth, Shannon entered the tunnel and descended the worn old steps. It was dank, and dark. Iris came behind her with a flashlight, but its beam barely penetrated the darkness. Cobwebs clung to her hair and her face. Brushing them away, she moved farther down the tunnel.

Paul's footsteps echoed behind her as they walked forward. The tunnel curved, then widened out into a small room. Shaking with terror, Shannon moved over to an old wood table standing against one wall. It had a battered lantern on it, but she barely registered its presence.

Iris swung the light around. "What a dump! I'll be glad when this is over." She frowned. "Idiot, you forgot the shovel!"

"Go back and get it!" Paul ordered.

Shannon leaned against the table to keep from falling. Her trembling fingers touched grooves in the wood, making out a pair of carved initials. *F. M., the runaway slave!* Long ago he'd been here, on his way to freedom. Maybe she could find the same strength and bravery to fight for her life. Her fingers moved and touched the lantern, closed around the handle and held on.

She was holding the lantern handle so hard her fingers ached. The tunnel was very dark beyond Iris's flashlight, but she had the oddest feeling someone else was there. Out of the corner of her eye she sensed movement near the wall past Paul's shoulder. Her heart leaped, and her mouth went dry. A tall man—*Mike!* He gestured for her to be still as Paul and Iris continued arguing about the shovel. "All right," Iris snapped, handing him the flashlight. "Shine it so I can see my way back up the tunnel."

Shannon, without pausing to think, threw the lantern at Paul's head. He never saw it coming, and it caught him over his left ear. A glancing blow, but he staggered; and she ran down the tunnel to Mike.

"Hurry!" he cried, grabbing her arm and pulling her along. They could hear Paul's footsteps behind them, and the crackle of a gunshot as it echoed off the rock walls.

"Damn bitch!" Paul yelled.

They rushed down the narrow tunnel, only steps ahead of him. Then cool night air brushed her face. She could make out a dim light overhead. Then stone steps, Mike dragging her upward. A blast of thunder shook the sky as they emerged. No time to shut the tunnel door. She found herself running through the woods, panting, her heart in her throat. Mike pushed her down behind an old stone wall. "Ssh. Listen."

Seconds later, Paul shone the light around as he stepped out of the tunnel. "Bitch, I'll get you!" His cold, hard eyes scanned the trees, looking for movement.

"Stay here," Mike whispered as he handed her a rock. "Toss this as far as you can." He moved to the far side of the wall and picked up another rock. A large, flat one.

Iris came out of the tunnel. "This way," Paul ordered, pointing left with his gun. They ran through the trees, Iris muttering that she was "cold, dammit!"

"Shut up!" Paul snapped. Suddenly, the ground gave way under his feet and he plunged downward, bending saplings that snapped back, whipping his head as he gave out a bloodcurdling cry.

*"Paul, what happened?"* Screaming, Iris looked down at him from the edge of the pit. He lay unconscious.

Shannon's heart seemed to stop as Mike rushed to grab the gun. Pointing it at Iris, he ordered, "Sit down! Shannon, go for the police."

For a long time, there was only the sound of rain and Iris's sobbing. Shannon headed back to her own house across the field; it was closer, and she knew she had two phone calls to make. The police, and then one to Palm Beach, to tell Linda of her sister's death.

The rain fell, and then, in the distance, came the sound of sirens.

SEVEN DAYS LATER, The Martian Spaceship Society called the weekly meeting to order at Nick's house. From downstairs came the smell of spaghetti sauce cooking. Andy said, "Let's take a vote. All in favor say 'Aye.'"

Chris and Nick solemnly said, "Aye."

"Motion passed," Andy explained. "Now we gotta figure out how to get my dad and your mom together for good."

"You mean 'married,'" Chris said.

"That's what I said."

"Did not."

"Okay, smartie." Andy pushed his glasses up. "You figure out how to do it, then." She didn't answer, so he said, "Anyway, it's too bad the Wagoners were only bad guys instead of vampires."

"Yeah," Nick agreed, flipping through the latest issue of his favorite comic, *Swamp Monster Meets Carrothead.*

"They could still be vampires," Chris said. "I bet they really are."

"Never mind them," Andy told her. "You've gotta go downstairs and pretend to be real sick like on TV. People are always falling in love when something awful happens, like some little kid gets sick."

"Yeah." Nick nodded. "Or a giant meteor hits earth."

"There isn't any meteor. We're stuck with her," Andy retorted.

"Want me to stick my finger down my throat and throw up?" she asked.

"Yeah," Andy said. "Like last Halloween when we wouldn't let you come trick-or-treating with us."

They crept downstairs and looked into the kitchen. Steam was rising from the pots on the stove. Shannon and Mike weren't stirring the sauce in the pan or straining spaghetti through the colander in the sink. They had their arms around each other and they were kissing.

For a minute or two, they stayed locked in each other's arms. At last Mike said, "Look in my eyes."

She raised her head. "You've got such wonderful eyes."

"Tell me," he said.

"Tell you what?"

"What I want to hear."

She kissed the corners of his mouth.

"Tell me," he said.

"I love you."

"Again."

"I love you, Mike. I really do." He kissed her and she said, "Mmm, that's nice. Mmm, I love you."

"Good, because that's just how I feel about you." He lowered his head again, and the only sound was the bubble of tomato sauce in the pan on the stove.

Andy pushed his glasses up, smiled and said, "Everything's gonna be okay, Chris. You don't have to throw up."

Nick grinned and said, "Yeah," and went back to his comic.

And Chris yawned. "Okay, but I can still do it if you want me to."

"Nah," Andy said. "Save it till we need it sometime."

Fifty red-blooded, white-hot, true-blue hunks from every
State in the Union!

Beginning in May, look for MEN MADE IN AMERICA!
Written by some of our most popular authors, these
stories feature fifty of the strongest, sexiest men, each
from a different state in the union!

Two titles available every other month at your favorite
retail outlet.

In July, look for:

CALL IT DESTINY by Jayne Ann Krentz (Arizona)
ANOTHER KIND OF LOVE by Mary Lynn Baxter
(Arkansas)

In September, look for:

DECEPTIONS by Annette Broadrick (California)
STORMWALKER by Dallas Schulze (Colorado)

**You won't be able to resist MEN MADE IN AMERICA!**

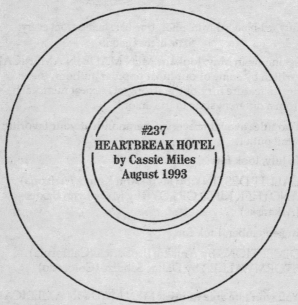

# HARLEQUIN®

# I N T R I G U E®

## "I AM BETRAYED"

In the still of the night, those were the words spoken to
Emma Devlin by her husband, Frank . . . from beyond the
grave. She'd given him no cause to doubt her devotion, yet he
haunted her waking hours and disturbed her dreams.

Next month, Harlequin Intrigue brings you a chilling tale of
love and disloyalty . . .

### #241 FLESH AND BLOOD
#### by Caroline Burnes
#### September 1993

In an antebellum mansion, Emma finds help from the oddest of
sources: in the aura of a benevolent ghost—and in the arms of
a gallant Confederate colonel.

For a spine-tingling story about a love that transcends time,
don't miss Harlequin Intrigue #241 FLESH AND BLOOD,
coming to you in September.

FAD1

THREE UNFORGETTABLE HEROINES
THREE AWARD-WINNING AUTHORS

# Untamed

## MAVERICK HEARTS

A unique collection of historical short stories that
capture the spirit of America's last frontier.

**HEATHER GRAHAM POZZESSERE**—over 10 million copies
of her books in print worldwide
*Lonesome Rider*—The story of an Eastern widow and the
renegade half-breed who becomes her protector.

**PATRICIA POTTER**—an author whose books are consistently
Waldenbooks bestsellers
*Against the Wind*—Two people, battered by heartache, prove
that love can heal all.

**JOAN JOHNSTON**—award-winning Western historical author
with 17 books to her credit
*One Simple Wish*—A woman with a past discovers that
dreams really do come true.

Join us for an exciting journey West with
*UNTAMED*
Available in July, wherever Harlequin books are sold.